CIVILIZATION

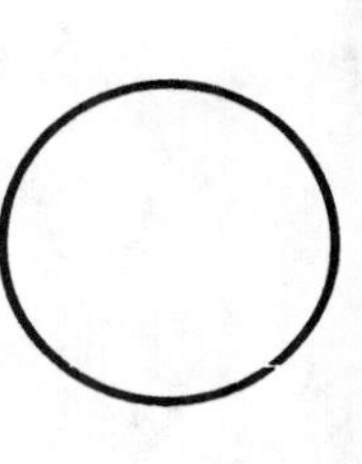

CIVILIZATION

V. F. LENZEN

STEPHEN C. PEPPER

GEORGE P. ADAMS

D. S. MACKAY

EDWARD W. STRONG

A. I. MELDEN

WILLIAM R. DENNES

UNIVERSITY OF CALIFORNIA PRESS

BERKELEY AND
LOS ANGELES

1959

University of California Press
Berkeley and Los Angeles, California
Cambridge University Press
London, England

Originally published as Volume 23
of the University of California
Publications in Philosophy

Second printing, 1959
(First Paper-bound Trade Edition)

PREFACE

IN THESE STUDIES, *first published seventeen years ago, the authors examined issues which in 1941 they judged to be fundamental in the twin enterprises of explaining and evaluating patterns of human social living. Their republication invites us to consider whether the processes of history during two turbulent decades, or the progress of philosophical interpretation and criticism, have either resolved or moved beyond the problems here discussed, or whether and in what respects the analyses are still relevant.*

If he were writing today, each author would want to take account of various new or additional materials. For example, Professor Lenzen would want to discuss the results of recent researches which have revealed the profound influence upon Galileo's work of the philosophical revision of Aristotelian physics that preceded it. In his essay he took pains to point out the limitations of any explanation of the development of science in terms of the influence of economic, political, and technological factors. He would now wish to explore more fully respects in which, for instance, the conceptual tools for the quantitative formulation of motion are to be found in Galileo's mediaeval predecessors. The scientific revolution, the occurrence of which certainly was aided by techniques and stimulated by practical problems of the era, required, Professor Lenzen believes, the prior philosophical decision to reject Aristotle's concepts and qualitative point of view for the geometrical methods of Pythagoras, Democritus, and Plato. Such additions would leave Professor Lenzen's principal theses intact. And although he underestimated in 1941 the bearing that microphysics was soon to have on military implements, and the influence of war pressures upon certain sorts of scientific development, it remains an impressive fact that such pressures seem not to have produced new breakthroughs in fundamental explanation comparable to those achieved by Einstein, Planck, and Bohr.

Professor Melden's enlightening examination of the confusions that result when the social context of inquiry is construed as constituting the meaning of explanatory hypotheses, carries further Lenzen's analysis and applies it particularly to the social sciences. The genetic fallacies of "sociologism" are probably as widespread today as they were when Melden wrote. As correcting these, as exposing various fashionable pseudo escapes from "relativism," and as exploring the conditions of objective judgment in the social sciences, his analysis is as timely now as when it was written.

Can communities of men organize to safeguard and promote the realization of intellectual and moral freedom, or is organization as such the enemy of freedom? The complex family of issues here involved have occupied philosophers since Plato, and we may be sure that they have been the practical concern of men from the beginnings of any life that we can imagine as human and social. The immense increase in the organization and control of research and of communication (to name only a few areas) in the years since Professor Pepper and the late Professor Mackay wrote, have made these problems more urgent and their theoretical analyses and practical suggestions of even greater importance than they were two decades ago.

Underlying most of these issues are the problems to which Professor Adams, Professor Strong, and the author of the concluding essay address themselves: Are norms of value presupposed even by the theoretical understanding of a civilization? What is the nature of such norms? And is it possible to establish one set of them as the "valid" or correct norms by reference to which the values of civilizations may be objectively measured? To these problems Professor Adams brings interpretations in which the spirit of Plato, and some of the insights of the classical objective idealists, are as fully embodied as in the work of any contemporary philosopher. Sympathetic to the values which Adams emphasizes, but skeptical of any absolute metaphysical grounding for them, Professor Strong explores what bases they may have in the natural needs and interests of men. The concluding essay is also naturalistic in its outlook, attempts to clarify the distinction between the descriptive and the normative use of various conceptions of civilization as actually developed by anthropologists, sociologists, historians, and moralists, and to resolve the alleged conflicts between natural and "spiritual" values. It is not for the authors to judge their success in these final undertakings. If they should in any way stimulate careful thinking by others on these fundamental issues they will consider their efforts well rewarded.

W. R. D.

March 31, 1959

CONTENTS

V. F. LENZEN:
Science and Social Context   1

STEPHEN C. PEPPER:
The Conditions of Social Control   25

GEORGE P. ADAMS:
The Idea of Civilization   45

D. S. MACKAY:
Organization and Freedom   69

EDWARD W. STRONG:
Civilizations in Historical Perspective   93

A. I. MELDEN:
Judgments in the Social Sciences   121

WILLIAM R. DENNES:
Conceptions of Civilization   147

V. F. LENZEN

SCIENCE AND SOCIAL CONTEXT

IT IS traditional that the ancient Greeks created science. Their predecessors observed the stars, devised procedures for measuring space, and invented machines for the constructive arts, but it was an achievement of the Greeks to form the concept of a system of knowledge that is sought for its own sake. The Ionian natural philosophers set themselves the problem of interpreting natural phenomena as the changes of permanent substance and created the theory of the elements. The Pythagoreans conceived of numbers as the essence of reality and thus laid the foundations for a mathematical description of nature. The mathematics of the Pythagoreans was extended in the Academy of Plato, who sketched a geometrical theory of the elements and called for a geometrical theory of the motions of the heavenly bodies. Guided by an ideal of systematic knowledge, the Alexandrian scientists organized the astronomical observations, rules of surveyors, and practice with machines of the Babylonians and Egyptians into Ptolemaic astronomy, Euclidean geometry, and Archimedean statics. After the practical and imperialistic Romans swept over the ancient world, the creative impulse of Greek science declined. Then Rome fell before the barbarians, and as western Europe became converted to Christianity the interests of man turned to salvation in a supernatural world, while Greek science was preserved by Islam. In the sixteenth and seventeenth centuries the idea of a rational theory of the universe was revived, and its realization has been the aim of modern science.

I

It is an interesting problem in the history of ideas to determine the influences that caused the revival of science in the modern period. Until recently, the orthodox view has been that the rebirth of science was brought about through the discovery by western Europe of the metaphysical doctrines of the Pythagoreans and Platonists. The essence of these traditions was the doctrine that the structure of the physical world is determined by numerical and geometrical relations. This doctrine had been transformed by the Neo-Pythagoreans into a numerological mysticism, the view that all is arranged by God according to measure and number, that life is an unfolding of mathematical relations. The historian of philosophy, Windelband, states that modern investigation of nature was born of empirical Pythagoreanism.[1] This thesis has been supported in detail by E. A. Burtt in his *Metaphysical Foundations of Modern Physical Science*.[2] Mr. Burtt asserts that a belief in a mathematical structure of the world, which was derived from Pythagorean and Platonic metaphysics, made possible such stupendous conquests of science as the Copernican astronomy and the Galilean dynamics. Burtt's interpretation has been criticized by E. W. Strong in his work *Procedures and Metaphysics*.[3] Mr. Strong has studied the Italian writers on mathematics and mechanics of the sixteenth century and finds that their starting point was the procedures derived from Greek scientists such as Euclid, Archimedes, Apollonius of Perga, and Hero. Concurrent with this inheritance of constructive mathematics there existed the metaphysical theories of mathematics created by Pythagoras and Plato and interpreted by Nicomachus, Theon, and Proclus. Mr. Strong contends that the constructive procedures of the mathematicians, rather than metaphysical theories, determined the scientific development which culminated in the Newtonian mechanics of the seventeenth century. Mathematics, Mr. Strong declares, marches by method and not by metaphysics.

In partial support of the doctrine of the metaphysical inspiration of modern science, I cite Edgar Zilsel's view that one should distinguish between influences on astronomy and on mechanics. Dr. Zilsel contends[4] that the outstanding contribution of Copernicus was a mathematico-geometrical one, and that it is sometimes not sufficiently noticed how far Copernicus still is from modern physical and especially mechanical thinking. In the first book of *De Revolutionibus*, in which Copernicus sets forth his basic ideas, Pythagorean and Scholastic ideas predominate. Thus, he uses the Platonic and Pythagorean idea that immobility is nobler than

---

[1] *History of Philosophy*, trans. by J. H. Tufts (New York, Macmillan, 1923), p. 387.

[2] New York, Harcourt, Brace, 1925.

[3] Berkeley, University of California Press, 1936.

[4] "Copernicus and Mechanics," *Journal of the History of Ideas*, Vol. I, No. 1 (Jan., 1940), pp. 113–118.

movement in arguing that the sun is at rest while the earth is in motion. He explains the spherical form of the universe as the form which is most perfect. Gravity is explained as a striving of the parts of the universe toward unity and wholeness by combining in the form of a sphere. Objects of the same kind are assumed to exert sympathetic influences on each other. Dr. Zilsel concludes: "Copernicus is interested in the exact formulation of the mathematical regularities of celestial movements; he is a Pythagorean, and advances not one real mechanical idea. Galileo, on the other hand, is a mechanist; in his dialogue on the theory of Copernicus he is so little interested in the exact details of the planetary movements that he does not even mention the laws of Kepler. Kepler, who was a contemporary of Galileo, was, as is generally known, at least as Pythagorean and thought at least as teleologically as Copernicus." Dr. Zilsel then declares that there seems to be a difference between astronomy and mechanics with respect to their historical evolution and sociological origins. "The very first astronomers were Babylonian priests and this connection with priesthood was never quite interrupted; and from antiquity through the Middle Ages up to the sixteenth century, astronomy belonged to the 'liberal' arts, contrasted with the 'mechanical' ones. This might explain why metaphysical, Pythagorean, and teleological ideas could persist in astronomy until Copernicus and Kepler." "It may be that in the modern era the experimental method and the elimination of teleological and animistic by causal thinking originated in the ranks of mechanicians and craftsmen. Certainly, scientific mechanics and physics did not appear in modern times before the way of thinking of the craftsmen was adopted by academically trained scholars of the upper class, as happened in the period of Galileo."

Thus Burtt is supported in his view that metaphysical ideas inspired the Copernican revolution in astronomy. Furthermore, it may be conceded that belief in a mathematical structure of the universe would justify the attempt to devise a mathematical description of natural phenomena. But as Zilsel suggests, the development of mechanics was primarily conditioned by problems of practice. Intellectual curiosity certainly was an important factor in the rise of science, but the mode of satisfaction of that curiosity has been molded by the technological problems that were rooted in the economic and social needs of the new era. In this paper I shall expound and criticize the doctrine that the principal stimulus to the creation of modern science has been the social context. Adopting a term introduced by Stephen Pepper, I call this doctrine an example of the contextualist theory of the history of science. The spirit of the contextualist theory is expressed in the following quotation from Hogben's *Science for the Citizen*.[5] "Whether we choose to call it pure or applied, the story of science is not something apart from the common life of mankind. What we call pure science only thrives when the contemporary social structure is capable of making full use of its teaching, furnishing it with new problems for solution and equipping it with new instruments for solving them."

II

With the foregoing statement of the contextualist theory as a background, I shall consider in some detail the social influences that stimulated the rise of modern science. The seventeenth century, in which modern science became of age, is marked by the publication of Newton's *Principia,* which marked the culmination of a development in mechanics. A study of the social context of this development furnishes instructive examples of the contextualist doctrine. As a basis for discussion I shall use the essay by Professor B. Hessen, "The Social and Economic Roots of Newton's Principia,"[6] published in 1931. This essay has contributed greatly to the contemporary interest in the social backgrounds of science.

The scientific developments that furnished the material for the synthesis set forth in Newton's *Principia* occurred during the transition from feudalism to an economic and social system characterized by the emergence of specialized manufacturing and trading classes. As the feudal system disintegrated, towns grew and entered into closer relations with one another, there occurred a division of labor in production between towns, and the need for money as a medium of exchange grew. National states were formed out of relatively independent communities and became instruments for almost continuous warfare. The technical problems of the rising capitalistic economy and the territorial ambitions of national states stimulated an interest in the solution of corresponding basic physical problems, such as those of transport, industry, and war. The

---

[5] New York, Alfred A. Knopf, 1938.
[6] In *Science at the Cross Roads* (London, Kniga).

spirit of enterprise broke the bonds of tradition and launched the Western world on its career of progress.

The development of capitalism created a demand for better means of communication between towns. Especial attention was given to water transport by ocean, river, or canal. An increase in the carrying capacity of vessels set problems in hydrostatics. Improvement of the floating properties of vessels required an understanding of the mechanical conditions of stability. The construction of canals demanded a knowledge of hydrostatics and of the efflux of liquids through orifices. The existence of these technical problems explains why physicists like Stevin and Pascal occupied themselves with hydrostatics, and why Torricelli was prompted to discover the law for the outflow of liquids from an orifice. Stevin became quartermaster general of the army of Prince Maurice in Holland, where an elaborate system of canals was early constructed; Torricelli, as well as his teacher, Galileo, was interested in the control of rivers, such as the Arno, in Italy.

The development of ocean transportation also required convenient and reliable means of determining position at sea. The use of the lodestone as a compass stimulated investigations of magnetism, and the discovery of the variation in declination inspired hope of using this phenomenon to determine longitude. The determination of longitude by the distance of the moon from the fixed stars stimulated observations of anomalies in the motions of the moon. The attempt to use the moons of Jupiter as a clock to determine longitude led to Römer's measurement of the speed of light. The desire to find a simple method of determining longitude stimulated improvements in clocks. The pendulum clock furnished Huygens with a problem that contributed to the advancement of the dynamics of rigid bodies.

But industry also set its problems for physics. During the fourteenth and fifteenth centuries mining developed into a great industry. The growth of trade increased the need of gold and silver. Explorations were stimulated by the desire for gold, both for itself and for the purpose of obtaining larger supplies of the medium of exchange. Firearms came into use and in the fifteenth century artillery reached a high level of perfection. In consequence there was an increased demand for iron and copper. Mines had to be exploited more effectively and ores raised from increasing depths. It is therefore understandable that problems of machines, the theory of which is formulated in statics, were studied by Leonardo da Vinci, Benedetti, Stevin, and others in the fifteenth and sixteenth centuries. As mines were deepened, problems of ventilation created an interest in the properties of air. The need of pumping water out of mines stimulated an interest in the problem of raising liquids in tubes. This problem led Torricelli and Pascal to experiment on atmospheric pressure.

I shall not refer in this context to the demands made upon chemistry by the reduction of ores.

New developments in the technique of war were initiated by the application of gunpowder to firearms. According to Hessen, heavy artillery first appeared in 1280 at the siege of Cordova by the Arabs. Artillery was improved in the fifteenth century when cannon were cast solid from iron and copper, and stone balls were replaced by iron. The development of artillery led to improvements in fortifications and this in turn led to new developments in artillery. J. D. Bernal has sketched in general terms the consequence of the introduction of gunpowder into Europe: "War became more expensive and needed far more technical skill, and both these needs played into the hands of the townsmen and the kings whom they supported against the nobles. Thus the introduction of gunpowder helped to bring on the economic developments which tended to the breakup of Feudalism.'" The new methods of warfare set new problems for science. The process of explosion set problems in the physics and chemistry of gases. The problem of the flight of a projectile stimulated investigations that finally resulted in the establishment of modern dynamics by Galileo.

I believe that it is of special interest to sketch the development which culminated in Galileo's discovery of the laws of falling bodies. This development, which illustrates how military problems have provided the stimulus for physical researches, appears to have started with Tartaglia.

In a historical introduction to his researches, Tartaglia says: "When I was living in the town of Verona in the year 1531, one of my intimate friends, master of ordnance at the old castle, a man of experience, very skilful in his art, and who was gifted with excellent qualities, asked me one day my opinion how to aim a

---

[7] *The Social Function of Science* (New York, Macmillan, 1939), p. 166.

piece of artillery to give it its greatest range. Although I had no practical knowledge whatever of artillery, for I have never in my life shot a single round with firearms, arquebus, bombard, or escopette, nevertheless, desirous as I was to be agreeable to my friend, I promised him shortly to give him an answer to this question....

"As the result of this I had the intention of writing a treatise on the art of artillery, and to bring it to a degree of perfection capable of directing fire in all circumstances, assisted only by a few particular experiments: for as Aristotle says in the seventh book of the Physica, Section twenty, 'particular experiments are the basis of universal science.' "[8]

Tartaglia then goes on to say: "But, since then, one day meditative to myself, it had seemed to me that it was a thing blameworthy, shameful, and barbarous, worthy of severe punishment before God and man, to wish to bring to perfection an art damageable to one's neighbor and destructive to the human race, and especially to Christian men in the continual wars that they wage on one another. Consequently, not only did I altogether neglect the study of this matter and turned to others, but I even tore up and burnt everything which I had calculated and written on the subject, ashamed and full of remorse for the time I had spent on it, and well decided never to communicate in writing that which against my will had remained in my memory, either to please a friend or in teaching of these matters which are a grave sin and shipwreck of the soul."

The imminent invasion of Italy by the Turks caused Tartaglia to change his mind. He says: "Today, however, in the sight of the ferocious wolf preparing to set on our flock, and of our pastors united for the common defense, it does not seem to me any longer proper to hold these things hid, and I have resolved to publish them partly in writing, partly by word of mouth, for the benefit of Christians so that all should be in better state either to attack the common enemy or to defend themselves against him. I regret very much at the moment having given up this work, for I am certain that had I persevered I would have found things of the greatest value, as I hope yet to find.... I hope that your Lordships will not disdain to receive this work of mine so as better to instruct the artillerymen of your most illustrious government in the theory of their art, and to render them more apt in its practice."

---

[8] Quoted by Bernal, *op. cit.*, p. 168.

Tartaglia expounded his theory of motion in his *Nuova Scientia,* which was published in 1537. He based the theory on a number of laws of motion. One of these laws states, "When similar and equal heavy bodies are projected with the same force, at different angles of elevation above the horizontal plane, the one whose path has an elevation of forty-five degrees will have the greatest range."[9] The truth of this theorem Tartaglia inferred from the fact that a shot fired vertically into the air has zero range, and likewise one that is fired horizontally. Halfway between these two, he concluded, must be the angle which gives the maximum range. This result is correct, but the reasoning was unsound. In 1546 he published a volume, *Questi et Inventioni Diverse,* which is largely given over to military tactics, munitions, and ballistics. A quotation from this book is: "The higher the angle of fire the less the curvature of path; but no part of this path is ever perfectly straight except in the two directions above mentioned, namely: directly upwards toward the heavens, or directly downwards toward the center of the earth; because in every direction, except these two, there is always some part of gravity drawing the shot out of its line of motion.... Whence it will be manifest that, in no other direction then the two mentioned, will a shot have any least part of its path along a perfectly straight line."[10] Henry Crew remarks, "At this late date, 1546, he occupied a position far in advance of the peripatetic school, and was indeed not far from understanding the composition of motions."

Tartaglia was criticized by Benedetti, who in 1585 published a treatise on mechanics. Benedetti partly anticipated Newton's first law of motion in that he recognized that inertial motion occurs in a straight line. He states, "Any heavy body whatever, whether in natural or violent motion, seeks of its own accord, a straight path."[11]

The correct theory of the motion of projectiles was finally given by Galileo. The essential step in his theory is the analysis of the motion into two components: a horizontal motion with constant velocity in accordance with the principle of inertia, and a vertical motion subject to the acceleration of gravity. The laws of motion of freely falling bodies are thus an element in the description of

---

[9] Quoted by Henry Crew, *The Rise of Modern Physics* (Baltimore, Williams and Wilkins, 1935).

[10] Quoted by Crew, *op. cit.,* p. 80.

[11] Quoted by Crew, *op. cit.,* p. 82.

the motion of projectiles. Throughout his work *Dialogues Concerning Two New Sciences,* published in 1638,[12] Galileo uses the motion of cannon balls in illustration. The subject of the dialogue for one day is the motion of projectiles. The work also contains a range table.

In view of the succession of treatises on the motion of projectiles during the hundred years from Tartaglia to Galileo's solution of the problem, I believe that Galileo's fundamental contributions to dynamics were the culmination of investigations that were initially stimulated by the desire to improve the accuracy of artillery fire. It may be conceded that Galileo sought a correct description of motion in order to satisfy his curiosity, but the background of his solution was provided by military problems.

Galileo's interest in military problems has been investigated by Leonardo Olschki.[13] This scholar reports that Galileo wrote two tracts on fortifications and intended to write a book for soldiers. Olschki states that Galileo's writings on military architecture and practical mechanics have not previously been investigated adequately. The tracts on fortifications are sequels to many works of this kind that were published in the second half of the sixteenth century and confirm the origin of modern dynamics out of military problems. Galileo, indeed, acknowledged the stimulus offered by military problems. The opening sentence of the "Dialogue on the First Day" reads: "The constant activity which you Venetians display in your famous arsenal suggests to the studious mind a large field for investigation, especially that part of the work which involves mechanics; for in this department all types of instruments and machines are constantly being constructed by many artisans, among whom there must be some who, partly by inherited experience and partly by their own experience and partly by their own observations, have become highly expert and clever in explanation."

Bernal states that except for a certain portion of the nineteenth century it may fairly be said that the majority of significant technical and scientific advances owe their origin directly to military or naval requirements.[14] However, it may be contended that under

---

[12] Trans. by Henry Crew and Alfonso de Salvio (New York, Macmillan, 1914; Evanston and Chicago, Northwestern University, 1939).

[13] *Galilei und seine Zeit* (Halle, Max Niemeyer Verlag, 1927).

[14] *Op. cit.,* p. 165..

contemporary conditions science is hindered more than it is stimulated by war. Fundamental physical investigation today is directed primarily to microphysical phenomena that are not likely to be immediately available for application in warfare. Under the pressure of war, fundamental investigation may be suspended in order to develop macrophysical implements the physical basis of which is already known. Technology may advance, but theoretical science languishes on account of the exigencies of war.

Having digressed on the influence of militarism upon science, I recall that the present topic is the social context of Newton's *Principia*. To conclude this discussion with a summary: In the period preceding Newton and contemporary with him the chief problems of physics were, first, the properties of simple machines which are the subject matter of statics; second, the motion of falling bodies and the trajectory of projectiles; third, the laws of hydrostatics and atmospheric pressure; fourth, the mechanics of the heavens and theory of the tides. The foregoing physical problems were determined by the needs of industry, war, and transport. The principles of statics contributed to the improvement of the lifting and conveying equipment used in mining and building. The theory of motion contributed to the improvement of artillery. The laws of hydrostatics and aerostatics were important for the design of ships, the building of canals, and the ventilation of mines. The mechanics of the heavens was of value to navigation in war and peace. It may be added that the prospect of using the declination of the compass to determine longitude stimulated an interest in magnetism, and that the invention of the telescope created an interest in the laws of refraction. It appears to me a justifiable conclusion that the scheme of physics was mainly determined by the technical tasks set by a rising capitalism and nationalism. But there should be some mention of the stimulus provided by the interest in art during the Renaissance. Leonardo da Vinci, Albrecht Dürer, and other artists investigated the laws of perspective and the structure of the human body in order to improve their representation of life, and thereby contributed to optics and anatomy.

The preceding analysis may be criticized on the ground that the scientific investigations may not have been undertaken for utilitarian purposes. No doubt, intellectual curiosity was the driving force in the solution of some of the problems. But in such a case the topic of research was a factor in the social context that had been created in response to economic or other needs. There is no reason why a technological problem should not be studied for its own sake.

III

Thus far the discussion has emphasized the social motives that stimulated the rise of modern science. But it should also be noted that the methods of experimental science developed from the techniques and ideas of craftsmen. This fact has been especially emphasized by Edgar Zilsel,[15] who has analyzed the work of William Gilbert. Gilbert's treatise *De Magnete,* published in 1600, is characterized by Zilsel as the first printed book, written by an academically trained scholar and dealing with a topic of natural science, which is based almost entirely on actual observation and experiment. Examination of Gilbert's work reveals his concern with the problems of mining and metallurgy. Some of his experiments merely repeat the working processes of the iron manufacture of the period. He acquired his habit of observing and experimenting from seeing manual workers, in accordance with the progressive spirit of the time, experiment with new processes. But problems of navigation and work with nautical instruments played an even greater role in providing a stimulus to Gilbert's scientific work. In this field Zilsel clearly demonstrates the influence of the craftsman by an analysis of the work of Robert Norman, a retired mariner, who had turned to compass making and had published the results of experiments in a book, *The Newe Attractive,* in 1581. In the work of this humble mariner and craftsman, in which are described many of the instruments and experiments of Gilbert's more famous book, are revealed the basic procedures of modern experimental science. That experience with practical problems can develop into knowledge for its own sake is demonstrated by the fact that Norman expresses "incredible delight" at his discoveries and that he performs experiments, such as on the ponderability of magnetism, which had no practical significance at that time. Zilsel concludes that Gilbert's method and independent attitude were derived not from ancient and contemporary learned literature, but on the one hand from miners and foundrymen and on the other from the navigators and instrument makers of the period.

---

[15] "The Origins of William Gilbert's Scientific Method," *Journal of the History of Ideas,* Vol. II, No. 1 (Jan., 1941), pp. 1–32.

The Middle Ages had inherited from antiquity a distinction in status between the liberal and the mechanical arts. Manual labor was considered to be beneath the intellectual classes. But in the dawn of the modern period superior craftsmen, like Norman, experimented and published their results in the vernacular. According to Zilsel, Gilbert was the first academically trained scholar who dared to adopt the experimental method from the superior craftsmen and to communicate the results in a book addressed not to helmsmen and mechanics but to the learned public.

Gilbert's field of interest was magnetism as manifested by the behavior of the compass. It was a problem of primary importance for the economic and defense interests of his native England. But it was not a subject that admitted extensive quantitative development without the prior development of mechanics. Zilsel remarks that, on the whole, Gilbert usually performs measurements only when he deals with quantities that are important in navigation. Gilbert does not contribute to the founding of mathematical physics. This science was born of mechanics. For the introduction of mechanical ideas into experimental science we must turn to Galileo, who is justly celebrated as the primary founder of modern analytical mechanics.

The development of the technique of experiment in the field of mechanics out of the procedures of craftsmen has been investigated by Leonardo Olschki, who has reported on the development from Tartaglia to Galileo. Tartaglia's ideas were derived from problems of practice; his notebooks record problems in calculation set for him by engineers, artillerymen, architects, and merchants. Galileo is frequently called the inventor of the experimental method. Examination of his preparation reveals the decisive influence of a technical background. Galileo's teacher of mathematics was Ostilio Ricci, who taught in an art academy in Florence and concerned himself with problems of technology. Under the stimulus of his teacher, who gave him a copy of Archimedes' treatise on floating bodies, Galileo published his first independent work on the determination of specific gravity by a hydrostatic balance. The practical import of this work is demonstrated by the fact that he gives numerical measures of the specific gravity of various metals and precious stones. I have already indicated the stimulus offered to Galileo by military problems. While a professor at the University of Padua, he maintained a workship in his house and gave private instruction in the theory of fortifications, perspective, applied mathematics, and so forth. His discoveries were made with instruments that he himself fashioned.

That the techniques of the craftsman furnished methods of experimentation has been commented upon by Clark, who states that one of the novel features of the new science was the experimental method and reports that this method was taken over, by long-continued contact, from art, from mining, and from the skilled handicrafts in general. To quote: "We can see this happening if we look in the diaries and correspondences of the scientists and see how they visited workshops, talked to artificers, wrote descriptions of industrial processes, used and adapted tools. Trial and error, verification by putting a theory into practice, which had always been the everyday procedure of craftsmen, became the everyday procedure of scientists."[16] In illustration, Clark cites Boyle: "Boyle, who was Bacon's most faithful follower, made it his business to carry 'philosophical materials from the shops to the schools.' He considered that 'in many cases a trade differs from an experiment, not so much in the nature of the thing, as in its having had the luck to be applied to human uses, or by a company of artificers made their business, in order to [increase] their profit; which are things extrinsical and accidental to the experiment itself!' He gave many convincing instances of ways in which craftsmen could improve the naturalist's knowledge, such as their ways of distinguishing what they call the goodness or badness of the things they handle, or their observation of the effects of time and the changes of seasons and the weather."

The fact is that the mathematical theory of a mechanics of nature developed in the seventeenth century was the outcome of the technological advances of earlier centuries. Franz Borkenau especially has expounded the thesis that the new system of nature was an attempt to comprehend the world after the processes of manufacture of the early capitalistic period.[17] Copernicus and Kepler had sought to achieve the Pythagorean aim of a mathematical theory of world harmony. The introduction of dynamical ideas

---

[16] G. N. Clark, *Science and Social Welfare in the Age of Newton* (Oxford, Clarendon Press, 1937), p. 76.

[17] *Der Uebergang vom feudalen zum bürgerlichen Weltbild* (Paris, F. Alcan, 1934).

derived from the procedures of craftsmen gave rise to the conception of the world as a mechanical system. Thus, Galileo theoretically generalized the experiences provided by technology. Lewis Mumford has described the mechanical clock as the most characteristic invention of the early technological era in the Middle Ages.[18] It is significant that a favorite analogy for the world machine was the clock.

The historical thesis that experimental methods were derived from the procedures of craftsmen can be supported by an analysis of physical concepts. In contemporary philosophy of science it has come to be accepted that physical concepts are to be defined in terms of operational procedures. The theory of an instrument or apparatus defines the meaning of a basic concept. Thus the compass is an instrument that serves to define the concept of magnetic field, the beam balance to define weight, a clock to define time, a thermometer to define temperature, and so forth. Basic concepts have been defined in terms of operations with apparatus inherited from a prescientific practice, and new concepts are dependent on technical advances. The relativity of physical concepts to concrete experimental situations thus explains the historical origin of science out of practice.

Not only were experimental techniques derived from the practical activities of the time; intellectual procedures also appear to have been conditioned by the qualities of mind required for economic enterprise. Werner Sombart, the historian of modern capitalism, has pointed out that an important element of the capitalist spirit is the capacity and habit of describing things in terms of numbers.[19] The description of values in numerical terms makes the art of calculation an essential factor in economic activities. The birth of modern capitalism was partly prepared by improvements in arithmetic and accounting. Commercial arithmetic was first developed in Italy. Leonardo of Pisa introduced arabic numerals in his book published in 1202, and during the thirteenth century the art of calculating made rapid progress. Sombart reports that in the fourteenth century there were six schools of arithmetic in Florence, a progressive center of commercial activity. Improvement in methods of calculation assisted in the mathematical de-

---

[18] In *Technics and Civilization* (New York, Harcourt, Brace, 1934).
[19] *The Quintessence of Capitalism*, trans. by M. Epstein (New York, Dutton, 1915).

scription of nature; quantitative procedure of business furnished
an example for the numerical representation of natural phenomena.
It is significant that Tartaglia, who was a pioneer in dynamics,
perfected the art of commercial arithmetic. Both economic rationalism and mathematical physics were manifestations of the spirit of
rationalism in the modern era.

The preceding argument is supported by Clark, who contends
that the habits of precision and economy fostered by economic
enterprise prepared the mind for the manifestation of the same
qualities in the study of nature. Concerning the positive, practical
spirit of the businessman, Clark asserts: "Indeed, this spirit even
helped science to hold fast that part of its method which seems at
first sight most high and abstract—the mathematical part. It has
long been recognized that the introduction of rational accounting
in business in the later Middle Ages was another result of the habit
of quantitative thinking which was married to experimentation in
the work of Galileo and Newton."[20] "Scientific method was thus
shaped and sharpened by what it took over from the arts and crafts
and from the practice of merchants."

I have now completed the analysis of the economic and social
roots of Newton's *Principia*. Let us examine his contribution.
Newton's achievement may be analyzed into two principal factors.
First, he formulated the laws of motion of a particle. Preparatory
work had been done by his predecessors, for Galileo and Descartes
had formulated a principle of inertia which was stated by Newton
in his first law of motion. Galileo had clearly recognized acceleration as a fundamental physical quantity—the law of falling bodies
is that the acceleration of gravity is constant—and thus had provided the conceptual tool for the second law of motion. Newton
rounded out the foundations of mechanics by formulating the third
law of motion. The second notable contribution of Newton was the
discovery that a mathematically simple law of gravitational force
sufficed to derive Kepler's laws from the laws of motion. Kepler's
laws had been formulated with respect to the sun as origin of the
frame of reference. The choice of this frame made possible the
application of the dynamics initiated by Galileo in the construction
of classical celestial mechanics.

Newton unified the mechanical discoveries of his predecessors

---

[20] *Op. cit.*, p. 78.

and contemporaries, partly with conceptual tools that they had fashioned in solving their special problems, and partly with concepts and methods that he developed. In his system of mathematical principles of natural philosophy the laws of statics constituted a limiting case of the laws of motion, and the motions of projectiles and the motions of the heavenly bodies were exhibited as in conformity with the laws of mechanics. In his theory of the properties of fluids he extended the principles of mechanics to continuous media. An analysis of the subjects of the *Principia* shows that they are the special problems which were of military, industrial, and transport interest in the period of the transition from the Middle Ages to the modern era. I do not assert that Newton specifically wrote the *Principia* in order to assist in the solution of problems of technology. It appears to me, however, that the material for his synthesis was derived from the solutions of technical problems in the social context of his predecessors. This is the meaning expressed in the title of B. Hessen's essay, "The Social and Economic Roots of Newton's *Principia*."

Newton's achievement illustrates the fact that once a science is founded it acquires a life of its own. An inner necessity impels it to strive for coherence. In the *Principia* Newton presented a systematic theory for the special mechanical problems solved by his predecessors and himself. He formulated the laws of mechanics that provided the foundation for a unified theory.

IV

In order to demonstrate the influence of social context upon science I have sketched the rise of modern science in a society in transition from feudalism to the capitalism of national states. The basis for science was furnished by inventions of the later Middle Ages such as gunpowder, the compass, and the clock. The scientific achievement of the early modern period was the creation of a mathematical system of mechanics. Galileo's contribution, for example, may be described as a theoretical generalization of the techniques of manufacture and warfare. The relative perfecting of the steam engine by Watt in the second half of the eighteenth century ushered in the Industrial Revolution and provided the stimulus for the development of classical thermodynamics. The steam engine was initially designed to pump water out of mines in England. In 1630 a patent was granted in England to Ramsay for "raising water with the aid of fire from deep mining works." In 1654 Otto van Guericke performed an experiment to demonstrate the pressure of the atmosphere. He exhausted the air from one side of a piston in a cylinder; the pressure of the atmosphere acting on the other side lifted a weight attached to the piston by a rope passing over pulleys. Huygens then attempted to apply this phenomenon in a motive-power engine, and constructed an apparatus in which a vacuum was produced under a piston by the explosion of gunpowder. Papin developed further the application of gunpowder, and then, in 1690, proposed to produce the vacuum by the condensation of steam. Newcomen applied the latter idea in 1712 to the construction of the first cylinder-and-piston engine of which there is any record. In 1711 a Society for Raising Water with the Aid of Fire had been formed for exploiting Newcomen's machine in England.

The steam engine was next used for providing motive power in factories. Attention was then directed toward reducing the cost of operations. Watt greatly improved the steam engine and made it more economical. His patent, taken out in 1769, begins thus: "My method of diminishing the consumption of steam in fire machines, and thus the expenditure of burning material, consists in the following basic propositions." The agreement which Watt and Bolton concluded with the owner of a coal mine provided that they be paid one-third of the saving of the expenditure of fuel accomplished by the use of a Watt engine.

In order to improve the efficiency of the steam engine, Watt investigated the properties of steam in the laboratory of the University of Glasgow, and thereby contributed to the foundations of thermodynamics. It is only fair to state that Watt utilized the results of researches by Joseph Black on specific and latent heats; but he extended the investigations. Carnot's important work on the motive power of fire was undertaken for the purpose of improving the efficiency of the steam engine. His conclusions constituted the first formulation of the second law of thermodynamics. Thus the development of thermodynamics proceeded in company with the problems of the steam engine.

The Industrial Revolution ushered in the machine civilization of the present era. It seems hardly necessary to point out that the increasing demands for energy and materials stimulated mining and thereby geology. The increase in population during the nine-teenth century made necessary improvements in agriculture and stockraising, and thereby stimulated biological research. Today the attempt to achieve national self-sufficiency is a great stimulus to chemistry and biology.

v

We have now examined the function of social context in the rise of modern science. As a test of our conclusions, it will be instructive to review the origins of science in ancient Greece. Theory and practice are alleged to have been separated in antiquity, and hence it might appear that rationalistic and metaphysical motives oper-ated independently of social context. However, as I have indicated in the introduction to this paper, the Greeks inherited fragments of science that were derived from the practical activities of the Babylonians and Egyptians. But the Greek creation itself was conditioned by the social context. Miletus, the seat of the first philosophical school, was a prosperous center of industry and com-merce. Hermann Diels in his book[21] on ancient technology expresses the opinion that the early Ionian philosophers, Thales, Anaximan-der, and Pythagoras, were excellent technologists. Archytas of the Pythagorean school is characterized as the first mathematician who especially developed mechanics scientifically. During the fifth century B.C. there was a development of artillery in the sense of apparatus for shooting arrows or hurling projectiles. Dionysius the Elder had the first effective artillery; it was devised with the aid of mathematical knowledge supplied by the Pythagorean society. Diels expresses the opinion that the scientific development of engines of war by Dionysius saved Sicily and Italy from falling to Carthage in that era. The catapult was used by Alexander, whose engineer Diades devised new engines of war.

The work of Archytas was carried on by Archimedes, who de-signed catapults and other implements of war for the defense of Syracuse. Archimedes represents the fruitful union of theory and practice. In the modern era, problems of the motion of a projectile have called forth the formulation of the laws of motion which have provided the basis of modern physics. The lever was an important part of implements of war in antiquity. It is not surprising that

---

[21] *Antike Technik* (Leipzig and Berlin, Verlag B. G. Teubner, 1920).

the primary contribution of ancient mechanics was Archimedes' theory of the lever. A classic illustration of the contextualist determination of science is furnished by Archimedes' discovery of the principle named after him. He was charged by Hiero to test the genuineness of a gold crown. Archimedes' apparatus consisted of his own body and a bath. The solution of the problem yielded a fundamental principle of hydrostatics.

VI

In order to complete our survey of the contextualist theory of science it is necessary to examine its limitations. In the first place, it must be recognized that philosophical and religious ideas have played a role in the development of science. The thought of the creators of modern science was evidently colored by the ideas of ancient philosophers. Copernicus and Kepler were influenced by Pythagorean doctrines, and Galileo was a Platonist in philosophical outlook. Adapting an expression of G. N. Clark, one may describe the creation of modern science as a process in which the new techniques of the craftsmen were grafted onto the mathematical and philosophical methods inherited from antiquity. The testimony of Burtt to the influence of the metaphysical tradition therefore contributes to a complete picture.

It is of interest to note that Newton was influenced by the religious ideas of his time. In a letter to Bentley he said, "When I wrote the third book of the *Principia,* I paid special attention to those principles which could prove to intellectual people the existence of Divine power." Newton maintained that in no case is it possible to explain the actual path of the planets or creation by natural causes, and that therefore an examination of the structure of the universe demonstrated the presence of an omniscient Divinity. The stability of the universe could only be created by a Divine Mind. Motion is not an inherent attribute of a body, but is produced by an external agency. God is required to give matter its initial momentum. Space is a receptacle with absolute properties and is independent of matter. Newton adopted the view of Henry More that space is the sensorium of God. It appears that Newton's religious ideas played a role in his science, like the Pythagoreanism of Copernicus and Kepler.

It might be contended by the advocates of the contextualist

theory that philosophical and religious ideas are factors in the intellectual atmosphere which is part of the social context. The proponents of historical materialism, according to which economic motives constitute the driving force of history, concede that life is influenced by political, religious and philosophical superstructures.

The doctrine that social needs determine the development of science is limited by some epistemological considerations. I assume it would be agreed that philosophy of science presupposes empiricism in theory of knowledge, at least in the sense that ideas are held to originate in experience. Even the Platonic theory that cognition is reminiscence recognized that recollection must be aroused by sense perception. According to Kant, it is on the occasion of experience that the pure concepts of the understanding become developed. Locke's criticism of the doctrine of innate ideas is correct so far as it implies that the meaning of concepts as distinguished from their validity is to be founded on experience. This acceptance of experience as the source of the content of knowledge presupposes the doctrine that in principle the discovery of fact precedes discernment of utility. In the last analysis, the instrumental function of science is based on causal relations between phenomena that must be observed prior to the appreciation of their value for the prediction and control of natural processes. To be sure, it has been maintained by instrumentalists that human beings institute their relations with the environment by functioning actively, by breathing, eating, drinking, and so forth. Practice thus precedes theory. But action that is determined in the light of consequences must be distinguished from the instinctive responses that maintain the life of the organism. The prevision of ends requires a discernment of relations founded on the analysis and synthesis of perceptions. This argument is supported by a distinction made by A. P. Usher between inventions of perception and of conception.[22]

The thesis that some knowledge must precede purposive action may be illustrated by astronomy. On the contextualist theory, the needs of an agricultural economy stimulated the invention of the calendar. In order that crops should grow to maturity it was necessary to plant in a specific season. A scheme for reckoning time was defined in terms of the positions of celestial objects by priests who made and recorded observations on them. The definition of a time

---

[22] Quoted by J. G. Crowther, *The Social Relations of Science* (New York, Macmillan, 1941).

system provided the basis for the law that crops grow in time under specific conditions. The calendar thus served as a frame of reference relative to which the appropriate times for the beginning of the life process could be designated. Since astronomical observation made possible the improvement of the calendar, astronomy served an economic need.

If one accepts the doctrine that the idea of utility stimulated the search for knowledge, one would expect that the concept of a law of correlation of positions of heavenly bodies and stages of a biological process should be formed prior to observation. But if one views the matter from the standpoint of empiricism, it is probable that the idea of control in terms of a calendar was founded on observations of correlations between positions of the heavenly bodies and biological processes. Crops that had been planted when the sun occupied a specific position in the sky were observed to grow to maturity. Once the idea of the correlation was obtained, it could be investigated for its practical value. Indeed, it came to pass that the calendar was revised in order to secure the invariability of the law of the dependence of growth on the seasons.

It may be argued that the crude observation of a correlation is not yet science, and that discernment of its value for prediction would inspire the refinement of observation characteristic of science. But crude observations of common experience that are made without intent of utilization are indispensable stages in complete scientific experience. The conduct of daily life is founded upon self-evident observations that have evolved from the status of discovery to habitual routine.

That scientific discovery has not been guided entirely by considerations of utility is confirmed by examination of historical discoveries for which all the conditions are known. Roentgen rays are used for discovering pathological tissues and broken bones, for destroying malignant growths in the human organism, and for determining the structure of matter. In view of the social value of this physical agent, the contextualist theory might lead one to entertain the hypothesis that the discovery of the rays was undertaken because medical men needed an instrument of diagnosis and therapy; but this was not the case. The discovery was an unexpected by-product of investigations of electric discharges through gases. Indeed, it has been called accidental. Accidental discoveries of unexpected phenomena demonstrate the absence of social control. Almost immediately after their discovery, the instrumental value of Roentgen rays was discerned and applied. The practical applications undoubtedly stimulated investigation of the phenomena, and to this degree the contextualist interpretation of the history of science is justified.

A developed science exhibits characteristics that can hardly be explained as determined by social demands. As I have remarked in the discussion of Newton's *Principia,* once a science has embarked on its career it acquires a life of its own and appears to be impelled by an inner necessity to strive for systematic coherence. The concepts of the exact sciences have been organized into deductive systems, not because this form is socially useful, but because reason strives to achieve unity in the structure of knowledge. It was of practical value for Archimedes to know the law of the lever in order to design engines of war, but it is difficult to see what contribution to immediate social welfare was made by the deductive theory of the lever. This contention should certainly be conceded by pragmatic philosophers who criticize the Greeks on the ground that they cultivated theory in isolation from practice. In the long run, perfection in the form of knowledge yields developments that are significant for practice, but historically the essential objective in building systems has been the realization of a rational ideal. I may add that J. G. Crowther explains the origin of generalized thinking among the Greeks by the necessity for persuasion in an equalitarian community. He views deductive proof as the systematization of the method of verbal argument by which one free man tries to change the opinion of another.[23]

It is difficult to explain the creation of constructive theories in terms of social needs. The purpose of such theories is to satisfy a rational demand for explanation. Meyerson especially has demonstrated that we not only predict phenomena with the aid of laws, but also explain in terms of a principle of identity. One may readily attribute an interest in macrophysical laws to the purpose of controlling phenomena, but this motive does not account for the original interest in the reduction of macrophysical laws to microphysical ones. Atomic theories, which explain phenomena in terms of the union and separation of entities that continue self-identical

---

[23] *Op. cit.*

in time, satisfy the rational demand that substance be conserved. Such theories were created by the Greeks for explanation instead of action. Contemporary microphysical theories are certainly of value for the prediction and control of phenomena, but I am confident that the driving force of creative minds in this modern field has been theoretical explanation.

The scientific interest in theoretical construction may be partly an expression of a spirit of play. Devotees of science often view it as a game that is played in accordance with rules. The dawn of modern science was characterized by mathematical tournaments and challenges to competition. Scientific apparatus has frequently been devised to serve as a toy. The steam turbine described by Hero of Alexandria was such a toy; on account of the aristocratic disdain for technology and the plentiful supply of slave labor in antiquity, the economic possibilities of this instrument of entertainment were not developed. The gyroscope was demonstrated for its entertaining behavior prior to the recognition of its great value for military and maritime purposes. It is beyond the scope of this paper to present a psychology of play, but the recreational aspect of some scientific inventions testifies to the existence of impulses to science that only by an extension of meaning may be called social. On behalf of the contextualist theory, however, it may be argued that prospects of utility are necessary to develop the full possibilities of the results of the playful activities of the scientist.

The preceding discussion has set forth the limitations of the doctrine that science is determined by social context. It is a historical fact that many developments in science have occurred without stimulus from practice. The decisive test of intellectual curiosity as a driving force of science is the existence of disciplines that are content to record the past and do not presume to predict the future from laws. The concern with the history of the remote past can be explained only as the expression of an interest in the panorama of history. Archeological investigations of the sites of Sumerian civilization of six thousand years ago could only with difficulty be justified in terms of their contributions to the welfare of society as it is usually conceived. The interest in such studies ultimately is to be explained in terms of the appreciation of knowledge as an intrinsic value. The deepest motive of science is the enhancement of man's sense of wonder concerning the environment in which he lives.

The disinterested cultivation of knowledge frequently yields unexpected results of social value. The best method of solving a vital problem may be found as an unexpected by-product of researches that have not been directed toward that end. Who could have imagined in antiquity that artificial illumination could be improved by investigating the properties of a piece of rubbed amber? Hence, even if one values science for its utility, long-range concern for the welfare of society should encourage disinterested inquiry. The creative activity of nature outstrips the imagination of man.

To conclude: The contextualist theory of the origin and development of science has focused attention on factors in the social environment that have not always been adequately studied. However, one must acknowledge the impetus to discovery that flows from the sense of wonder, the need to explain, the demand for unity. The development of science is molded primarily by the technical problems originating in the economic and social problems of its environment.

In broad outlines the history of science exhibits an interaction between observation and action, between description and prescription, between theory and practice. Primitive observation, whether incidental to response to an environment or intentional, furnishes the basis for primitive description and practice. The requirements of practice stimulate observations that provide a basis for the refinement and development of the concepts employed. The technique of practice itself calls for conceptual analysis and thereby inspires theory. The theoretical interest yields explanation and unification. The impulse toward theory feeds on itself; indeed, theory may become almost dissociated from practice. In the long run, the perfecting of theory is likely to yield material as well as spiritual benefits. As N. I. Bukharin has remarked, "Great practice requires great theory."[24] But in the last analysis the impetus to science comes not merely from man's efforts to adjust himself to his material and social context, but from the urge to survey that context throughout its extent in space and time.

---

[24] "Theory and Practice from the Standpoint of Dialectical Materialism," in *Science at the Cross Roads*, p. 21.

STEPHEN C. PEPPER

THE CONDITIONS OF SOCIAL CONTROL

To LISTEN to some people, one would imagine that the actions of society were haphazard and as unpredictable as the throws of dice. Every historical event, we are told, is unique. History never repeats itself. One event emerges from another, each new-born and without heredity, in successive redirections in which there is no direction.

Reflecting on such utter social and historical skepticism, one marvels that he can count on receiving his mail next day, getting his salary check next month, finding his dividend check next quarter, getting his income-tax blank at the beginning of the year, voting for his President the next fourth year, or appealing to the Constitution as the supreme law of the land for another decade.

Certainly, tomorrow there may be an earthquake disrupting the mail service, or a fire destroying a factory and resulting in a passed dividend, or a collision of the earth with some stellar body wiping out the human race and the American Constitution. These things might happen. Nevertheless, I do surely predict the receipt of my mail, salary check, dividend check, income-tax blank, and the rest of these social occurrences with as much confidence as I predict most of the physical occurrences of my environment about which this high skepticism is now rather antiquated and ridiculous. Actually we see, if we look around us, that there is about as much control of social events as of physical events, for the very good reason that all our practical predictions of physical events are made with a view to the control of social events. What else is the significance of engineering, agriculture, and medicine?

Pessimism regarding social prediction and control is not seriously a denial of its occurrence, but disappointment over its extent. Men wish there were more of it. In this paper I shall briefly survey the extent of present social prediction and control and the prospects for its greater extension. Control is, of course, not the same as prediction. A war may be predicted and yet be beyond control. But the two are closely related, since all control depends upon prediction, and where there is prediction some degree of control is generally available. By prediction I mean a warrantable statement about future events based on evidence; by control, the application of predictions to the attainment of human purposes.

What, then, is the extent of our powers of social prediction?

For convenience, let us arrange them in three levels. (A) First, we have what we may call the natural-science level. All the regularities of physics, chemistry, and biology are at society's disposal, and are systematically prepared for social utilization in the applied sciences of engineering, agriculture, and medicine. (B) Second, there are the regularities of individual behavior. These are not so fully systematized as those of the A level, but many of them are dependable. They are scattered through the techniques of various professions and employed in such services and institutions as schools, conservatories, journalistic enterprises, the movies, publicity services, salesmanship, industrial efficiency, social welfare, psychiatry, criminology. All these techniques for influencing or handling men have various degrees of reliability, and most of them go back to regularities which it is the task of psychology to systematize. We may call this the psychological level. (C) Third, there are regularities which apply to social groups. We may call this last the sociological-ethical level.

It appears from this classification that the main issue over social control arises in the sociological-ethical level. No one seriously questions the existence of what I have called the natural-science and psychological regularities of the A and B levels, and consequently no one seriously questions the possibility of controlling social actions by means of these laws and techniques. What is often seriously questioned is the possibility of any further control along the lines of level C regularities. This question is serious because unless there is control, or at least prediction, of the course of activity of social groups as wholes, our control of activities by A- and B-level regularities may be largely wasted. To possess the engineering formulas for the planning of powerful battleships, and to have the educational techniques for training men and the efficiency techniques for organizing them into shops and yards for the rapid production of such ships, means little in the end if the end is to plunge human society into disaster and misery. The serious question is not whether we can control social activities—of course we can!—but whether we can control them as a whole.

There seem to be three types of theories regarding the possibility of the control of society as a whole: First, the sort of theory which affirms either that the behavior of a society is a resultant of A-level and B-level regularities, and that from a sufficient knowledge of these regularities we could predict the course of social behavior as a whole; or that in social behavior there are emergent laws dependent upon and therefore controllable by the lower-level (A and B) regularities but not as resultants. Let us call this sort of theory, in either the resultant or emergent form, the functional theory of social control. It asserts that group behavior is a function of individual behavior. The group behavior may be directly predictable from the properties of individual behavior as a resultant—which would be the extreme mechanistic view; or the group behavior may be an emergent law with properties unpredictable from individual behavior but nevertheless correlated with individual behavior and controllable through it—which would be the emergent view. Both these views agree in the basic mechanistic assumption that social behavior is controllable through individual behavior.

Second, there is the sort of theory which holds that there are distinct social laws independent of individual behavior. Not that society is not composed of individuals, nor social behavior not made up of individual behavior; but that a law directly determines the course of society either by supervening upon individual acts or by operating in partial independence of them. We may call this sort of theory social determinism. By this theory, social events should be predictable. As to control, that would depend on the law; but some degree of control might be possible, as we shall see presently.

Third, there is the sort of theory which maintains that there are certain social or ethical ideals which should be striven for, and that a society may be controlled by inducing it as a whole or through its members toward the realization of these ideals. We may call this the exhortational theory of social control.

I find that the evidence for these theories weakens as we proceed. The probability that there are social regularities as resultants or emergents from level-A and level-B regularities seems very great on the analogy of similar regularities accepted within the lower levels. In chemistry there is great confidence in regularities of the properties of compounds, based on regularities of the properties of components. This sort of confidence runs right up through the natural and biological sciences. If there is knowledge of the regularities of the components of a whole, there is reason to anticipate regularities in the properties of the whole. Whether these regularities of the whole can be predicted from the properties of the components is a secondary matter. But if we have complete or partial control of the parts, we expect to have a proportionate control of a whole composed of such parts, even though the regularities of the whole are unexpected and therefore emergent in respect to the properties of the parts. This anticipation has been so often confirmed in sciences where such control is attainable that it may be set up as a general hypothesis with a high degree of probability. Applied to social behavior, it means that, so far as we are assured of natural and psychological regularities as components of social behavior, we have good reason to expect some regularities of general social behavior correlated with these components. The probability, therefore, of some degree of social control through functional laws of social behavior seems very great.

There is also a degree of anterior probability for the theory of social determinism. The line between an emergent law and a formal law such as is presupposed by any common type of social determinism is not an easy one to make in practice. The difference can, however, be clearly defined. An emergent law is one in which the properties of the higher-level regularity are directly, and, if there are quantitative factors, quantitatively, correlated with the properties of the lower-level constituent regularities. Thus in the vector law of composition of forces in mechanics the direction and quantity of the resultant force is directly correlated with the directions and quantities of the component forces, and in chemistry allotropes such as diamond and graphite are correlated with different degrees of energy content. But a formal law is one in which the properties of the higher-level regularity are not directly correlated with the properties of the constituent regularities. Within certain limits, a formal law is said to hold—that is, its properties are regarded as fixed—irrespective of modifications of properties occurring in the materials in which it holds.

Biology seems to offer us abundant illustrations of such formal laws in the laws of growth for the various biological species. Every individual peach tree is different from every other, but the stages of growth of a peach tree from the sprouting stone to the bearing of mature fruit is a law which holds of the species irrespective of accidents or peculiarities in each particular tree. The mechanist tends to interpret this law as a statistical resultant or emergent from physicochemical regularities. The formist, however, interprets it as a fixed law of normal growth for the species and explains the variations as due to the interference of other laws or to accidents. He carries the same interpretation down into physical and chemical laws, so that what is involved is in part an issue over the interpretation of scientific results, but in part also a matter of direct evidence concerning the probability of the special operation of such laws. In the social-deterministic theories that we shall consider, the question rests mainly on a judgment of direct evidence regarding the probability of a destiny for society indicated by such laws. All I wish to point out at this moment is that there is a certain antecedent probability for the existence of such laws or, at least, for the interpretation of laws in this sense, and consequently a possibility of social prediction and even control by means of them.

But as for the exhortational theory of social control, there is no analogy in any other fields of inquiry, so that there is no antecedent probability whatever for its validity. On the contrary, there is definite improbability.

It is not even easy to state the exhortational theory clearly, despite the fact that it appears frequently in our cultural thought and literature. The underlying idea seems to be that certain individual or social ideals are real in some ultimate sense, and that men may attain or approach them, and that in proportion as they are attained society can be relied upon to run smoothly, and that men should be persuaded or compelled to seek them. The crux of this theory obviously lies in the reality of the perfectionizing ideals. In one common form the perfect ideal is conceived as an ideal social structure, a perfect state. Men are to be exhorted to attain this state, with the assurance that once this state is attained all will be well. The difficulty is, whence this assurance. If it is an empirical assurance, this theory resolves itself into the functional or social-deterministic theories—that is, the ideal resolves itself into a hypothesis of social control based upon observed regularities of social behavior. But if it is not an empirical assurance, then it must be authoritarian, *a priori*, or fictitious—that is to say, in one word, fictitious. For there seems to be plenty of evidence today to discredit purely authoritarian or *a priori* claims to matters of fact.

Sometimes it is insinuated by exhortational theories that only if there is a gap between the empirical world and ideals can there be any ideals, and that an empirical theory of social control implies the denial of the reality of ideals. This is, of course, preposterous, for the reality of credible ideals can only be established (apart from the rejected methods of supernatural authority and *a priori* asseveration) by empirical methods. No one dreams of appealing to supernatural or *a priori* authority for the description of an ideal automobile, violin player, baseball team, office force, or city management. Why, then, of an ideal society? What may be the status of a credible ideal is an arguable question, but arguable only on the basis of evidence, never of fiction. It is no recommendation for an ideal that there is no evidence for it—though people often talk as if it were. They often talk as if faith itself could establish an ideal; whence exhortation becomes very necesary indeed, for the less the evidence the greater the need of emotional persuasion.

But if to exhortation is added social compulsion through hope and fear and other well-known empirical means, then it can no longer be said that the society is being controlled by the aspiration for ideals at all. Certainly, arousing hope through depiction of glowing ideals is one of the regular empirical means of influencing and to some degree controlling the social actions of men. And another way is to threaten men if they falter in their beliefs. But the control in these instances is not literally through the ideals (which are generally fictitious), but through the empirical psychological agencies of the emotions and their stimuli.

Thus either the exhortation theory boils down to propaganda, which is certainly empirical enough but not on the level supposed, or it resolves itself into the search for empirical social laws of kinds already described. I shall maintain that there is no evidence for the exhortation theory of social control, widespread though it is both in pure and in various adulterated forms.

We turn now to the theory of social determinism. We are dealing here with a frankly empirical theory, so that we do not have to be concerned with the legitimacy of the basis for the theory. The questions we shall have to ask are, first, whether social control is possible under such a theory (for prediction is possible by definition as soon as the law is known), and, second, whether there is adequate evidence to give us any great confidence in the theory.

There are many varieties of this theory. Some evolutionary views, such perhaps as Comte's or Spencer's, suggest a social-deterministic motive. Hegelian theories of progress through a dialectical movement are social-deterministic. And so also are all social theories stated in terms of Aristotelian or Platonic forms. How rigidly a social-deterministic law will be applied to society for predictive purposes will depend partly on the theory, partly on the evidence. It should ultimately, of course, depend entirely on the evidence. If it is not rigidly applied, such a law is very difficult to distinguish in practice from an emergent law for which the lower-level correlates are only imperfectly known. For clean-cut illustrations, therefore, we should examine men who are exponents of a rigid social determinism. For this purpose I suggest Spengler in his conception of cultural cycles and the Marxians in their conception of dialectical materialism.

Spengler in his *Decline of the West* is quite unambiguous in his method and predictions and consequently the better man to begin with. He calls the operation of the social law "destiny," and contrasts it with causality, which he regards as a natural-science concept of no importance in social prediction. Destiny is the inevitable cycle of stages which a culture must pass through. He constantly refers to the life cycles of plants and animals by way of empirical analogy. As man has his inevitable cycle of infancy, youth, maturity, age, and death, so "every Culture," he writes, "every adolescence and maturing and decay of a Culture, every one of its necessary stages and periods, has a definite duration, always the same, always recurring with the emphasis of a symbol. . . . As the plant's being is brought to expression in form, dress and carriage by leaves, blossoms, twigs and fruit, so also is the being of a culture manifested by its religious, intellectual, political and economic functions."[1]

Spengler elaborates upon the stages of a cultural cycle. There is first the patriarchal or feudal stage, highly religious, "rural intuitive," with a vigorous primitive art; second, there comes an aristocratic stage, class-conscious, absolutistic, with urban and critical stirrings, and a matured flowering of art in "the Great Masters";

---

[1] *The Decline of the West*, trans. by C. F. Atkinson (New York, Knopf, 1926; 2 vols.), Vol. I, pp. 109–110.

third, a democratic stage, governed by the masses who are dominated by money, in which economic powers permeate political forms and authorities, and in which great cities develop with outlying provinces, and art is exhausted of creativeness and oppressed with art problems, but in which there is great intellectual creativeness and much work in mathematics and philosophical system-building; finally, the dictatorship stage, Caesarism, in which force is victorious over money, leading toward an inward decline of nations into formless populations held together by an imperial machinery of gradually increasing crudity of despotism, followed by a gradual enfeeblement and breaking down of the imperial machinery under pressure of "young peoples eager for spoil." After that the culture cycle begins anew.

For evidence of the operation of this cycle Spengler amasses quantities of material from the history of art, religion, economics, and politics and spreads it out in vast parallelisms to demonstrate the existence of a number of these culture cycles within the period of recorded history. There is an Asiatic Indian and also a Chinese culture cycle, but those upon which he spends most time are the Egyptian (2900–1205 B.C.), Classical (1100 B.C.–300 A.D.), Magian or Arabian (1–1000 A.D.), and Western (900 A.D. on). Within this final Western culture we are ourselves caught in the last declining stage.

So far as he establishes his culture cycle, predictions are easily made. As he points out,[2] we can not only predict our yet unfulfilled social destiny, but we can reconstruct the history of cultures the archeological and literary remains of which are fragmentary, just as a paleontologist can reconstruct a prehistoric animal from a few bones. He takes, however, a very fatalistic view of our human powers of control over society as a result of the inevitability of the cyclic stages. His great book ends with these lugubrious words: "For us, however, whom a Destiny has placed in this Culture and at this moment of its development—a moment when money is celebrating its last victories, and the Caesarism which is to succeed approaches with quiet, firm step—our direction, willed and obligatory at once, is set for us within narrow limits, and on any other terms life is not worth living. We have not the freedom to reach to this or to that, but the freedom to do the necessary or to do nothing.

---

[2] *The Decline of the West*, Vol. I, p. 113.

And a task that historic necessity has set, *will* be accomplished with the individual or against him."[3]

We shall for the moment accept his evidence for a rigid culture cycle. Let us within this limitation inquire whether on his own evidence so submissive an attitude toward destiny as this last quotation demands is required—whether some degree of human control is not possible and profitable. First, let us suppose that nothing can be done about altering the culture cycle; it would still seem, on his evidence, that we could do a good deal about ordering our individual and social lives within the limits of our destiny. If the cycle exists, we as reasonable men should obviously control our individual lives and our social actions to conform to its successive stages just as we all individually adjust our lives to the stages of the individual life cycle. A man of fifty may wish occasionally that he had the characteristic properties of the age of twenty, but he does not literally try to be twenty; he prepares to be fifty-five. We should do the same if we were as convinced of a cultural cycle as we are of our own life cycle. Moreover, on Spengler's own evidence every stage but the last one has its amenities. Even this last might be enjoyed if we should adjust to it and enter into the pomp and power of Caesarism or watch the stirrings of the "young peoples eager for spoil" who are harbingers of the new cultural cycle about to begin. We should, after all, be in the worst of it and should know that it will be better for our children or grandchildren inevitably, and that all we have to do is to bear it out as anyone would do if caught in a storm. Some of us might even gloat about it, as Spengler quite obviously does, repeating "How tragic! How tragic!" So even the declining stage of the culture cycle has its amenities.

A great deal of individual control would therefore be possible within a rigid cycle. And similarly there would be control of social policy. For clearly, if we had confidence in Spengler's cycle, we should not be vainly attempting to preserve our democracies which are nearly over now, but should be preparing for Caesarism as the next stage and arranging conditions for a dictator of our own if we could make one, or bracing ourselves to submit to an outsider if we could not.

But why, on Spengler's own evidence, should we not go farther and see if we cannot control the cycle itself? The last stage is

---

[3] *Ibid.*, Vol. II, p. 507.

apparently the objectionable one. The first three stages have each their respective cultural glories in religion, art, and knowledge. Then let us bend our efforts to shorten or avoid the last, declining stage. That a stage may be altered in its period and activity Spengler makes perhaps unwittingly clear in his treatment of the Arabian culture, which was "cheated of its maturity," he says, "like a young tree that is hindered and stunted in its growth by a fallen old giant of the forest."[4] The giant was Rome in the declining stage of the Classical culture, which held the Arabian culture in check for several centuries so that in one century alone of intense Arabian expansion there was "compressed the whole sum of passions, postponed hopes, reserved deeds, that in the slow maturing of other Cultures suffice to fill the history of centuries."[5]

If one culture cycle can modify another in this way, many possibilities of control of a culture cycle begin to dawn upon us. May we not modify a cycle by directing one cycle upon another? In the instance cited, the younger culture was nearly cheated of one whole stage by the older. The outcome might by chance have been reversed. The Classical culture might have been cheated of its final stage instead of the Arabian culture of its mature stage. Trees often die before completing their life cycle. Young animals in nature often kill old animals that get in their way. If the last declining stage of a culture is objectionable, shorten it or dispense with it by directing it across a younger culture and having everybody step off the older culture and onto the newer one. Had the Romans known Spengler's law, they could have abandoned their old decaying culture and stepped onto the vigorous growing one, as three hundred years later they stepped off the end of the Classical culture and onto the beginning of the Western in the normal course of Spengler's events. For there is this difference between a plant and a social culture: the cells of a dead plant rot and perish with the death of the plant, but the individuals of a culture go on living in another culture when a culture dies. So, there is really no tragedy in the death of a culture so far as individuals are concerned; nor so far as a culture is concerned either, unless a culture has a consciousness of its own, which Spengler never asserts. So obviously the thing to do is to kill off one's culture before the last stage and get onto a fresh young one. Here is a formula for eternal cultural youth.

---

[4] *Ibid.*, Vol. I, p. 212.   [5] *Ibid.*, p. 213.

If Spengler objects that the cultural forces are too strong to be controlled in this way, the onus of proof is on him. We ask why not? If men do not like the last stage, if they know the law of the cycle, if they know how the cycle can be modified, what is to stop them from modifying it? The knowledge of the law itself is a force.

The basic point, of course, is that we are not convinced of the law. The evidence he presents is insufficient and too selective, and bears too much the stamp of a single man's bias under the strain of a single set of influences in a single nation in a single century. It is eloquent of the German state of mind in the early twentieth century—the drive for power and the secret sense of its futility. His evidence is insufficient to demonstrate his law of social determinism for all men.

Much the same may be said of the Marxian law of social determinism—the inevitable sequence of social states from the slave state, to the feudal, to the bourgeois, to the dictatorship of the proletariat, to the ultimate communistic utopia. There are two sides to the Marxian argument: the one side, a detailed criticism of the capitalistic economy and its social consequences and causes; the other, a statement of a law of social determinism. The two are inconsistent with each other, for the critical analysis is in terms of resultant regularities. Such and such interests (low-level regularities) lead to such and such social resultants. The conflict of labor and capital results in consolidations in each, which accentuates the conflict and results in further consolidations. Extrapolating from these resultants, it is possible to predict a breaking point which will bring into society a new force—a dictator. For some reason, probably bias for the labor interests, this dictator was predicted to be a labor dictator; for the same causes indicated the equal possibility of a capitalistic dictator. Events in recent years have verified the prediction that dictatorships were imminent in the conditions. But this prediction was based on a realistic study of human interests and depended upon a belief in the constancy or regularity in human behavior which is colloquially called human nature. Psychological regularities were such, human nature was such, that the conflicts of interests must necessarily lead to a breaking point under capitalistic conditions; whence the inference to a dictatorship. But when the Marxians come to predicting the eventual utopian state of communism, in which men will be so well adjusted to their special duties in the complex economy of the state that no strong power from above will any longer be necessary and every man will do his part voluntarily, they must abandon their belief in the constancy of human behavior and argue for an amazing amount of modifiability—no less than would convert human nature into something like an ant. It is at this point that the Marxians appeal to their law of social determinism, through which they predict the inevitable coming of the last, harmonious state of society, whatever the present nature of human beings may be.

There is thus actually less evidence for the Marxian law of social determinism than for Spengler's. For Spengler adduces many instances of his complete social cycle, while there has never been an instance of Marxian communism, and our knowledge of human nature which the Marxians so astutely employ in their negative criticisms is such that their communistic man would be impossible. For Spengler's law there is only insufficient evidence, but against the Marxian law there is direct contrary evidence, since from such knowledge of psychological regularities as we do possess we may definitely predict that the communistic state will not exist. Man is not so far modifiable. And if he were, why wait for communism? Why go through the miseries of the revolution and the miseries of the dictatorship of the proletariat? Why not modify men at once to contentment in the capitalistic system! Their only answer, of course, is that certain *basic* interests cannot be satisfied.

As a parting shot at theories of social determinism, I cannot forbear pointing out that the Spenglerian and Marxian laws of social determinism are inconsistent with each other, so that whatever evidence there is for each is evidence against the other.

It would be going too far to say that there are no laws of social determinism, but we may safely say that we know none sufficiently well evidenced to be taken as bases for either individual or social policy, prediction, or control.

When we turn to resultant or emergent functional laws, we are better rewarded. I wish to call attention to five such laws, so well evidenced that a great deal of social control goes on in terms of them in the various modern societies.

They are the economic law of supply and demand, the system of social techniques known as centralized government or centralized management, the system of social techniques known as representative government and parliamentary procedure, the law of satisfaction of interests in its social bearing which I shall call the ethics of freedom, and the law of biological evolution in its application to societies, which I shall call the ethics of security.

The law of supply and demand I merely mention in order that we may be reminded of its limitations. I believe there is evidence enough in economics to regard this as a genuine resultant law based on the operation of the acquisitive interests. It states roughly a functional relationship among supply, demand, and price as follows: $SP/D = $ const. But it holds only under conditions of free competition, and where no other interests but the acquisitive are involved. Where these conditions are lacking, the law does not hold.

It was the basis of the hope for a *laissez-faire* utopia, the idea of which was that if the acquisitive interests were given free play the production of goods would be automatically controlled by the demand for them, to the maximum benefit of society and individuals. The simple principle of social control was to provide for a minimum of government, just so much government as would be an adequate check to attempts at government interference—the principle of "government out of business." But the experience of the nineteenth century, when this principle was tried out as completely as possible in Europe and America, has shown that the acquisitive interests themselves consolidate into monopolies and labor unions which cannot be held in check except by a powerful central government which is driven to a degree of regulation that completely neutralizes the automatic working of the law. That is to say, laws of social organization combine with the law of supply and demand to produce a result that throws society as a whole completely out of control unless a central government again takes control in terms of these very laws of social organization which interfere with the free action of supply and demand. The hypothesis of a *laissez-faire* utopia conceived the problem of social control in much too simple terms, and this error has been experimentally demonstrated in the social experience of the last century.

The social laws neglected by this hypothesis were those of social organization, the techniques of centralized organization and representative organization, especially the great power of the former in the guise of business management. The extreme example of the centralized organization, however, is the military structure of stratified commands. Examples of representative organization are familiar to all of us in any parliamentary institution, with its methods of electing representative delegates and the methods of decision by voting. It is not sufficiently recognized that these two forms of organization actually constitute resultant social laws or regularities. Under the conditions of the institution of these forms of organization certain types of social action can be predicted. It is precisely because predictions can be made through these social organizations that they are instituted for social control. For instance, it can with high probability be predicted from a well-established centralized organization that an order given at the top will be executed at the bottom. And from a well-established representative organization it can be predicted that the arbitrary will of no one man or small group of men will result in general social action without the persuasion of a majority in the representative group authorized to act for the society as a whole. If these forms of organization did not act as social laws from which probable predictions could be made, they would be useless techniques. They are the result of long social experience, and are resultants of many psychological regularities of behavior summarized as discipline or tolerance.

It should also be noticed that these two resultant social laws in their application as social techniques are opposed in their social action. The centralized technique is a way by which the will of one man or a small group of men may be quickly and effectively executed in general social behavior. The representative or decentralized technique is a way in which it may be guaranteed that precisely this will not happen and that only those acts will be executed which are, in a complicated sense, the desire of the whole social body. The one is a social technique for drive, the other for restraint. If the two are combined, the one works as a social engine, the other as a social brake.

The two in practice generally are combined in some degree. Even a very highly centralized organization generally has advisory councils in which the representative form is employed in principle. And a decentralized organization from which any considerable action was expected could not function without a subsidiary executive organization based on the centralized form.

We have, therefore, in the combination of these two techniques of organization a remarkably flexible and effective potential instrument for social control. Like mechanical parts, they can be put together in a variety of ways to achieve a variety of results. If we want society to go fast, we will put in mainly centralized techniques. If we want to slow it up, or loosen it up for the freer independent actions of the constituent parts, we put in mainly decentralized techniques.

Within certain psychological limits—for it takes a certain time to train men or educate them into these techniques, and there are also limits beyond which both discipline and freedom will not work—it would appear that by means of a skillful distribution of these two techniques, one as a drive, the other as a brake, men could have about anything they wanted in the way of social structure and action. Society, in other words, is highly controllable, and we have the whole requisite range of techniques for controlling it.

Why, then, are we still disturbed about social control, with an ear for dubious Spenglerian and Marxian destinies? Why do we listen to such fantastic prognostications, when we have well-evidenced predictive techniques right in our own hands, which we use every day, and need only to use more intelligently, it would seem, to direct society where we will, almost as surely as we direct our car with accelerator and brake?

The answer seems to be, "Because we don't know where to go." Spengler and Marx are attractive to our age chiefly because they settle that question. They offer us a destiny which we can accept, bitter though the prospect is—for the one tells us we are in for a decline, and the other that we are in for a revolution and a dictatorship, and amazingly some of us immediately start using the empirical techniques of organization which we have found to be actually effective in prediction to plunge society toward these ends, which we do not want. Why not use these techniques of control to get us to ends that we do want?

Well, what do we want? Are there any regularities or probable hypotheses from which we can predict human ends or social aims? Anything empirical we can rely upon in these regards?

There is. And, here again, they are so familiar and close at hand that we do not notice how important they are or how they can be integrated with the social techniques of which we were just speaking.

One of these regularities is that men desire the satisfaction of their interests. This is so highly attested that it is taken as almost axiomatic. It spontaneously develops into the hypothesis that the aim of society is the maximum possible satisfaction of human interests. This hypothesis has a long history under the names of hedonism, utilitarianism, and interest ethics, which differ with respect to a variety of minor issues but are well agreed on the main principles. The general hypothesis may be called the ethics of freedom, since its aim is consistently to free individuals for the attainment of as much satisfaction as possible. It is a systematization of the nature and kinds of human interests, their ways of combining which tend to increase or decrease the total satisfaction, and a description of various techniques which may be expected to increase total satisfaction. This ethical system has a strong affinity for the decentralized form of social organization, since this form tends to increase the range of individual freedom.

But another regularity that bears on the problem of social ends is the biological law of evolution in its application to social survival. It is clear that the law applies to societies as well as to individuals of a species. The two are not altogether separable. The structure of a society is to a large degree (perhaps entirely) a resultant of the structure and consequent potentialities of behavior of the individual. So far as a society is stronger than an individual, those individuals who have characteristics which result in effective social behavior will tend to survive in competition with unsocial individuals. The same process continues with respect to types of social structure. The stronger the society in competition with other societies, the greater its chance of survival. And this social competition reflects back on the individuals within the societies, since those individuals who are so constituted as to produce the stronger society will tend to survive as against individuals otherwise constituted. Unsocial individuals in terms of the stronger social structure will find themselves in precarious situations. This biological drive for survival thus pushes right up into societies and makes itself felt there irrespective of the interests of individuals, and determines another empirical social aim, namely, social survival.

This aim has exhibited itself in another ethical system with a long history. It is the ethics of duty, loyalty, conscience, reverence for the law, rationality, organic structure. It also has many varieties and is, as we might expect from its rather hidden origin, rather uncertain about its aim. It tends to identify its aim with supernatural authority or *a priori* truth, and often deteriorates into an exhortational theory. But there is a system of empirical material in this type of ethics which is fairly well agreed upon and could be still more effectively ordered if the underlying aim of the ethics were brought out into the open. It may be called the ethics of security, since its aim is to integrate the individual into a social organization which will be strong enough to make him secure against the dangers of social competition. It consists in a set of empirical observations on the dangers of self-indulgence, the techniques of discipline, and the integration of desires, and hypotheses regarding effective and secure forms of social organization. It has an affinity for the centralized form of social organization, since this is the form conducive to a swift and firm concentration of power for social action either for attack or defense.

Now these two empirical social aims—the one based solidly on the psychology of individual behavior, the other quite as solidly on the social application of the biological law of evolution—are directly opposed to each other. This opposition does not limit itself to the relations between nations; it appears equally in the relations of groups within the large political units—in industrial and labor groups, educational groups, social groups, art groups, and families—though it comes to a special head in the political groups having control of the ultimate instruments of social force such as armies, navies, and police.

When we talk about lack of social control, it is the apparently fortuitous operation of these conflicting aims in social history that we have in mind. For, as we have seen, we have all the social means necessary to get what we want, but we cannot seem to want what we want. Does this, then, represent the limit of social control? Must we leave social ends to chance, catch the drifts of social movements whatever these may be, and organize our societies to make the best of them? Since our earlier examination gives us no confidence in the social-deterministic hypotheses about social trends, must we conceive these trends as fortuitous, unpredictable, and uncontrollable? Are there no better-evidenced hypotheses for the control of social ends?

I believe there is one, an empirical hypothesis of the resultant type. It is a statement of a law regarding the interplay of the two kinds of social aims—interest value and survival value—which we have just described. These may be brought together through the mediation of a concept which I shall call social pressure. By social pressure I mean the total amount of frustration of satisfactions endured by the individuals of a social group. The pressure may de due to environmental agencies such as inadequate food supply and neighboring competing societies, or it may be due to internal friction between individuals or between subordinate groups within the society. The hypothesis is that, on the one hand, with increasing pressure the society tends to centralize and assume the properties of a security ethics. Failure to do so threatens the survival of the society and, in the long run, that of its members. In other words, in the long run, social pressure through the agency of a security ethics and its centralized forms of organization tends to eliminate unsocial interests and the kinds of individuals who inherently embody them. Survival value thus periodically takes precedence over interest value by eliminating individuals of a type not conducive to the survival of the society as a whole. On the other hand, with decreasing pressure, the society tends to decentralize and assume the properties of a freedom ethics. Failure to decentralize in proportion to a decreasing pressure produces what may be called an artificial pressure, which leads to revolts which in turn may so disrupt a society as to produce an actual condition of increasing pressure, whence the cycle commences again.

On the basis of this hypothesis, it is possible to make rough predictions, and we apparently do so. We hear such predictions daily—that the United States must centralize under war pressure or run the risk of perishing, and that freedom will consequently be restricted; that if the totalitarian governments win they must moderate their forms of government or face revolts and disruption; that the totalitarians expect to forestall these revolts by keeping the working populations at just the level of comfort where revolt will not be worth while; that the days of small nations are over, since these lack the power to survive.

In proportion to our confidence in such predictions we should have confidence in the possibility of social control in terms of the laws by which the predictions can be made. We seem to have considerable confidence in such predictions, and well we may, for they appear to be based in a law which combines the empirical observations of two long-tried and opposed ethical hypotheses. The desirable social aim on the basis of this law may be condensed into the maxim, Make your social organization conform to the social pressure. That means centralize when the pressure increases, accepting as far as necessary the characteristics of the security ethics; decentralize when the pressure decreases, taking on as much as possible of the characteristics of the ethics of freedom. What we gain by such control is riddance from all unnecessary frustrations arising from a belated acceptance of change in either direction or from excessive swings from one pole of social organization to the other. The aim may accordingly be even more briefly stated: Keep the social pressure down to a minimum.

GEORGE P. ADAMS

THE IDEA OF CIVILIZATION

IT IS impossible, under present circumstances, to reflect on the theme of civilization without constantly keeping in the focus of our minds the haunting sense of the tragedy which has engulfed our own world. In one sense, not to be forgotten, the present war is a civil war. The peoples of western Europe, Englishmen, Germans, Frenchmen, and Italians, belong to the stream of European civilization. This central fact is brought home to our minds by the following words of Tawney: "The societies composing Europe are in varying degrees the heirs of the first great age of western civilization; nor was the partnership dissolved when that age was wound up. Greek philosophy and literature, Roman law; the long adventure of Christian missionaries; the medieval church; feudalism; the Renaissance, the Reformation and Counter Reformation; the Revolution—all these and much else have directly or indirectly set their stamp on all. Different countries have reacted differently to the great crises of European history; but all have reacted to them. Their religion, their literature and art, their science, their economic systems are a cosmopolitan creation, to which all have contributed and all are in debt. Such things, it is true, do not in themselves create unity, but they create the conditions of it. They cause Europe, amid all its feverish jealousies and terrors, to be a single civilization, as a contentious family is still a family, and a bad state remains a state. They make its culture one, its crimes domestic tragedies, its wars civil wars."[1] The betrayal of this common heritage of European civilization, from whatever quarter it may have sprung, has come from within. Western civilization is not being assailed from without, and, if it perishes, it will be because of some fatal internal malady and disruption.

Toynbee, in his monumental history, has arrived at the conclusion that, in fourteen of the sixteen historical, individual civilizations which have perished, the end has come as a result of internecine warfare between states, "in which a single surviving state is left staggering, half dead, among the corpses of its fellow combatants."[2]

---

[1] Introduction by R. H. Tawney to J. P. Mayer and others, *Political Thought: The European Tradition* (New York, Viking Press, 1939), pp. xii–xiii.

[2] Written in 1938.

But what is to be understood by a historian's observation that, in the career of humanity, individual civilizations have arisen, have flourished with expanding vigor and vitality, and then have collapsed, disintegrated, and died? What are we to envisage when we contemplate the possibility and the danger of an impending doom which shall bring our own civilization to an end? Life and death are, primarily, biological concepts. Individual organisms—plants, animals, and men—are born, they live, and they die. Likewise species have an origin and a history in time. They come into being, and innumerable species of living forms have perished. Yet life, we say, goes on. The time span alloted to life itself is so enormous as to be virtually incommensurable with the span of life of individual organisms or even of species. Life goes on in spite of and even because of the death of individuals and species. Can we say the same of civilization? Have we grounds for saying that civilization endures throughout a long time span punctuated by the rise and fall, the life and death, of individual civilizations? If we have, whatever may be the fate of our own individual species of culture, we need harbor no fears for the continuance of civilization as such. If we suppose otherwise, if we identify the collapse of our civilization with the death of civilization as such, are we not identifying an instance with the type, confusing the values and treasures denoted by civilization as such with the particular features of our own parochial landscape? In like manner, we speak of dead languages, but language as such does not perish with the death of any one language.

But we can hardly remain content with the assurance that, no matter what may be the fate of our civilization, men will still go on living and human life will far outlast the particular forms of living which chararacterize our own civilization. For civilization is not coincident with human lfe. On the other hand, the historian will warn us against identifying civilization with any one individual civilization, with its relatively restricted time span. This means that we may not yield to the belief that the fate of civilization is dependent upon the fate of any one specific way of life which is our own. If English is our mother tongue, it does not follow that, if and when English shall become a dead language, civilization will have died. Dare we affirm that this or that particular feature of our way of life, comprising the civilization to which we belong, is so essential for the continuance of civilization as such, that, when it is threatened and impaired, the very essence of civilization is undermined? Can we say this with reference to our particular political or economic organization, our system of property ownership, our procedure in law and education, in industry and administration? Is there anywhere in our civilization any settled habit or pattern, any specific body of beliefs and ideas, which is indispensable to civilization as such, so that, in seeking to defend or to perpetuate it, we are at the same time upholding the cause of civilization as such? If we avow this, anywhere along the line, are we not guilty of the monstrous fallacy of identifying the ecumenical and universal values of civilization as such with some local, historical, and parochial structures which happen to be our own? Dare any one epoch, any one class, nation, or race affiirm that, in struggling to maintain this or that specific way of living, it is serving the cause of civilization? Along this path there appears to lie bigotry, arrogance, all the marked accompaniments of any holy crusade, the zealotry and fanaticism of him who believes that the sword he is wielding is veritably the sword of the Lord. Is this the implication of taking seriously the notion of civilization as such, an essential and substantive civilization, distinguished from the many patterns of civilization spread across the pages of history?

To this there is one radical alternative, the only one which may appear to avoid the hazards and difficulties which arise whenever anyone invests the ends and values which enlist his energies with an alleged absolute or universal worth. The alternative lies in the avowal that such and such a way of life is cherished and is to be struggled for and defended because it chances to be the manner of living which is our own. It expresses what we ourselves are. It utters the habits, the structures, the energies which comprise the fiber of our being. To renounce, or not to defend, our way of life, if it is threatened with loss or destruction, would be tantamount to the renunciation and relinquishment of ourselves. We cherish the privilege of speaking in the English tongue, not because we vainly imagine that English, rather than French or Sanskrit, is the one indispensable vehicle for furthering the universal ideal of a rational or humane civilization, but simply because English happens to be our mother tongue. The habit of using English has fashioned the very substance of our minds. That such is the case is a contingent fact, a historical accident. It might have chanced otherwise, and then no doubt we would have felt the same way about French or Hungarian. For what we are, the bent and bias which happen to be ours, determines our likes and dislikes, our preferences and aversions. How could it possibly be otherwise?

Now, the perspective within which this appears plausible and convincing is one in which civilization is assimilated to life. We expect a wolf to defend his way of living which is himself; we expect a she-wolf to defend her cubs because they too are of her; and we expect nothing more. Let the human way of life of any tribe or group, or class or nation, differ in any way one pleases from the manner in which wolves live their lives; if the human group cherish and defend their way of life simply because it is their own, because, being themselves, that is what they perforce happen to like, they are doing, in principle, nothing other and nothing more than wolves do. It is in terms of this perspective that one asks whether anyone can seriously entertain the notion that the animal, man, is able to transcend the limitations and specifications which define the particular pattern of wants and interests, habits and desires, comprising the substance of his life. These dictate what man will cherish and defend. No radical displacement, no new dimension or principle, puts in its appearance at the human level of life. There are, of course, distinctively human interests and action tendencies, just as each animal type has its specific preferences for food and habitat, determined by the bent of its own nature and internal structure. But the tale to be told of the life of man is but another chapter in the tale of life itself. This may indicate my meaning in speaking of this as a perspective in which civilization is assimilated to life. It is the same general perspective as that in which mind is assimilated to behavior. The alluring spectacle of an unbroken continuity, embracing all knowable entities within the matrix of nature's events, comprises the core of such perspectives as these. They generate a naturalistic interpretation of life, mind, and civilization.

Upon premises such as these, what meaning will attach to the concept of civilization in the singular, to civilization as such? The answer is, I think, that the only legitimate use of the term civilization on these premises is to denote the class of civilizations. What exists and is actual is always some particular pattern of human life and society, a persistent set of institutions, habits, and interests. Each concrete civilization is a historical episode. It is a theme exemplified within certain boundaries of historical time and geography. The boundaries may be imprecise and vague rather than sharp and clear. The transition from one culture epoch to another may be slow or rapid, gradual or revolutionary. Mingled with the distinctive traits of a new civilization will be strands of life and thought inherited from earlier cultures. Cultural diffusion and osmosis endlessly complicate the historian's task of delimiting any one specific civilization. But it remains true that there are diverse and distinguishable civilizations in the plural, for the historian to describe as best he may. And, on this showing, what can civilization, in the singular, mean except the class of all such individual civilizations? It will denote ingredients shared in by all, a least common denominator. That the resulting concept of civilization is bound to be something pretty thin is obvious; as meager, for instance, as the notion summarized by the writer of the article "Civilization" in the *Encyclopaedia Britannica* when he says that "man is a seeker after the greatest degree of comfort for the least necessary expenditure of energy"—as if man were a kind of steam engine and the only important thing were the ratio between the energy which was used and that which the mechanism of the engine made available.

Now, if civilization be taken primarily or exclusively as a class term, one thing at least is clear. It will then be quite meaningless to entertain any notion that it is incumbent upon any one concrete historical civilization, such as our own, to further the ends of civilization as such, to devote its energies to the realization of any ideal denoted by the term civilization in the singular. That term is the name of a class, and a class name is not to be confused with any type of prescriptive ideal or principle. The class of Airedale terriers includes all individual dogs having certain common characteristics. It is not incumbent upon any particular Airedale to approximate to or to incorporate in his own structure or behavior an Airedale ideal. Each dog is what he is. The class is *ex post facto,* descriptive of results attained, not of ends or ideals to be achieved. If there are any ideally desirable features denoted by the Airedale type, they owe their existence to the *de facto* preferences of human breeders and owners. The point which I would here note is the correlation between the view that a term such as civilization is nothing but a class term and the view that the source of all prescriptive ideals is to be looked for in what somebody happens to like. A nominalistic theory of universals goes hand in hand with a naturalistic theory of value. Now, by far the majority of common nouns are class terms. They denote nothing in the shape of intrinsic or objective standards or ideals. To accord to such terms as civilization a different nature and status introduces discontinuity and interferes with our deep-seated and naturalistic penchant for continuity. If Airedale terrier is a class term, why not civilization? In the end, the answer to this question hinges upon the weight we shall assign to whatever it is which distinguishes man from dogs and wolves.

For civilization is a human achievement: it pertains to the energies and the life of man, of man as viewed not by the biologist, but by the historian, the humanist, and the moralist—in the unpedantic sense of this last term. But in saying that civilization belongs to the historical life of man, in dealing with the concepts both of life and of civilization, we have to face at the outset a question with many long-range implications. Life, in the broadest generality, means two things, discrepant and contrasted. There is life as it is lived, and there is life as it is observed. Life as lived is life felt from within, primarily one's own life, pulsating with activity, interest, zest, joy and sorrow, failure, tragedy or triumph. Life as observed is, in the first instance at least, the life of other living creatures; the rhythm, span, and continuity of life as observed or observable is far wider and more inclusive than the narrow range of life which is lived and felt from within. Let it not be hastily inferred that, in making this distinction and in stressing its importance, I am going to plunge into the abyss of a Bergsonian romanticism and mysticism. What I would wish to make of this distinction lies in quite another direction. But some such distinction is, initially, inescapable. It may well happen that life as observed, taken in all strict literalness, deliquesces into something that isn't life at all; that, in the last analysis, everything observed or observable is motion, displacement in space and transition in time. In any case, the observed and observable is objective and phenomenal. It is the home of evidence, of verifiability, of fact. It is the area to which description, prediction, and scientific hypothesis are relevant. It is the field of scientific knowledge, and for an age and an intellectual climate with a theoretical heritage derived primarily from science it is the field to which everything which purports to be knowledge must refer. When the rhetorical question is propounded—as it was recently by Sabine[3]—where in this phenomenal, objective world will you ever find evidence for a value pronouncement, a preference, the answer is obvious. Nowhere. Where, in all the world, viewed as the totality of observed and observable phenomena, will you find life as lived, mind as experienced, pulsating with felt activity, diffused with qualities and values, love and hate, the warmth and intimacy of felt attractions and repulsions? Let the answer come from the biochemist and the strict behaviorist, and if behaviorism isn't pretty strict, it is lax, loose, and unscientific.

Civilization falls in with life in this respect, at least. Here likewise are two dimensions. There is civilization as being lived and enacted, civilization in the making, viewed from within as an affair of pursuing ends, making policies, practicing arts and techniques. This is the civilization which we are living and making. It is our actual, present civilization. There is also observed civilization, many diverse civilizations, to be surveyed and studied by the historian. Most of these are dead. There is nothing further to be enacted in their finished and completed careers.

Now, it is to be noted that when civilization, in the singular, is taken as a class term, it is civilizations *as observed*, taken phenomenally, which comprise the relevant universe of discourse. The historian stands outside of several cultures spread before him for his scrutiny. They are objective data, factual structures and processes, to be reported and described. In such a survey, the historian will include his own civilization, placing it alongside of other civilizations and eliciting the common, class characteristics of them all. As such an observer of civilization, as factual phenomena, the historian is detached. As such, he is no longer living within the living currents of his own civilization, participating in its vital concerns, under the necessity of making decisions with respect to the better and the worse; it is only as active participants in the life of a civilization still being enacted that values as such enter into the picture. It is only in this context, within civilization

---

[3] Cf. the Howison Lecture for 1941, by George H. Sabine: "Social Studies and Objectivity," Univ. Calif. Publ. Philos., Vol. XVI, No. 6 (1941).

as being lived and enacted, that civilization in the singular acquires a meaning other than that of a class designation. There is now the possibility that civilization names a significant ideal rather than a neutral class. Within this action perspective, it becomes pertinent to ask whether the form being taken by our own civilization, whether the issue and import of our decisions and policies and attitudes, are contributing to the fruition of these values and ideals denoted by civilization as such.

What is here said of civilization, in the large, applies equally to those ingredients of civilization which we designate as science, morality, law, religion, the arts and technologies. None of these are exclusively descriptive class names. They become such only when looked at from without—when viewed, phenomenally, as observed facts. Science as lived, produced, and enacted stands for an ideal, of which this, that, or the other scientific procedure or result is a more or less adequate embodiment and realization. In the light of the ideal denoted by the very idea of science it is possible to appraise and criticize some specific level of scientific attainment. It is this which gives backing to the statement that the vocation of science is a significant human enterprise, enlisting the coöperation of scientific workers in building up the edifice of science transcending the efforts and achievements of any one scientist. The scientist is the servant of a cause which claims his energies and his devotion. The value current runs here not from likings, interests, and preferences to some object which but expresses a contingent and arbitrary bias; it runs in the opposite direction, from objectively significant ideals and contents which make a rightful and rational claim upon the expenditure of human energies. What is true of science holds equally for the other contents comprised within the idea of civilization. It is upon some such premise as this that our own civilization will be seen not merely as one instance of a common type, but as the guardian and spokesman for values and ideals the validity of which is in some significant sense objective and universal, and which are comprised within the idea of civilization as such.

Civilization, then, is not a biological category. It is no universal ingredient or aspect of life, as is, say, metabolism. It denotes something which supervenes upon the life common to man and animal. It belongs to human life, and then only to a certain stage or level of the total life history of man. And this implies that an understanding of civilization is contingent upon our success in singling out those powers and proclivities in the nature of man which comprise his distinguishing traits. In the tradition of Western philosophy these specific characteristics of man have been comprised under the rubric of reason. I shall not here recount the serious questionings to which this version of man's nature has been subjected, particularly by Hume and his many followers. They are familiar—all too familiar—to a disillusioned age which has witnessed the decay and the collapse of so many cherished institutions and beliefs. Perhaps the term reason had best be allowed to lapse into obsolescence, provided we can succeed in catching, once more, some of the concrete ingredients and aspects of man's life and experience which the term may originally have denoted.

There is one such to which I would here refer and follow for a bit in some of its implications. It is familiar enough. It is spoken of as tradition, as social or cultural inheritance. There is something carried along, transmitted from one generation to the next. Arts and techniques, language, institutions, beliefs and ideas, are not transmitted biologically, through germ plasm, but otherwise: through imitation, training, and education, handed on throughout a sequence of generations. The temporal boundaries of a specific civilization are marked by the origin and persistence of such a body of cultural capital. It is not suggested that it is anything inert and unchanging, a mere dead weight. It is, metaphorically, a living thing, both in the sense that it is recaptured and relived by individuals belonging to many generations, and also in the sense that it undergoes cumulative change and development, involving both growth and decay.

I mention this fact and this process of social inheritance not so much for its own sake—important as it is—as for another reason. Nothing could be carried over from the life and experiences of one generation to succeeding generations unless in some manner it should become detached from the setting in which it was first incorporated. Pythagoras is said to have been the first to have clearly formulated and demonstrated the geometrical proposition called by his name. The formulation and demonstration of this theorem by Pythagoras was an incident in the life history of the individual man Pythagoras. It was something lived through in the actual experience, in the mind, of a single individual. That experience of Pythagoras was an actual occasion or series of actual occasions. Twenty-odd centuries later a schoolboy comes to understand the Pythagorean proposition. He does not relive the experience of Pythagoras and resurrect the actual occasion through which Pythagoras lived when he first came upon this demonstration. He cannot literally reënact the living mind, the actual experience, of the individual man Pythagoras. But he can understand the Pythagorean demonstration. The *content* of the experience of Pythagoras has been loosened and set free from its original embodiment in the concrete, actual occasions comprising the experience and the mind of Pythagoras. A content is separated from its original container. It becomes common property, and renders possible that sharing in common of contents which underlies all communication and coöperation at the typically human level.

It is not here being suggested that such detachable and detached contents maintain any ghostly, completely unembodied, existence, floating by themselves in some vacuous empyrean. They are incorporated in signs and symbols, above all in language. This fully justifies the statement of Whitehead that "human civilization is an outgrowth of language. We are thereby released from complete bondage to the immediacies of mood or circumstance. . . . Language has gradually achieved the abstraction of its meaning from the presuppositions of any particular environment."[4] The meanings which attach to language symbols—vocal sounds and marks—are not imprisoned within their phenomenal containers. Were such the case, there could be no such thing as translation, metaphor, tradition, or communication. But, although meanings and ideas do not float freely, although they are incorporated in objective symbols, they come to life and become realized only when they become the contents of some mind, some living actual experience. The meanings which slumber within the printed pages of closed books require an understanding and living mind if they are to be aroused from their somnolent states and enter into living, actual experience. There are many accounts of mind in terms of the interplay of symbols, as if the meanings incorporated in objective symbols were able to generate their own comprehension and understanding once

---

[4] A. N. Whitehead, *Modes of Thought* (Cambridge Univ. Press, 1938), pp. 49–53.

the situation in which they function should become sufficiently problematic and complicated. This seems to me like supposing that a mechanical signal device for controlling traffic suddenly turns into a traffic officer when the highway crossing becomes sufficiently congested. Mead's illuminating account of the mechanism of social communication stops just short of the crucial point. When one self assumes the attitude of another, makes similar gestures and utters similar sounds, nothing which we know as mutual understanding or sympathy will arise unless some content, lived through in one individual context, is transferred to another self and enjoyed and actualized in his living experience. A description of the mechanism of communication in behavioristic, phenomenalistic terms is one thing. An understanding of the content communicated is quite another thing.

Now, a distinction similar to this needs to be made when we are dealing with civilization; for we apply the term to two distinguishable sorts of things. On the one hand, the term denotes the way in which a society is organized, the political, legal, and economic structures and relationships characteristic of men's lives and behavior. On the other hand, by civilization we may indicate the meanings and values which are incorporated within such structures. These comprise the content of men's lives and institutions. These contents are not observed and observable phenomena as are institutional patterns and behavior habits. These contents are discernible, they come to life, only within the perspective of human life as being lived and civilization as being enacted. An insect colony is a kind of social organization. The behavior habits of individual insects are the meeting point of various pressures, habits, and automatisms. We have no grounds for supposing that the machinery of insect life and of insects incorporates a content— let alone a detachable content—of which individual insects may be consciously aware. Their life has no meaning in the sense in which the civilized life of human beings may have a meaning. Insects live on a one-dimensional plane. Civilization has two dimensions, with resulting strains and tensions of which animal life and the state of nature are quite innocent.

In speaking of civilization as the *content* of such life as is typically human, I intend deliberately to stress a dimension of human experience which has little or no analogy in physical nature, in animal life, or in the long stretch of man's career before the possibility of realizing the values intrinsic to civilization as such dawned upon his mind. The metaphor of a content and its container is, to be sure, derived from physical situations and transactions. I can pour the liquid contents of one vessel into another. It may well be that most of the words used in reflective thinking hark back originally to some elementary physical content. But the story of language, as of man's experience and civilization itself, is the story of the "etherialization" (to use Toynbee's term)—the metamorphosis and the metaphorizing of symbols, as primitive meanings are stretched farther and farther to encompass new vistas and dimensions. What social structures contain, the meanings which they incorporate and convey, may bear little enough resemblance to the filling of a tooth. Yet some distinction between the container and the contained is indispensable, and the notion of a content applied to civilization is instructive. A description of the mechanisms of society, of historical processes in terms of the relaxation and intensification of social pressures, leaves quite untouched the content, the actualization of which gives point to and makes significant the operation of the social machinery. Civilization denotes the content of human life and society as well as its structure and its machinery. This is why I think that Mr. Pepper's discussion was concerned less with civilization than with the interplay and balance of social forces. The truth about the nature and significance of civilization is to be discovered through a scrutiny and understanding of civilization itself. There are no antecedent probabilities, such as Mr. Pepper looked for, derived from a survey of nature and individual behavior, prior to the advent of civilization itself, which are likely to have much relevance. What are the antecedent probabilities derived from an acquaintance with the correlations of nature's events outside the history of music, which itself belongs to civilization, that Beethoven would create the Ninth Symphony?

Every civilization has its characteristic social structures, its habits and routines of behavior, its regularized procedures. The totality of these comprise the institutional pattern of relationships in which individuals stand to one another and to their world. Forms of government, the state of industrial arts, the manner in which legal and moral sanctions are enforced, the organization of individuals into schools, churches, labor and business associations, families, tribes and nations, urban and rural communities—all such, and many more—are aspects of social structures and institutions. They name the ways in which any one society, as a going concern, is organized. Historical and social studies, descriptive and explanatory of the factual organization of society, are concerned primarily with such as these. Organization is not, of course, a privileged prerogative of human societies. Living organisms, too, are organized structures and processes. And atoms, molecules, and inorganic compounds exhibit their own characteristic modes of organization. If it makes anyone happy, as it apparently does, to reflect that everything, everywhere and everywhen, is organized in some fashion, so be it. That leaves us just where we were before, profoundly interested in discovering the objective differences between organization and disorganization, between order and chaos. And this difference is to be looked for, I think, in the fact that it takes a certain kind of structure and organization to house and embody certain kinds of significant contents. A disordered mind is one with a structure and order inadequate to serve as the vehicle of logically coherent ideas and contents. A chaotic society is one with a type of organization which bars it from incorporating significant ideas and values, such as justice and freedom. The question whether you are confronted by order or disorder, civilization or barbarism, has nothing to do with subjective preference. It is the question of the objective adequacy of a container to its contents, of a body to its soul. In short, the institutional organization of any society is not the totality of its civilization. For these human and social insitutions have a content; they are the vehicles through which something gets expressed. They comprise the body and not the soul of civilization. For the purposes of this discussion, I am ready, wholly unabashed and unrepentant, in spite of all the warnings and critical refinements of Ogden and Richards, to say that human institutions and social structures embody, incorporate, and contain meanings. And I think that you haven't come in sight of the essential aspect of civilization so long as you confine your attention to the machinery, the organization, of social structures and processes, the interplay of social pressures, and the balance of powers. It is not enough to say that social structures—the state, industry, universities, and the like—perform certain functions, in the sense in which the nerve ganglia of mollusks perform a function. No doubt they do; but that is not their distinctive trait. The new, utterly unique, and momentous thing about the functions performed by social structures is that the individuals belonging to these institutions can become aware both of the social machinery and of the ends which it may serve, the significant contents and meanings of which the social machinery is but the vehicle. The mollusk, presumably, just lives. Civilized man lives, too; but woven into the texture of his living are awareness, ideas, thought, and mind. Ideas supervene upon animal and subhuman life and behavior. The structures which arise in history and society are now invested with a meaning of which men may be aware. These meanings are the contents of social institutions and the entire machinery of government, industry, law, and education.

I am afraid that I am getting dangerously near that third type of social theory and social control which Mr. Pepper so cunningly dismissed by giving it a bad, a very bad, name. In calling it an "exhortational" view he dismisses it not even with faint praise. Exhortation is a practical art, with its own skills and aptitudes, suggestive of emotional ebullition of a rather low grade and with a considerable smatter of coercive practices. When brought to a certain degree of refinement and purged of all the accessory and arbitrary sanctions which exhortation employs, exhortation passes over into persuasion. And persuasion is the only type of control which is suitable to a mind. It is the polar opposite of coercion. It operates in a dimension which has nothing to do with social pressure. It is what transpires when a mind or a self is confronted by an idea the meaning, significance, and validity of which elicits free and unconstrained assent—unconstrained, that is, by everything except the intrinsic nature and worth of the idea itself. Mr. Pepper's own exhortation was a delightful instance of high-grade persuasion setting before us certain ideas and exhorting (or persuading) us to assent to them. Only such ideas as are freely accepted and acknowledged can become the viable contents of minds. This principle of persuasion, as I would call it, is the central core of democracy and indeed of civilization itself. Here is the one categorical imperative laid upon minds: Accept only those contents, those beliefs, convictions, and loyalties, which have a significance and validity that you are yourself persuaded of. It is this imperative alone which warrants our concern for free inquiry, freedom of thought and of discussion. This alone makes possible science and morality, art and religion. You must not treat a mind as if it were the behavior of a body the motions of which in space and time are to be controlled, in direction and velocity, from without. But one small letter, in the middle of the alphabet, separates "idea" from "ideal." Perhaps it is the part of wisdom now to eschew this term "ideal," and to attempt a description of the defining principle of civilization, and the central persuasion of the metaphysical tradition of European philosophy, in other terms. *Corruptio optimi pessima.* A kind of Gresham's Law governs the fate of words. Adulterated, debased, and sentimentalized usages of terms drive out more profound and subtle connotations. Words are subject to processes, both of etherealization and vulgarization, and we have to make the best of the verbal instruments at our disposal. Let me depict the kind of situation to which the term ideal seems to me to be relevant and applicable to our central themes.

The machinery of social organization, methods of social control, of government, administration, industry, and social institutions, incorporate meanings; they are the bearers of contents, instruments for actualizing and realizing values. This implies, as an ideal, that the individuals whose lives are determined by such institutional patterns will not accept them and conform to them unless (1) they are persuaded that the content embodied within all this social machinery is humanely significant and valid, and unless (2) they are likewise persuaded that these institutional structures are tolerably adequate embodiments of such values and meanings. The external shell and body of civilization should be fashioned to house the soul of civilization. Is this proposition an inductive inference, vouched for by empirical, historical evidence? Yes and no. A social behaviorist will admit as evidence only observed and observable structures and events. He will be impressed by the striking and essential continuities of animal and human behavior. He will note the fundamental resemblance between human and animal intelligence and shrewdness. The employment of symbols, particularly linguistic signs, will permit an enormous extension of conditioned reflexes and the operation of methods of control over an ever-widening front. There is observable evidence for all this, and for very much more of the same kind. But try to place yourself in the position of a scientist engaged in making his observations and inquiries, of a statesman deciding upon policies, of a citizen participating in a discussion and voting, of a creative artist struggling to express an idea—try, in short, to regard civilization as something being enacted and lived, and you are moving in a different dimension. Now you are confronted by a meaning, an idea or ideal, which you are seeking to incorporate in action, in life and in some structure or institution. Civilization as lived springs from the incessant and perennial tension between the machinery, the organized structures, of society and a content of values and meanings which ought to be actualized and embodied in institutions. This is, if you will, a metaphysical hypothesis. Its evidence lies in the way it may begin to make sense of some large-scale aspects of human history and human achievements. Evidence is never, I think, more than a hint, a clue; to restrict a theory to a description of evidence is always to deprive yourself of an interpretation of the evidence, an understanding of what the evidence means.

Now, the detachment of a content from a concrete, particular instance occurs along two different paths. One of these leads to the formation of class terms and most common nouns. This particular piece of paper is blue. The concrete item, here and now before me, has a character, a nature, which can, in idea, be detached and abstracted from this particular instance. It is relevant to and descriptive of other items. It has a wide range of applicability. The class of blue objects is large and varied. Any one particular member of the class is the container of a content, a character in terms of which the class is defined. But observe that along this path there is no possible warrant for saying that any one member of the class is a bad or inadequate container of the content which defines the class. It either belongs to the class or it doesn't. If it doesn't, then it is lacking in the content under discussion. If it belongs to the class, it possesses that content, and there is nothing more to be said. This would be the situation with respect to civilization if civilization were a descriptive, class term.

There is another and different direction, which leads to the detachment and abstraction of a content from some one of its particular, concrete vehicles or containers. An illustration will here best serve my purpose. Consider that stage in the history of religion which is spoken of as totemism.[5] Here you have some plant or animal species occupying a unique and privileged status. It constitutes the focus of ritual procedures, fraught with tremendous moment for the life of the groups. It is the subject of taboos. It is invested with a wealth of meaning and significance, sacred, numinous, and awe-inspiring. It is the container and the vehicle of a significant content. As long as totemism endures, no incongruity is felt to exist between the observable, phenomenal animal and the meanings incorporated in such an object. The totem is a container adequate to its content. But let there arise a felt discrepancy between this kind of object and the meanings which it ought to sustain and embody, and totemism is, in principle, done for; the totem is no longer able to sustain the weight of meaning with which it is invested. The content of which the totem is the bearer is not a class idea. It is an ideal, and it provides a criterion by which to measure the adequacy of the object which is its vehicle or embodiment. The *content*—the sacred, the awesome, or the numinous—is wrenched free from its incorporation in this kind of object, and the search for a more adequate container of this meaning, this content, is under way. Of course, the content does not itself remain unchanged. It undergoes deepening and refinement as it is carried over from one concretion and embodiment to another. Is this myth and sheer metaphor? Perhaps; but I think this kind of metaphor is a better container of what it is that civilization means than the metaphors lifted out of mechanism, as if some Boyle's Law could be found to expose the secrets of the life of civilization.

Totemism is here cited only as a typical illustration of the kind of thing which everywhere confronts the student of human civilization. It has a sweep and a universality within this domain, analogous, say, to the generality of motion in the physical order. The totem is the actualized embodiment and concretion of a wealth of meaning. That meaning is the content of which the phenomenal object is the bearer and the vehicle. A time comes when the meaning outgrows its visible embodiment. The totem is then seen to be a bad container, no longer suited to its content. The content is loosened and detached from its original container, and the search

---

[5] This illustration was suggested to me by A. A. Bowman's *Studies in the Philosophy of Religion* (London, Macmillan, 1938), in which the distinction between a "container" and its "content" is applied, in an illuminating and penetrating manner, to a study of religious development.

for a more adequate container is again begun. The machineries of human society, resulting in some here-and-now structure and organization, in politics and industry, all of man's institutions, may be viewed as analogous containers of meanings. They are vehicles through which such things as are abstractly denoted by economy, security, freedom, and justice become practically incorporated within the actual structure of human living. But these contents, these ideal meanings, outgrow the body, the visible, organized social structures, the institutions, which are the containers of these meanings.

This is made possible because some meaning, idea, or principle is pried loose from its concrete embodiments. As thus abstracted, it is discerned to possess a scope and a validity independent of the particular, concrete setting in which it is here and now, or then and there, incorporated. In the etymological sense of the term it has become absolute, absolved and loosened from its concrete and particular setting. Its being set free is just the correlate of the processes whereby its particular embodiment is discovered to be an inadequate container.

Mr. Lenzen directed our attention to the fact that science, whatever may have been the technological interests which determined the field of inquiry, whatever may have been the social context in which science originated,—that science, once born, comes to live a life of its own. This is the point of the following quotation from G. N. Clark (to whom Mr. Lenzen also referred). He is speaking of the great cumulative movement of modern physical science. "The scientific movement," he writes, "was not the mere aggregate of the efforts of many individuals, each one of whom can be explained in terms of his social position. It was a common enterprise, partially incarnated in each of them, but having its own existence and nature."[6]

This is to say that significant contents and meanings get themselves detached from the particular circumstance and perspective in which they first happen to be incorporated; they are dissolved and absolved from the local and the parochial and become, in this sense, absolute. They now function not as class terms, but as ideals, in the light of which this, that, or the other institutional pattern

---

[6] G. N. Clark, *Science and Social Welfare in the Age of Newton* (Oxford, Clarendon Press, 1937), p. 87.

may be judged inadequate and consequently a bad container. It is observed, in passing, that the kind of content or meaning which here comes into view has not only to be distinguished from that represented by logical classes and common nouns; for it is also different from another kind of meaning, which in many quarters is taken to be the original and norm of significant meanings throughout. I refer to the kind of meaning which a particular thing has so far as it points, or leads, to some other particular thing. Smoke means fire. It does so because we have generally found that these two particular items, smoke and fire, are in close temporal and spatial proximity to one another. To act intelligently is to act in view of such probable space and time proximities or continuities. This sort of meaning might be spoken of as nominalistic or pragmatic; it leads to specific, practical mastery and control. To ascribe this sort of meaning to any particular item is a matter of shrewd inference, based upon specific evidence. We are moving entirely within the dimension of prediction and verification, of specific leadings and operations. And usually, when one asks for the evidence in support of any value judgment, one is also moving entirely within this dimension, one is but going farther along the path marked out by animal intelligence. That along this road one scarcely comes in sight of the distinguishing features of man's life and his civilization is what I have wished to indicate.

Science is an affair of knowledge, and we expect knowledge to be concerned with objectivity. Is there any analogous objectivity which belongs to the other major ingredients of civilization, those which pertain to men's actions and preferences, to politics, economics, and morals? Are there any significant contents here, objective and detachable, transcending the play of interests and pressures which determine the patterns of life and history?

Let one recall that the meaning and possibility of attaining objectivity even in the domain of knowledge has been one of the central problems of modern philosophy. What can objectivity possibly mean, in view of the forces and pressures which play upon our human minds and bodies? Our sense perceptions are caught up within chains of causal processes, physical, biological, and psychological. These appear to be the sole determining factors. Social and historical studies have likewise discerned the subtle ways in which all our ideas and beliefs are conditioned by the social context within which they have originated. And so objectivity within the domain even of knowledge itself, so far as man's experience as cognitive and theoretic is concerned, is seen to be something extremely problematic. No wonder, in these circumstances, that the problem of knowledge should have thrust itself into the foreground of reflective thinking. But notwithstanding this, and with perhaps diminishing concern for all these philosophical doubts and queries, the march of science has been steady and progressive. The discovery and acknowledgment of matters of fact, the utilization of evidence, specific verifiability and controlled procedures—these familiar traits of science do admittedly define a universally significant kind of objectivity. That scientific objectivity implies something other than the acknowledged preference of matter of fact can, I think, be shown. Science when viewed within the perspective of civilization denotes a significant content, yes, an ideal, the meaning and validity of which become detached from the contingent circumstances of its origin. There is here a dimension of objectivity different from that of matter of fact.

But let one now turn his attention from knowledge to life, from theory to practice, from intelligence to volition and decision, from facts to values. What strikes me, both as I survey some of the institutional patterns of modern society, particularly nationalism and individualism, and as I try to take stock of some of the deeper currents of modern ideas, is the complacency with which we have come to accept a radical cleavage between the requirements of knowledge and the exigencies of living. The idea and ideal of objectivity is domiciled within knowledge, within science. The idea of knowledge spells control by something which is objective and independent, whether we think of this as sheer matter of fact or as a significant content set over against the contingencies of sense experience and the interplay of social, historic forces. But what, we ask ourselves or our philosophy, can a purpose, a plan of action, a vital commitment or loyalty, a choice among competing ends or parties which may solicit our devotion,—what have such as these to do with any kind of objective value? Of course, once some end or purpose, some ideal or practical direction for our expenditure of energy, has been chosen, then knowledge and control by the objective results of scientific inquiry come fully into play. Here intelligent action is guided by knowledge. But how can any objective authenticity attach to the inclusive and ultimate organizing principles of conduct, life, and civilization where the choice of realizable values rather than the description of fact are at stake? If the theoretical proclivities bred by modern experience and ideas have made knowledge problematic, how much more problematic have the structures of our value pronouncements and of our accepted institutions come to appear! This is not surprising, for modern men set out to achieve both knowledge and freedom, and while knowledge means submission to and control by something objective, freedom is taken to mean the maximum degree of release from any objective control whatever. The concomitant pursuit of knowledge and freedom, on these premises, may be said to define the specific nature of the modern enterprise and experiment. It has introduced a bifurcation into the heart of our world, more disconcerting, I think, than the cleavages and divided loyalties alleged to have been injected into man's life by the dualisms of nature and supernature, characteristic of older cultures. For, on the one hand, there is employed the possibility and the necessity of agreement and coöperation in building up the structure of knowledge. Only that is fitted to enter the edifice of knowledge, of science, which is verifiable by any disciplined observer. Here is a structure open and public, universal and sharable in common. The content of knowledge is an objective focus, independent, in principle, of the idiosyncrasies and divergences of private perspectives. The methods of scientific procedure are devised in order to make due allowances for subjective bias and to discover the distortions which derive from it. This all spells objectivity. On the other hand are all the divergencies and conflicts of human desires, the interests of particular groups, classes, and nations, the struggle for existence and for power, the forward thrust of life itself, dispersed in sullenly diverse and competing units. Here is the domain of conations, desires, interests. It is the world of the will, the will to live and the will to power. Values are now seen to be the declaration and expression of specific conations and interests; values are generated by the particular bias and direction in which some vital force is moving.

Here is the polar antithesis of knowledge, objectivity, a common focus; here can be no content detached from particular interests, whether those of an individual or of some specific social and historical context. Any such detached and objective content, asking, as it were, to be acknowledged, would appear to bind the will, to impose claims upon energies which demand freedom from any such objective obligation. Our interests and desires do, to be sure, encounter objective facts. They sometimes meet with obstacles which prevent, and sometimes with means which insure, their fruition. Both obstacles and pliant means are objective matters of fact. This realm of knowable, objective matter of fact holds no seat or source either of values or of valid claims made upon the will. Something like this is, of course, the naturalistic theory of value. It accords with that common sense which comprises the tacit premises of our living and our thinking, the deposit left in our minds both by the institutional patterns and by the ways of thinking to which modern men have become increasingly habituated. No displacement of this, our common-sense perspective, would seem even intelligible. Every college freshman knows that facts are objective and values subjective.

In the terms which have been employed in this discussion, this means that in the organization of man's experience as practical, in life and art, in politics and industry, and in the impact of nations upon one another, there is no significant content which can be detached from the interplay and the conflict of particular pressures and interests operating here and now, there and then. No plan of action, no social philosophy can or should do more than express the contingent configurations of interests which characterize a specific individual, class, race, nation, or individual cultural epoch. Take, as an instance, the body of ideas and persuasions comprised within liberalism and the liberal tradition. An astute and learned scholar has this to say about the origin of European liberalism: "What produced liberalism was the emergence of a new economic society at the end of the Middle Ages. As a doctrine, it was shaped by the needs of that new society; and, like all social philosophies, it could not transcend the medium in which it was born. Like all social philosophies, therefore, it contained in its birth the conditions of its own destruction."' That all ideas and ideals are born in the medium denoted by the interplay of human needs and interests may be admitted. Does it follow that there is no detachable

---

' Harold J. Laski, *The Rise of European Liberalism* (London, Allen and Unwin, 1936), p. 17.

content, no ideas or principles which transcend the concrete historical circumstances in which they originate and which acquire thereby a validity that is, in a crucial sense, objective? A wide range of the institutional patterns of human action, and the tacit premises of much of our thinking, have answered this question in ways which we know. We have given knowledge a monopoly of all available objectivity, and we have undertaken to release the springs of action and the choice of ends from the control of any significant, objective content. This answer to the question, in the light (or darkness) of all that is now transpiring, cannot but evoke a further question. How adequately does the accepted framework of social organization incorporate the idea of civilization as such? How good a container of the content denoted by civilization as such is the particular civilization which is, or has been, our own? Perhaps we are now witnessing the answer being given to this question.

D. S. MACKAY

ORGANIZATION AND FREEDOM

IN HIS later disillusionment about the future of science in civilization, Renan used to contend that the sole purpose of universal education is to protect an enlightened minority against the fanaticism of the masses. The intensive culture of the few is inevitably diluted when widely distributed among the many. The education of the masses is therefore desirable only in order to promote tolerance toward ideas and values which most are unable to appreciate, but which they may nevertheless be taught to respect and defend.

There is a measure of truth in this contention, and we may accept a version of Renan's argument without his aristocratic disillusionment. The civilization of the masses is indeed for the sake of preserving and promoting the civilization of the few. But we must add the proviso that the few in question need be no elite class with a monopoly upon the higher values of civilized life. Let us admit that these achievements can be fully appreciated only by a minority, and that civilization of the many is justified by its contribution to the few. But the minority, apart from political discrimination, is a variable class to which all are eligible in *some* respect, since there is no individual or group within a civilized society that is incapable of appreciating one or another of its skills. Only a few are capable of understanding higher mathematics or enjoying the music of Bach, but it is no less true that only the few are capable of appreciating good craftsmanship in carpentry or good care of the soil in farming. These concerns are equally ingredients of civilization and expressions of its intrinsic values. The greater variety of skills an individual is able, not necessarily to master and make his own, but at least to appreciate aesthetically and with intensive insight, the more highly civilized is the man.

Civilization is thus both means and end. It is a continual means to its own ends, justified only by the achievements and enjoyments of individuals, although, as means, it is the collective concern of all. Civilization is that which "enables mankind to progress independently of heredity and of mere natural selection."[1] It is also that

---

[1] D. G. Ritchie, *Natural Rights,* p. 54.

which justifies the progress mankind has been able to make, since any conceivable goal of progress is the enhancement of some type of civilized existence.

Considered as means and as end, civilization has two diverse though closely related meanings. In the latter sense, we are apt to think of civilization as a single whole, whereas in the former sense it is civilizations in the plural, or a particular civilization, that we have to consider. As means to an end, a civilization is a domain of facts and events. It is a *culture,* in the geographical and anthropological senses of the term. Such a culture exhibits a spatial or extensive order of human and physical relations. It occupies a definable area on the face of the earth, and it endures for a limited period. Yet the duration counts for less in the character of a particular civilization than does the succession of events within that duration, however long or short it may be. Each civilization comprises recurrent patterns of human behavior. A civilization is essentially temporal and its "time" may be defined as "succession in duration."[2] But it is the repetition within the succession of events, and not the duration, that counts in this connection. Athenian civilization in antiquity had less than one-third the duration of Egyptian civilization, and yet it achieved a more highly developed and significant type of culture. The character of a civilization, considered as a means, depends on the fact that its language, customs, and institutions have spread and prevailed over certain territories. It depends on the fact that skills and techniques have been invented and improved by successive generations, so that greater numbers of human beings and wider regions are continually brought within that type of culture. And, finally, the character of a civilization depends basically on the ways of replenishing the food supply and on the essential materials and modes of production. In this aspect, considered instrumentally, a civilization has its own characteristic although changing elements of material culture. It involves a process of assimilation from other cultures, as well as exclusion and elimination, but it is a process of continual expansion or else decay.

---

[2] This conception of time is applied by Alexander to the problem of freedom in *Space, Time and Deity,* Vol. II, bk. iii, chaps. ix, x. The ethical and social implications of his doctrine of time and freedom were anticipated in his earlier work, *Moral Order and Progress.* My indebtedness to Alexander in both of these works, as well as to Bergson, will be obvious in the ensuing argument, in spite of my disagreement on the values of *organization.*

In the other aspect, civilization as an end consists of ideas, beliefs, and aspirations which reflect the values of its particular material culture, but which also give new direction to further changes in that culture. How accurately the ideas reflect the actual situations, and how realizable the aspirations may be, are questions of the first importance in the analysis of civilization, if only because of the discrepancies between its two aspects. The ideal claims for civilization as an end do not jibe with the attainments of any particular civilization as means. Anthropologists have rightly insisted that the economics and the social organization of a tribe, however primitive its culture may be, are not intelligible apart from the ideas of the individuals who participate in them. The implements of a material culture do not manipulate themselves. The production and use of artifacts requires not only technical knowledge, but also ideas of their social functions, and these ideas are closely connected with a practical discipline that has its sources in legal, moral, and religious beliefs. Thus, a material culture has its setting in what Mr. Dewey has described as "the occupational psychosis" of the group. The division of labor, as between the sexes, and among different age groups and other classes, involves generally accepted beliefs about the several occupations, their purposes, and their comparative social importance. The organization of families and similar social units is in accordance with general ideas about their management and interrelations, however much the conduct of individuals may vary in detail. The life of a tribe or a nation is civilized so far as its organization is *rationalized*. This means that common standards are explicitly recognized in the management and interrelations of social units. To what extent the practice actually agrees with the recognized standards in a given state of society is a question for the anthropologist, the economist, and the social psychologist to decide. A philosophical analysis can scarcely be expected to contribute anything of positive value on that question. Here, instead, we are concerned with the differences and conflicts involved in the conceptions of civilization as means and as end.

There are, then, as Mr. Adams has suggested in the previous lecture, two diverse meanings of the notion of civilization. The traits of civilization as means are the traits of an organized society, possessing its own solidarity of interests and a morality that is, in

Bergson's sense, "static" rather than "dynamic."[3] Its cohesiveness is the result of social pressure instead of individual aspiration. The organization of a society which is primarily instrumental and utilitarian involves an extensive order of relations, deployed in space, temporal only in the sense that there are successive repetitions of a spatialized pattern within that order. The traits of civilization as an end, on the contrary, are the traits of initiative, intelligence, insight, and creative effort. It is an intensive and qualitative order of duration, linking aspiration with memory, social purpose with tradition, an ideal future with the funded experience of the past. In this aspect, civilization means freedom rather than social organization. Its obligations arise from the claims of individual aspiration, and not from the demands of social pressure. In this "dynamic" aspect, civilization suggests a realm of ends that may be shared by all humanity—an "open" instead of a "closed" society.

The main theme of this argument is that all social organization tends to become a "closed" society, in Bergson's sense of the term, and that this tendency is the collective effort of a group to acquire an independent, corporate existence as such. In other words, any form of social organization, from a family to a nation, tends to become exclusive rather than inclusive of interests that happen to lie beyond the immediate pressure of its obligations. There is, indeed, no such thing as a social organism, with its own individuality. Nevertheless, every organization from family to nation has a tendency to behave *as if* it were or could eventually become a social organism. It is only the plurality of organizations, with coördinate interests and aims, that prevents a given group from acquiring independent, corporate existence, and so functioning as an organic whole. I shall therefore reject the prevalent theory that the development of an organized society is a process of increasing *differentiation* and *integration*. This theory identifies an organized society with a social organism, and the identification rests on a false biological analogy. The conception of "organization" has been borrowed from physiology and applied to the study of social order and change. The underlying assumption is that the ordering of a social group resembles the growth of an individual organism, and that the adaptation of a group is like the integrated response of an

---

[3] Henri Bergson, *The Two Sources of Morality and Religion*.

organism to its environment. Well, the resemblance is there, but we have been looking for it in the wrong place. An organization resembles an organism where each is *least* purposive in its behavior, and *most* automatic in its defensive or offensive reactions. It resembles an organism when its members begin to behave as though they were molecules in the cells of a single body instead of acting as free individuals.

The idea of evolution is said to have been itself evolved from the idea of progress, as "a gift from the philosophy of human nature to the philosophy of all nature."[4] Whatever truth there may be in that remark, it aptly describes the development of thought in Spencer's philosophy of evolution. Today, most of those who speak glibly about the progressive organization of social groups as a process of increasing "integration" are evidently unaware of the source of that doctrine, since they so emphatically reject Spencer's views and hence deny the only cogent arguments in favor of it. It is well known that he derived his formula for evolution from von Baer's embryology, but it is not so well known that Spencer first accepted this formula under the influence of Schelling's philosophy of nature as this had reached him through Coleridge.[5] Spencer's theory of evolution is the metaphysical doctrine of organism applied to the dogma of social progress in the nineteenth century and translated into Darwin's theory of natural selection. But Coleridge had presented this metaphysical doctrine in a way more congenial to the temperamental empiricism and individualism of the Anglo-Saxon mind, and to Spencer's in particular. "Organic Nature is in every class and everywhere tending to Individuality," said Coleridge; "but Individuality actually commences in man." Life itself is simply "the principle of individuation."

If life is progressive individuation, what is the basis of cohesion in an organized society? Coleridge answers in terms of Kant's principle of teleological judgment: organization of life, whether individual or social, is a product of nature, in which all the parts are reciprocally end and means. The principle of such organic unity, internally purposive, is a regulative and not a constitutive

---

[4] A. W. Benn, *History of English Rationalism*, Vol. VI, p. 13.

[5] In his *Social Statics* Spencer explains that Coleridge had first brought to his attention the principle of individuation. In a later edition Spencer notes that he had previously been unaware of the fact that Coleridge owed this conception of universal evolution to Schelling and the *Naturphilosophie* of the post-Kantians.—*Social Statics* (4th ed.; New York, 1892), p. 256 n.

idea. It points to the idea of nature's teleology—a system of ends
to which all of nature's mechanism is subordinate. In the same
vein, Coleridge argues that the organic unity of a society is not a
constitutive but a regulative principle. The notion of a social contract, considered as a concept of the understanding, is "at once
false and foolish," incapable of historical proof. But as a regulative
idea or ideal of reason there is an "ever-originating contract" in
all social organization—a standard of free association for common
ends and "the final criterion by which all particular frames of
government must be tried." Rousseau had been right in asserting
that the General Will is more than a mere aggregate or sum total
of particular wills. But he was wrong in supposing that it resides
in the motives or inclinations of individuals. The General Will is
not an empirical object in any sense. The motives of the masses are
never at one moment sufficently rational to express the General
Will. Rousseau had been under the illusion that all human beings
are equally interested in what is to their equal interest. The logical
consequence of that doctrine was communism, according to Coleridge, and not the sort of republican society that Rousseau had
in mind. But the General Will, as an "ever-originating contract,"
presupposes a Universal Reason or a Transcendental Mind, of
which the consciousness of each individual member of society is an
integral part. The whole of a society is more than the sum of its
parts. Through his membership in an organized group the individual acquires new traits, assumes a different character from that
which he had previously or which he could have had apart from
these social relations. Hence, the process of individuation, which,
according to Coleridge, is life itself, finds its most adequate expression in the organic unity of human society. The more conscious
he is of his relations to others, those in the past as well as those in
the present, the more complete is a man's individuality. "Each man
in a numerous society is not only co-existent with but virtually
organized into the multitude of which he is an integral part. His
idem is modified by the *alter*. And there arise impulses and objects
from his synthesis of *alter et idem,* myself and my neighbour."[6]

The celebrated debates between the philosophical idealists and
naturalists of the nineteenth century have obscured the underlying
agreement between the metaphysical doctrine of organism, on the

---

[6] Quoted by J. H. Muirhead, *Coleridge as Philosopher.*

one hand, and the evolutionary doctrine of social organization, on the other. Each applied biological analogies to societies, and each entertained the optimistic faith in the indefinite perfectibility of human nature, taken over from the rationalism of the preceding century. Besides individual enlightenment there was to be increasing collective solidarity, so that however ignorant, acquisitive, or diffident men might be as individuals, they would eventually be wise, generous, and confident when large enough numbers of them should act together in unison. Spencer's normative ideal of "the perfectly adjusted man in the completely evolved society" was Coleridge's perfection of the process of individuation in the synthesis of *alter et idem.* It is significant that Coleridge should have provided Spencer with his strange designation of ethics as "Transcendental Physiology."

Running through the entire social philosophy of the nineteenth century was the illusion that individuals can be collectively compelled to be free. This had its practical counterpart in the policy of imperialism, with its assumption that backward peoples of Africa and Asia could and should be forced to become civilized, whatever their preferences for civilization might have been. It had its counterpart also in the later policies of liberalism, or better, "libertarianism," which assumed that democracy could and should be forcibly imposed upon other countries, even though they might be reluctant to live under democratic forms of government. There was general agreement about the dependence of freedom on social organization, whether men were compelled to be free by the persistence of an inscrutable force in social evolution or by the authority of a Transcendental Reason in the state. In spite of Spencer's policy of *laissez faire* and his repugnance to "the sins of legislators," he was of the same mind with Comte and Hegel and other philosophers who thought that freedom was a function of social organization because it is supposed to be a process of increasing differentiation and integration.

There were, however, a few who challenged this dominant faith in freedom and individuality through social organization; but their protests had little effect upon the general trend of thought. Ironically, the thinkers who most clearly exposed its fallacies were the men who unintentionally supplied the most plausible arguments for freedom by means of regimentation. J. S. Mill had made it clear in his essay *On Liberty* that, if human beings could be free, this was in spite of social organization, not because of it. But his arguments were unfortunately used as reasons for the free enterprise of powerful organizations in their vested interests, thus in effect justifying greater regimentation in order to preserve economic freedom. There is no greater irony in the history of ideas than this perversion of Mill's arguments in behalf of individual liberty, unless it is the current attempt to justify governmental monopolies in the name of constitutional rights.

From opposite and more radical extremes there were harsher voices challenging the faith in freedom through organization. Nietzsche, from the standpoint of his "aristocratic radicalism," protested against the belief that individuals could become free and strong through the herding of the weak into social and political organization for the sake of their own security. "The apparently crazy notion that one should consider the act he performs for another to be higher than the act he performs for himself ... has its own reason : namely, the gregarious instinct which rests on the valuation that individuals as such are of slight importance, although collectively their importance is great. It is assumed that they all constitute a community with a common feeling and a common conscience. My thought : goals are lacking and *these must be individuals*. We see the general trend : each individual is sacrificed and serves as a mere tool."[7] Marx and Engels, from the opposite extreme of democratic radicalism, challenged the assumption that there is a rational basis for social organization, such that class conflicts could be resolved through an essential community of different interests. On the contrary, the basis of social organization is an irrational conflict of economic forces. The only freedom that is achieved through organization is the ability of a stronger class to exploit the weaker until the latter through organization deprives the former of its specious liberties, and so on to the goal of a genuinely free society. Such a free and classless society will obviously require a minimum of organization. "As the basis of civilization is the exploitation of one class by another class, its whole development moved within a permanent contradiction. Each advance of production ... is a step backwards in the position of the oppressed class, that is, of the immense majority. Each benefit

---

[7] *Der Wille zur Macht*, Vol. I, p. 269.

for some is necessarily a disadvantage for the others; each new liberation of one class is a new oppression for another class."[8]

Mill, Nietzsche, and Marx are here grouped together, in spite of their different motives and presuppositions, because they all attacked the centralization of authority in the modern nation-state as a new form of tyranny. They attacked it in behalf of what Croce has called "the religion of liberty" in the nineteenth century. It was, as he says, a genuine religion or a common faith of the age, possessing its own ethic and its own form of aspiration. "Its significance lay solely in the goal at which it aimed—that human life should draw breath more freely, should grow deeper and broader."[9] And it was shared by countless thousands who knew nothing of philosophy. What needed to be challenged was the complacent assumption that a more liberal and highly civilized type of life would be inevitably evolved through the increasingly complex organization of modern society. In other words, it was assumed that greater freedom was in store for human life by continuing along the same lines of national and imperial expansion. The doctrines of Mill, Nietzsche, and Marx, different as they may have been in all other respects, were in a common revolt against the identification of liberalism with the tendencies generally regarded as progressive. But the conviction that human freedom increases with the organization of society outlasted the efforts of its critics. The strength of this conviction is exemplified today in the various attempts to justify a more highly centralized economic organization under political autocracy—and this in the name of new freedoms, under some travesty of arguments from Mill or Nietzsche or Marx. Thus, "the impatience for liberal institutions has given rise to open or masked dictatorships everywhere. Liberty, which before the war was a static faith or a practice with scant faith, has fallen from the minds of men even where it has not fallen from their institutions, and has been replaced by activistic libertarianism, which more than ever dreams of wars and upheavals and destruction, bursts out into disordered movements, and plans showy and arid works."[10]

---

[8] Engels, *Origin of the Family* (quoted in Burns, *Handbook of Marxism*, p. 336).

[9] Benedetto Croce, *History of Europe in the Nineteenth Century* (London, Allen & Unwin, 1934), p. 13.

[10] *Ibid.*, p. 352.

The first half of the present century may perhaps be remembered as the period in which nations set out to commit all the mistakes which the previous century had betrayed in its philosophy. The rapid advances in economic and political organization—"the machine age," "the rise of nationalism"—had been favorably interpreted as continuous betterment and "the evanescence of evil." This material progress, as social change in the external and spatial order of civilization, was likened to the process of growth and learning in an individual organism. What empirical evidence is there for the theory that the progressive organization of a civilized society is a process of increasing differentiation and integration, and that the outcome is more freedom and individuality? The growth of an individual from its embryological stage through infancy and youth to maturity is evidently a development from the comparatively simple to the comparatively complex, and perhaps also, if the terms are carefully defined, from relative incoherence to coherence, and from homogeneity to heterogeneity. Human learning is like that: there is transformation from a vague, homogeneous totality of experience to a clarified and coherent state of knowledge, with concomitant differentiation of its terms and relations, and progressive integration of ideas. The development of character is like that, and the progress of science exhibits the same principle. Stout has called it the principle of indeterminate apprehension. But this process of differentiation and integration pertains to the qualitative and intensive dimension of life as lived through its span of duration. It pertains to the careers of minded individuals as enacted historically, and not to the extensive, spatialized interrelations of those careers within a social order. Presumably, freedom and individuality are achievements of the moral and intellectual growth of human beings as they reach maturity. But where is there any evidence of greater freedom and more highly integrated individuality in the behavior of social institutions and organizations as they grow older? I can find nothing to support that assumption except metaphysical speculations about the "organicity" of society.

The fiction of a primitive state of nature survives in the theory that civilization advances from the simple to the complex. In first-hand reports of primitive societies by competent students, there is little to indicate that the life of savages is simple, undifferentiated, or even incoherent. The order of their social organization of marriages and families, of food getting, handicraft, religious ritual, political administration, and the like, seems not less complex and heterogeneous, but rather another kind of complexity and a differentiation less familiar to ourselves. In certain respects the organization of tribal life seems more complicated, more highly differentiated, and more unified than that of a civilized community. The daily life of the savage is circumscribed and minutely regulated in ways that make our civilized life seem relatively disorganized and haphazard. Furthermore, it would be impossible to account for the origin of complex social orders in civilized life unless there were at least as much complexity in the original materials or "contents" out of which the civilization developed. Tracing back the history of organized society, we are led not to a simple and undifferentiated beginning, but to other sorts of complexity and differentiation.

Durkheim was correct in asserting that the primitive societies possess a *mechanical* instead of an *organic* type of solidarity. The former, with its ensemble of customs, beliefs, and sentiments, has less specialization of skills and less division of labor, but more similitude of thought and conduct. For that reason Durkheim considers this solidarity to be mechanical, whereas the solidarity due to division of labor and specialization is organic. On the one hand, the mechanical solidarity of similitude involves human laws that are essentially retributive. The sanction of this type of law is the punishment of an individual for violating the collective conscience of the group. The organic solidarity from division of labor, on the other hand, involves a type of law that is not retributive, but *restitutory*. Its sanction is essentially a simple act of reparation or restoration (*remise en état*). The violator is not condemned to suffer the same evil that he has inflicted on others. The sanction of restitutory law is rather "a means of turning back upon the past in order to restore it as far as possible to its normal form."[11] My disagreement with Durkheim is only with respect to what has been said before concerning the "organic" character of society. If its organization resembles that of an individual organism, it is not in its actual structure, but in its "inclination to seek power after power." Division of labor and specialization of aptitudes in groups

---

[11] Emile Durkheim, *De la division du travail social*, 2d ed. (1902), p. 79.

are the conditions, not the consequences, of "organic" solidarity. They are the features through which the organization of a group is able to give direction to the behavior of its members, as motivated by merely gregarious impulses, and so to control the chance juxtapositions that produce "mechanical" solidarity. To illustrate the contrast: when every able-bodied man in the neighborhood is called out to fight a forest fire, there is little time or occasion for division of labor in accordance with special skills. There is, of course, a certain amount of organized direction and the assignment of men to particular jobs. But the direction of activities is determined for the most part by *similitude* of human capacities in a common emergency, and not by difference of capacities for a variety of situations; the assignment to particular jobs is largely a matter of chance in the *proximity* and *number* of individuals at hand. Coöperation of that sort is "mechanical," in Durkheim's sense, and it was probably the type of solidarity that prevailed among primitive groups, faced with common dangers. In contrast to this, consider the manner of dealing with fire hazards in a modern city. The police and fire departments, the architects and builders who devise fire protection, the underwriters of fire insurance, and other agencies, both public and private, represent specialized services for providing security against fire. The more highly organized this work becomes in its various branches, through increasing division and specialization, the more it tends to produce an "organic" instead of a "mechanical" type of solidarity.

This tendency is not, as Durkheim supposes, in the direction of more inclusive interests, wider sympathies, and greater freedom. On the contrary, it is toward a more exclusive or "closed" type of society, in which restitutory laws are intended to preserve the corporate identity of the organization, with shared responsibility, instead of merely exacting penalties for particular acts. Thus, restitutory or reparative law, expressing the organic type of social solidarity, is directed not primarily against individual culprits, but against the alleged hostility of minority groups to organized society as a whole. Instead of the primitive belief that the act of a single individual contaminates his whole tribe, there is the reverse assumption that individuals are contaminated because of their membership in groups or classes opposed by dominant interests in the nation. With more rigorous political organization, laws are interpreted and enforced less with regard to relations between individuals and more with regard to the interrelations of organized groups. The organic tendency in social change is toward more collective discipline and less individual freedom.

To sumarize: In spite of increasing division of labor, social organization is inherently opposed to the kind of organization that pertains to individual growth and learning. The familiar analogy between the specialization of organic functions and the specialization of social functions is essentially misleading. Social organization is the reverse of physiological and psychological processes. Instead of differentiation, there is increasing *uniformity,* and instead of integration, there is, not indeed disintegration or dissolution, which is the concomitant of growth and evolution, but *elimination* of interests that are not exclusively devoted to the survival of the organization. As a political party, a labor union, a private club, a university, or whatever other sort of human association, becomes more highly and effectively organized, the importance of administration increases. Authority is centralized. Archives and precedents accumulate. The whole becomes greater than the sum of its parts. At the same time, the corporate identity of the institution, with its particular pattern of activities, becomes less a means of promoting the tastes and pursuits of individual members, and more an end in itself. The organization tends to become self-sufficient, independent, and exclusive of all other interests, so far as this is possible within the limits of its social environment. To use a colloquial phrase, each social organization tells the rest of the world, "Watch us grow!" Since nothing *can* grow except individual plants and animals, the social organization strives to become as like a growing organism as possible. Not being able to grow, it expands. Having no capacity for differentiation apart from the lives of its members, it strives to be different by means of its self-imposed uniformity. Unable to achieve any genuine integration apart from the integrated minds and characters of its members, the organization tries to eliminate variety and raise its own prestige. It strives to be viable in its own separate and corporate character.

In order to analyze the relation of freedom to social organization, I shall return with Coleridge to Kant's conception of nature's teleology. I shall take as a clue the following statement from the

Critique of Judgment: "Only organized matter, as in its specific form a product of nature, necessarily demands the application of the conception of natural end. But this conception, when once obtained, necessarily leads to the idea of the whole of nature as a system of ends, and to this idea all natural mechanism must be subordinated in accordance with principles of reason."[12] We need not debate here the alleged necessity nor the transcendental principles of reason to which Kant alludes. For purposes of the present analysis we may substitute the idea of an organized society as a whole for "the idea of the whole of nature." The relation of freedom and organization is to be analyzed in terms of the Kantian conception of a system of ends, to which the mechanism of organization may be (not "must be") subordinated in accordance with "principles of reason."

The conception of *organization* has two distinct ingredients: the notion of the elements or constituents that are brought together as a whole, and the notion of a structure or pattern of relations in which these elements stand to one another. This is true of any type of organization, whether it be the organization of cells and tissues in a living organism, the organization of facts and ideas in a system of knowledge, or the organization of individuals in groups, and of groups in states. There is, first, material to be organized, and second, the forms or patterns of organization.

With social, economic, or political organization there is a significant difference. Obviously, its constituents as human beings are, to a certain degree, free to go their own ways apart from the particular organization in question. A member of a business firm may also be a father, a house owner, a tennis player, a Republican, and the chairman of a Committee to Aid the Eskimos. He may have a variety of interests, personal tastes, and associations that do not depend on the structure and character of the business firm to which he belongs. Hence, not only are the individual differences of the human material in a social organization independent variants, but they may point in opposite directions. For example, members of a labor union may have individual interests contrary to the accepted policy of the organization during a strike, and so they may have an allegiance divided between their responsibility in collective bargaining and the desire to support their families or the desire to maintain amicable relations with the management.

---

[12] P. 391.

As individual differences are intensified in the functioning of an organization, the stability of its structure is likely to be weakened. Conversely, the more secure and permanent the structure, the less effective will be the individual differences. In theory, if not in practice, the demand for greater freedom of action on the part of individuals or groups is a constant threat to *some* form of organization, although it may also be preliminary to another and a more vigorous form. A freedom opposed in principle to *any* further organization of human activities would mean social nihilism and systematic disintegration of a community.

These were the main grounds of philosophical criticism against the rationalism of the eighteenth century. It was generally agreed that the thinkers of the Age of Reason, as well as the subsequent leaders in the Revolution, had so greatly exaggerated the importance of the individual that they were blind to the need of social organization. The earlier thinkers had conceived of knowledge as solely the product of individual experience and reason. They had attempted to establish the state on a basis of individual rights without regard to moral and political obligations. They had conceived of justice in terms of self-interest or "egotism," not in terms of collective welfare or "altruism."[13] The principal problem presented to the early nineteenth century was a problem of *restoration:* how to reinstate the intellectual, moral, and religious values of the old regime without giving up the recent gains in human freedom during the Revolution. Out of the traditionalism and romanticism of this period of restoration came the organic conception of laws and institutions, in which the restitution of social order was brought into a new (if not a "higher") synthesis with the ideal of individual liberty. Comte could insist, with more confidence than evidence, that progress was henceforth to be the achievement of freedom *through* order. The synthesis, indeed, was less a solution than a definition of a problem. But it was a problem that was to become more urgent with the increasing complexity of organization, leaving its aftermath in the social revolution of the present century.

It has been convenient to distinguish, with Windelband and others, two general philosophical approaches to the study of civili-

---

[13] Critics of rationalism in the nineteenth century were guilty of at least one exaggeration: they exaggerated the faults of the eighteenth century.

zation. One approach is from the standpoint of the natural sciences, the other from the standpoint of history. Any theoretical solution of the problem of freedom and organization presupposes some conception of the relationship and differences between these two approaches. There is an instructive ambiguity in the term *natural knowledge*. In one sense, knowledge is "natural" because it is a science of nature, "that which we observe in perception through the senses." The objectivity of nature, as we know it, is expressed by Mr. Whitehead in the statement that "we can think about nature without thinking about thought."[14] In another sense, knowledge is "natural" because it develops out of conditions that Mr. Dewey has called "the existential matrix of inquiry."[15] Any piece of knowledge has its natural history, biological and cultural. Knowledge is natural in the sense that it is continuous with organic life. Inquiry, like the rest of life, is a process of activity that involves environmental factors and also effects further changes in the environment. Knowledge is conditioned by, and in turn effects changes in, a social as well as a physical environment. The existential matrix of inquiry, through which knowledge is achieved, is a cultural context of language and traditions. But Mr. Dewey is careful to point out that, although inquiry, like all organic behavior, "is a strictly temporal affair," the terms of the propositions in the knowledge resulting from inquiry do not themselves stand in a temporal relation to one another. The temporal phase of knowledge is expressed in language as *narration,* while the spatial phase is expressed as *description.* But no subject can be narrated without also being describable, nor can there be description without narration being taken for granted, since "what is described exists within some temporal process to which 'narration' applies."[16] Although there is no separation between the spatial and temporal phases of judgment, there is a significant difference in the analysis of descriptive and narrative judgments. In the temporal and historic phase of judgment, subject matter is characterized in terms of *direction* of change. Narration signifies change *from* something *to* something; its terms are events. Now, an event, which is literally

---

[14] A. N. Whitehead, *The Concept of Nature* (Cambridge Univ. Press, 1920), p. 3.

[15] John Dewey, *Logic: The Theory of Inquiry* (New York, Holt, 1938), chaps. ii, iii.

[16] *Ibid.,* p. 220.

the *outcome* of a process, involves a telic reference: the process can be narrated only in terms of a beginning, an interval, and an ending. But events not only occur in time; "they also take place somewhere, and the conditions of this 'somewhere' stand in co-existence with one another and also with things taking place elsewhere."[17] Events, in an order of coexistence, are describable in terms of interaction, and mechanism is simply a name for the descriptive explanation of interactions. Hence, in its spatial and descriptive phase, judgment abstracts from the telic reference to endings or consummations, and emphasizes mechanism. The model for the spatial determination of subject matter in descriptive judgments is mathematical physics.

Mr. Dewey's instructive distinction between judgments of narration and judgments of description helps to make clear the relationship and differences between the two approaches to the study of civilization. There are three major differences.

1) The method of the natural sciences is *experimental*. Every proposition, theory, or formulation of a law is hypothetical and subject to modification in the light of further evidence. Historical judgments are also hypothetical, but for different reasons. Scientific propositions are means to further experimental transformation of their subject matter, whereas it is obviously impossible to experiment on things in the past. Historical judgments are hypothetical in the sense that their confirmation is contingent upon the discovery of further evidence. We do not predict or control events in history. The ideal of historical knowledge is, instead, to determine the continuity of the present with the past, or the development of a more recent from a more remote past. The subject matter of historical knowledge is to be found in traditions, not in observations, and, while observations can be repeated, no two traditions are the same. The value of an observation is to serve as a basis for scientific generalization. But generalizations from history are seldom instructive and always dangerous.

2) In the descriptive propositions of natural science, classification is nominal and more or less conventional. There is a valid distinction between "natural" and "artificial" classifications, but it is a difference in degree, not in kind. Scientific classifications are deliberate constructions, with an arbitrary element in them, where-

---

[17] *Ibid.*, p. 239.

as "nature knows no classes." Hence, hierarchical conceptions are out of place in scientific description. There is no ultimate subordination of the lower to the higher. Natural phenomena do not belong on different levels of importance or perfection. The study of history, on the contrary, is concerned with materials inherently and inevitably classified. The classification is not designed for the convenience of the student, but is discovered in the historical subject matter itself. There are classes of rulers and their subjects, of nobility and peasants, groups differing in nationality, in occupation, and in property rights. Here, classification is both the cause and the effect of social organization. It represents real historical entities and actual forces of social change.

3) Finally, the natural sciences are indifferent to values, or at least to any value except the truth of warranted judgments. In physics, the behavior of molecules, atoms, and electrons is neither right nor wrong, neither good nor evil. Chemistry does not decide that one element is more beautiful than another. But historical interpretation implies a theory of social values. A "scientific" historian may have the ideal of a wholly disinterested, objective attitude toward the past, without any moral approbation or disapprobation of its events. Nevertheless, the subject matter with which he deals involves moral and aesthetic values, since it consists of the conduct and attitudes of passionate human beings, as well as the purposes of their laws and institutions. History is not adequately narrated unless the historian takes human volitions and preferences into account. "Those who boast that they are not, as social scientists, interested in what ought to be, generally assume that the hitherto prevailing order is the proper ideal of what ought to be. . . . A theory of social values like a theory of metaphysics is none the better because it is held tacitly and is not, therefore, critically examined."[18]

The distinction between scientific and historical knowledge, both in subject matter and in method, is no arbitrary or subjective division. The differences between description and narration reflect basically diverse phases of civilization, having to do with its instrumental and intrinsic values. As neither narration nor description is possible in complete separation from the other, so it is with the

---

[18] Morris Cohen, *Reason and Nature* (New York, Harcourt, Brace, 1931), pp. 343, 349.

two phases of civilization. There is no civilization as end without some particular civilization as means, and no technique of civilization as means that does not involve the intrinsic values of civilization as end. The diversity of the two phases does not imply a separation of means and end. Narration of the history of civilization involves at every step the description of a particular material culture. We cannot suppose, and there is no reason to suppose, that by the nature of our judgments we are obliged to think of civilization differently from the manner in which it is, whether as extended in space or enacted in history. If, then, there is this marked diversity between the scientific and historical accounts of civilization, it is reasonable to infer a corresponding diversity in its spatial and historical phases. In what does this diversity consist?

Mr. Leonard Woolf has recently attempted to analyze the "anatomy of civilization" into its essential elements, and while he has not entirely succeeded in this ambitious attempt, he has at least indicated the sources of the most serious tensions in civilized life. "There are," he says, "three main factors, which determine the nature of all social life and on which, therefore, the preservation or destruction of civilization depends," namely, *power, economics,* and *ideas*.[19] Although there is wide disagreement about the means of preserving or advancing civilization in the various countries, Mr. Woolf argues that ideas about the ultimate end of civilization differ very little from those expressed in the speech of Pericles twenty-five hundred years ago. Hitler, Mussolini, and Stalin have voiced essentially the same ideas of the ultimate end as those of Mr. Churchill or President Roosevelt. They may hold antithetical opinions about the right way of realizing this end, but in their utterances they all at least profess agreement with the Athenian ideal of civilization in the speech of Pericles. As Mr. Woolf defines it, "the ultimate end is the widening and enrichment of the individual's existence, the creation of an association in which the free development of each is the condition for the free development of all."[20] However, when there are today such conflicting means of promoting "civilization" in Europe, it is difficult to see how there can be more than verbal agreement about its goal.

---

[19] *Barbarians Within and Without* (New York, Harcourt, Brace, 1939), p. 112.

[20] *Ibid.,* p. 54.

Opposition of social organizations and technologies puts a radically different content into the idea of civilization as end.

Tension and conflict within modern civilization result from discrepancies among the three main factors of economics, power, and ideas. In social organization the main factor is *economics*, in technology it is *power*, and in the significant growth of individuals it consists of *ideas*. When ideas lag behind the development of organization and technology, these two latter factors pull in opposite directions. The employment of power in human society belongs to the descriptive and extensive phase of civilization; the organization based on the factor of economics, to its historical and intensive phase. The tendency of the effective use of power is the mechanization of society, and thus mechanism becomes the model for all descriptive and technological knowledge of energies in a spatio-temporal order. The tendency of economic organization is the organic unity of society, and thus the model of historical knowledge is a universal system of social, political, and economic forces, working toward some sort of world-wide unity. But civilization is threatened with overmechanization on the one hand and with overorganization on the other. The former leads to a rapid acceleration of material progress that increases insecurity. The latter leads to social stagnation, preventing the betterment of living conditions. Hence, in order to escape the anarchy of mechanization, society organizes; and in order to escape the tyranny of organization, society mechanizes.

The conflicting tendencies of mechanization and organization may be illustrated in the present dilemma of agriculture throughout many parts of the United States. The use of the tractor, harvester, and other machinery on the farm has resulted in a large increase in its productivity and the efficiency of farm labor. At the same time, it has resulted in the displacement of large numbers of agricultural workers, with a consequent loss of security. "Overmechanization" in this connection means the substitution of machinery for human beings to their own detriment and without sufficient compensation in the welfare of the rest of society. Where displacement of farmers and increased unemployment lead only to greater profit for the few remaining owners of the land, with a "surplus" of undistributed farm products, the tendency may be regarded as overmechanization. In order to counteract this tendency various private and governmental agencies of organization are set up, such as means of "freezing" prices, of withholding products from the market, of persuading or compelling growers to reduce their crops, or of keeping the wages of agricultural workers at a minimum. In the voluntary associations of owners on the one hand, as well as in governmental regulation on the other, there need be no question of motives, but there is an evident tendency toward "overorganization" or "regimentation," preventing further progress.

Between the limits of complete mechanization and total organization is the field of freedom. There is no real freedom independent of the factors of economics and power; that is to say, apart from organization and mechanization. But organization is free when the idea of mechanism is subordinated through intelligence to a social purpose. It does not follow that a human society ever has been or ever might be completely mechanized, any more than it ever has been or ever might be totally organized. These conditions are ideal. They represent limits to which social development may approximate in one direction or the other. Durkheim was correct in supposing that the process of civilization tends to transform an instinctively mechanical solidarity into a consciously organic solidarity. In a primitive society, as in any mechanical system, interactions can be understood in terms of mere relations of resemblance and contiguity in space and time. As civilization advances with the increasing complexity of its economic factor, social interactions are no longer to be understood merely in terms of resemblance and contiguity; face-to-face relations and direct use of material power by individuals become of less importance in the organization of society; division of labor and its specialization involve more remote interdependence of individuals and more indirect use of power for human purposes; and, thus, relations in a civilized community involve a higher degree of organic solidarity. But these two tendencies are correlative, even though they point in different directions. The contrast and the correlations between them have been reflected in the categories of different metaphysical interpretations. Materialism reflects a state of affairs in which the influence of mind and conscious design is at a minimum, while idealism reflects a state of affairs in which their influence is at a maximum. Each interpretation suffers from the illusion, inherited from the prevailing optimism of the nineteenth century, that the more we advance in organization, or in mechanization, or in both together, the greater is the amount of human freedom. Modern war has most effectively punctured the bubble of that illusion. The region of freedom lies neither within the sphere of organization and the economic factor nor the sphere of mechanization and the power factor. Freedom lies in the process of *communication,* and ideas may be regarded as the primary factor of communication.

Coleridge's notion of the General Will as an "ever-originating contract" signifies one of the essential conditions for a free society. The several forms of freedom—freedom of thought and speech, of tastes and pursuits, of assembly and worship—depend upon the mutual adjustment of interests that is symbolized by a *contract.* But there is no need of assuming a Universal Reason or a Transcendental Mind in society in order to account for its "ever-originating contract." Freedom exists neither as a result of higher social organization nor as a result of more efficient mechanization. Freedom exists *in spite of* these efforts for greater security and material progress. The question whether the two factors of economics and power in civilization have a rational or an irrational basis can be given only a qualified answer, relative to different historical conditions. It is not a question of whether Kant was right or wrong in his teleological conception of organization, with power rationally subordinated to a system of ends. It is rather a question of when and where and to what extent this conception does or does not apply in the history of civilization. Society becomes *rationalized* when the management and interrelations of its institutions are controlled by general conceptions or standard meanings. But society only becomes *rationally free* when and where these general conceptions are directed toward the idea of civilization as an end.

Mr. Woolf has designated *ideas* as the third main factor in civilization, but he seems to have regarded ideas as elements in an ideology that seeks only to organize the economic system and to control mechanical power. I agree that ideas are developed primarily as instruments for economics and power. But the function of ideas as instruments depends on something more than their technical fitness to accomplish a specific end. The function of ideas in civilization depends also upon the fact of communication. Ideas are communicated not only through the medium of spoken or written language; they are also communicated through trade and travel, through sport and recreation, and through the unspoken suggestions of the visual arts and music. Forms of communication, then, acquire intrinsic values over and above the instrumental values of the ideas that are communicated for immediate ends. The idea of civilization as end is the normative conception of free communication in all of its various forms. Freedom is essentially the intelligible communication of ideas, in spite of the barriers of economic or political organization and in spite of the constant pressure of expanding material power. The problem of civilization as an end is to overcome the economic barriers and the political pressures that hinder free communication of ideas, but without thereby forfeiting the security gained by social organization.

EDWARD W. STRONG

CIVILIZATIONS IN HISTORICAL PERSPECTIVE

IF CIVILIZATION were not a time-continuant character of some human societies and if these, as civilizations, were not subject to alteration in their temporal courses, fears about the future of civilization and summons to preserve it from peril would be misplaced. Civilizations have perished. Whether the civilized be contrasted valuatively with the barbaric or temporally with societies less advanced in their cultivation, men are so contrasted because they have become civilized. The practices that are civilized in character or civilizing in their effects have beginnings and perpetuations, and are, by the same historical token, subject to discontinuations. Clearly, the idea of civilization is not divorceable from a historical context of discussion. The designation "civilized" pertains to several societies, the several civilizations in their temporal occurring. Were all these civilizations arrayable as stages of one continuous process of transmission and inheritance, we should be warranted in using "civilization" for the unilinear development and "civilizations" for the societies in sequence. Today, with societies linked in world communication, there may be such warrant for viewing civilization as a unitary diffusion and development with respect to further continuation. In the past, however, there have been civilizations isolated in space from each other. Moreover, there are temporal discontinuations in the lapsings and innovations by which the nucleus of one society disintegrates and that of another becomes formed. Finally, what is transmitted from an earlier and inherited by a later society is a fund with a currency of meaning and value which does not remain constant. A single development and unitary meaning predicable as a sequence and common content of civilizations is not a warranted assertion. Our description of civilizations remains pluralistic.

The concern of this lecture is to examine the consequences for valuation of this pluralistic description. The rejection of a unitary description of civilization is also the rejection of a standard value or unitary norm of civilization-as-such by which the several civilizations are to be judged. The irreducible pluralism of civilizations obligates relativity in our value judgments. The argument of the essay is that this historical, valuational relativity cannot be escaped or transcended. Valuation is with respect to a perspective and involves a standpoint. This would mean only a diversity of representations of a common subject or content if the unitary description of civilization were legitimate; but, for a pluralistic description, diversity pertains to the historically situated content of judgment. For unitary description, relativity characterizes points of view but not the subject viewed. The relativity entailed by pluralism denies a common denominator and admits a radical disjunction of valuations.

Through participation in a civilization a man comes by the estimations and preferences expressed in his valuations. If his civilization were indeed the inheritor and perpetuator of preceding civilizations so that their contributions were accumulated in it, furthered in degree but not differing in kind, he could subsume them under a single standard of worth. The term "perspective" would designate no more than a time when and a place where a participant should come to make value judgments. The relativity of his participation would not thereby be a relativity of the civilization participated. The conditions of person, time, and place would simply be the relational situation of a judger. To take this as tantamount to relativity of content would be to confuse conditions of comprehension and judgment with what was comprehended and judged. For if, as the unitary view asserts, civilization is all of a piece though with many strands woven into its fabric, the manifold perspectives would have a common subject.

It is the irreducible pluralism of civilizations that puts sting into the use of the term "perspective." The value judgments engendered within any one civilization are not applicable to all others. *Within* the compass of any one civilization, meanings and valuations will vary from one generation to the next and between groups; but these variations are none the less conjunctive by a fund of common conviction and acceptance. It is perhaps this limited prevalence which has led to the supposition of universal prevalence, men finding it difficult to conceive of incentives and purposes radically different from those resident in their own society. Pluralism admits only the limited identification of valuation with one or another civilization as lived and enacted. The disjunctions of these identifications alienates one perspective from another and forbids us to claim more than a limited or relative scope for our ideals.

I

The unitary view of civilization embraces two main ideas. The first is the idea of a unilinear development or universal progress of mankind; the second is the idea of a content detached from its original investment in a society and inherited as a fund of culture common in meaning to both original and subsequent societies. One may proceed to argue from the belief in a master continuity or main stream of history to a belief in a common content carried forward and conserved by successive societies. Yet the latter belief does not depend upon the former. Rejection of the idea of universal progress takes away a support for the idea of a common content but does not thereby render the second idea untenable. No continuity of practice or of institution is required for inheritance of art and literature. In this first section, the criticism of the unitary view is concerned only with an analysis of valuation based on the idea of a unilinear course of civilization. We will consider the second idea, asserted as independent of the assumption of universal progress, when we come to examine the attempts to transcend valuational relativity.

In taking up an example of contemporary valuation based on the idea of unilinear development, a word of introduction is in order. The idea of civilization itself has a history in which the word has acquired the predominantly historical signification it now has in common usage. The word still carries with it a value connotation first attached in the eighteenth century when to the idea of civilization as *l'état social* was added the idea of progress. A progress of civilization (or even civilization as progress) was conceived as a single development of the human mind through successive stages of advancement. The unilinear sequence appeared plausible within the provincial scope of Condorcet's *Esquisse*. The nine epochs of his history delineate man's intellectual history leading up to the age of French enlightenment which is to usher in the tenth epoch of liberal humanization. The history of mankind is the course of development sketched for European societies from ancient to modern times. Universal progress was the assumption of a purpose or direction common to all these societies, each a stage in advance toward, or of temporary hindrance and recess from, a goal.

To accept Condorcet's assumption today, when the volumes of Toynbee's *Study of History* would alone discredit it, would be an anachronism. Yet the anachronism may escape detection and criticism when clothed with appeals to which we are sympathetic, and may even be taken as an argument which establishes a unitary, all-inclusive concept of civilization on the basis of an assumed continuity culminating in our valuations. As an example, I refer to the essay by William Henry Chamberlin entitled, "Europe's Revolt against Civilization."[1]

Chamberlin opens his essay with the announcement: "Within the short span of a single generation, between the beginning of the first World War and the present time, Europe has experienced the most formidable breakdown of civilization since the collapse of the Roman Empire in the fifth century A.D." He characterizes this breakdown by saying, "It is a revolt against civilization from within, a systematic destruction of cultural and humanistic values first through revolution, then through war and conquest." Russia and then Italy and Germany have been "lost" to European civilization. "All were completely and avowedly amoral, all were implacably hostile to any categorical imperatives, to any conception of the unity of European civilization."

Chamberlin goes on to say that "civilization of course is a broad term. But before 1914 there would have been fairly wide agreement among educated Europeans of all nationalities that freedom of speech and press and conscience and research, legal security of persons and property against arbitrary state action, some form of popular participation in government, freedom of travel, limitation of the death penalty to extremely grave offenses, if not its total abolition, would have been the distinctive characteristics of the civilized, as against a barbarous state. With all due allowances for exceptions and setbacks, liberalism was the strongest trend in the civilization of the nineteenth century; and a definition of civilization in liberal terms would have commanded more general agreement than any other definition." The "distinctive characteristics" of liberalism are further called "standards." "Now, measured by any of these standards, the record of the Communists in Russia, of the Nazis in Germany, of the Fascists in Italy is one of

---

[1] *Harper's Magazine*, December, 1940.

profound retrogression." The judgment of retrogression by liberal standards follows, according to the author, from viewing "what has happened in Europe . . . in a time perspective." So viewed, each of these three regimes which emerged after World War I "is a challenge to and a negation of the traditional European civilization." The consequence of this negation of liberalism is the return to barbarism: "Europe, cradle of so many civilizations, is becoming uninhabitable for civilized men."

As a limited identification or a valuation within one civilization as lived and enacted, the appeal to a fund of common conviction and acceptance is legitimate. Chamberlin's interpretation of history is addressed to a civilized audience; civilized, that is, in conforming to liberal characteristics and in advocating these as standards of conduct. For this audience, actions which challenge and negate a tradition of individual rights, of legal security of person and property, and of political consent and representation are retrogressive. They do not move in the direction desired by those who identify a civilization by the presence and perpetuation of liberal values. It is Chamberlin's universalization of this limited identification that is illegitimate as based on an idea of unilinear development.

Singular and plural usages of the word civilization remain free from ambiguity provided that one or the other of the two following distinctions is being maintained. There is, first, the descriptive contrast between two types of society, one civilized and the other primitive or savage. Anthropologists have not found this contrast very useful as a working distinction and have preferred the use of the term "culture" for that which is produced and transmitted by men. It remains feasible, however, to study a number of societies called civilized in an attempt to derive a set of traits common to all. These common traits, if established, would then be the defining characteristics of civilization used as a class term. Similarly, another set of traits established from the study of societies called primitive would establish the species with respect to individual instances. The generic term in this differentiation of civilized and primitive is mankind, humanity, or the human race. Once the two classes are established, a possible usefulness of a descriptive definition would be that of typing further instances for purposes of investigation.

The second distinction is the normative contrast between civilization and barbarism. Men defined as civilized, in terms of the first distinction, have asked themselves the question, Are we civilized? The question directs attention to what associations of men *ought* to be in order to be worthy of being called civilized. On this approach, one first sets forth an ideal of civilization. This ideal of a societal life worthy to be lived by men is then employed as a standard for judging how far societies that have existed, or that now exist, approximate to the normative conception. Instances of oppression and exploitation of some men by others in the working of institutions are brought into contrast with the ideal, with what men would do if they were "really" civilized. This way of judging lends itself to a Rousseauan reversal if we now introduce the first distinction, the contrast between civilized and primitive. The inhumanities and vices inhering in institutional practices are pointed out as the moral scandal of our civilization. These practices are the ignoble, the morally barbarous, as compared with the innocence of the noble savage. We have here the theme of primitivism which celebrates a simpler life as the better one, or which imagines an earlier time to have been a golden age in contrast to this age of iron.

More characteristic of modern valuations is the alliance of civilization with the idea of progress. Civilization as it should be is the future goal of reformatory or revolutionary change of existing societies. Compared with the ideal, these societies are not yet civilized; but the historical period of human life demarcated from the prehistorical, primitive period is, for purposes of historical description, still called a period of civilization. Advances in the direction of fulfilling the ideal are then a progress of civilization. With the judgment of progress, historical interpretation goes beyond description in making a claim about the desired or desirable direction of development. The argument is now but a step removed from the fallacy of converting descriptive classification into an interpretation of history by which to justify and support the preferred ideal. This fallacy consists in converting an abstraction, the generic term mankind, into a unity developing through time.

The unity of civilization, for classificatory description, is synonymous with the set of defining characteristics asserted as common traits of all civilizations. Interpretation proceeds without any warrant whatsoever in converting this unity into a temporal continuity. When this is done, the generic term of the definition, mankind or the human race, is taken as the continuant which develops through a succession of civilizations toward the realization of some master purpose. Each society is then treated as a stage in a total progression and is called a civilization so far as it can be assigned a place in a single, cumulative development—the universal progress of mankind.

Undoubtedly, the persistence of the human race on earth is the biological condition and continuity for all other human continuities. Such persistence, however, does not constitute any identifying nucleus of social relations with respect to which cultural transmissions take place. Philosophers of history have, indeed, been aware that it was illegitimate to assert mankind as a continuant linking a temporal sequence of societies. Either the idea of universal progress was thereby illegitimate, or it was saved by recourse to a metaphysical fiction. Hegel's World-Historical Spirit is such a fiction. The Spirit first dwells in the Oriental world and, having actualized all the inherent potentialities of that society, it journeys into the lives of men in the Mediterranean Basin. This continuity by metaphysical fiat becomes acutely embarrassed by mention of the Mayan society. On the unilinear interpretation of history, we must either deny that this society was a civilization at the expense of a descriptive classification, or else strain credulity by an Atlantic leap to save continuity in Spirit where it cannot be shown in evidence.

We are now ready to examine Chamberlin's argument and value judgment. When Chamberlin asserts that "Europe has experienced the most formidable breakdown of civilization since the collapse of the Roman Empire in the fifth century A.D.," he designates "Europe" as a continuant, and civilization as progressing, retrogressing, or breaking down. The "many civilizations" of which Europe has been the "cradle" are then interpretable as a succession of stages by societies or by centuries. The latest stage and trend is identified as liberalism. Individuals, groups, and nations opposed to liberalism are, by his valuation, opposed to civilization. Their opposition is what Chamberlin calls "Europe's Revolt against Civilization." What supplants liberalism is barbarism, and the revolutionists are the barbarians.

Chamberlin characterizes the revolutions in Russia, Italy, and

Germany as all "implacably hostile to any categorical moral imperatives." He does not state what these imperatives are. If it be assumed that they have to do with the defining traits of liberalism when asserted as standards of conduct, the moral imperatives pertain to the course a society must take if it is to be called civilized. Chamberlin might have held that the revolutions in Europe are a breaking with a liberal tradition of what is proper and ideal in human conduct and, following the precedent of Greek usage, declared that this defection is barbarian in the sense of being *immoral* from the point of view of men who adhere to this tradition. Instead, he designates the new regimes as being "completely and avowedly *amoral.*" They break not just with a European civilization defined in liberal terms. They are not barbaric relative to alienation from and negation of a liberal tradition. They are absolute barbarism. Their histories constitute a "profound retrogression" from all civilization and not simply from a civilization. The absolute valuation rides upon the back of a unilinear concept of Europe's civilization. A unity, actual or ideal, of European civilization is a categorical imperative which has its definition from liberalism but its presumed authority from history itself as a single tradition. Any break with this tradition is retrogress. With the foundering of the unilinear concept, Chamberlin's absolute valuation is dismounted. The most that he is entitled to assert is a limited or relative judgment.

II

If the civilization in which we live is only one of several actual and possible civilizations, we should initially be on guard against the assumption that our preferences and ideals have a privileged historical status. Our interpretations and valuations of histories would then be seen to involve a time-place content of what we are concerned to live and enact, and thereby the relativity of our perspective. This historical pluralism does not encompass nonhistorical questions with respect to which perspective is irrelevant, questions that do not implicate the questioner's historical situation as ingredient to and involved in his answers. The valuative contrast between civilization and barbarism, however, is a historical question; and the attempt to discriminate a superior from an inferior civilization is a historical problem. If time-place situations of historical comprehension are pluralistic with respect to the subject or content comprehended, value judgments can make only a limited and never a universal claim to acceptance.

There are, in principle, three ways in which historical interpretation starting from a pluralistic description can seek to escape from valuational relativity. The first consists in the claim of a time-free perspective, an insight that transcends the time-place limitation of judgment lacking this higher vision. The second attempts to establish an objective scale of valuation based on factual indices by which to discriminate the more advanced from the less advanced societies. The third holds that there is an ideal content of civilization which is itself absolved from local limitation and which is absolute and not relative for its participants. I will discuss each of these attempted escapes, beginning with the first, the claim of a time-free perspective as made by Oswald Spengler in *The Decline of the West*.

Spengler early in his book criticizes and discards the unitary interpretation with its subdivision of history into ancient, medieval, and modern periods. "The most appropriate designation for this West-European scheme of history, in which the great Cultures are made to follow orbits around *us* as the presumed centre of world-happenings, is the *Ptolemaic system* of history. The system that is put forward in this work in place of it I regard as the *Copernican discovery* in the historical sphere, in that it admits of no sort of privileged position to the Classical or the Western Culture as against the Cultures of India, Babylon, China, Egypt, the Arabs, Mexico—separate worlds of dynamic being which in point of mass count for just as much in the general picture of history as the Classical, while frequently surpassing it in point of spiritual greatness and soaring power."[2]

Spengler's pluralism maintains a radical discontinuity between individual societies in regard to the motivations and purposes within each society. Such life experience is individual, unique, and noncontinuable beyond the death of a society, even though many

---

[2] *The Decline of the West,* trans. by C. F. Atkinson (New York, Knopf, 1926; 2 vols.), Vol. I, p. 18.

Since Spengler maintains that every great culture is followed by its own civilization period, neither "culture" nor "civilization" can be employed, if we adopt his usage, to designate the time-extended occurrence which is the beginning, continuance, and ending of an ethnographic complex called by anthropologists a culture and by historians a civilization. I will therefore use the word "society" throughout the discussion of Spengler for this more general designation, to avoid confusion with his special meanings.

of its products are inherited and some of its relationships persist and overlie the development of a subsequent society. Yet though each society is a unique "organism," he holds that the sequence of developments from beginning to ending follows an irreversible, necessary order of occurrence. This necessity is inherent in the structure of each society but is the common morphology, or "organic-logical sequel," of all.[3] The sequence of periods is metaphorically likened to the four seasons in the comparison of spiritual epochs. The myth and religion of a Springtime period are followed by the Summer of high culture, this by an Autumnal period of intellectual analysis, and finally by Winter, the civilization period in which, all intensive possibilities having been fulfilled, only the extensive possibilities of conquest and empire remain to be enacted.

Having asserted a life, soul, or idea unique to each society, Spengler is faced with the problem of understanding the "soul" of societies other than his own. If it is only in the Western society that Faustian man conceives of his life as through-and-through temporal, this temporal perspectivity is then peculiar to our society and to no other. For the Western historian alone does it become possible to assert the destiny of his own society by analogy with past societies. Yet how is the historian to "penetrate" into the feel and go of the perished societies? How is he in a position to recreate the idea of another Culture as "the sum total of its inner possibilities"?

Spengler does not bypass the problem by ignoring the relativity of historical perspectives. On the contrary, he makes out so good a case for relativity that his own asserted transcendence has no ground to stand on. "It is a quite indefensible method of presenting world-history to begin by giving rein to one's own religious, political or social convictions and endowing the sacrosanct three-phase system with tendencies that will bring it exactly to one's own standpoint. This is, in effect, making of some formula—say, the 'Age of Reason,' Humanity, the greatest good of the greatest

---

[3] Vol. I, p. 112. "I hope to show that without exception all great creations and forms in religion, art, politics, social life, economy and science appear, fulfil themselves and die down *contemporaneously* in all the Cultures; that the inner structure of one corresponds strictly to that of all the others; that there is not a single phenomenon of deep physiognomic importance in the record of one for which we could not find a counterpart in the record of every other; and that this counterpart is to be found under a characteristic form and in a perfectly definite chronological order."

number, enlightenment, economic progress, national freedom, the conquest of nature, or world-peace—a criterion whereby to judge whole millennia of history. And so we judge that they [men of other societies] were ignorant of the 'true path,' or that they failed to follow it, when the fact is simply that their will and purposes were not the same as ours."[4]

In opposition to this indefensible method, the Copernican pluralism leads to the assertion of the "historically relative character" of data as the "expression of one specific existence and one only." It follows that our standards of political and moral valuation are not universally valid in providing for "the" solution of "the" problem of property or of marriage. As pluralists, we are only entitled to speak of "a" solution of "a" problem, a limitation not recognized by Ptolemaic historians and philosophers.[5] How, then, is one to deal with the pluralism of many questioners and many answers? Spengler replies, "... it is only by obtaining *a group of historically limited solutions* and measuring it by *utterly impersonal* criteria that the final secrets can be reached. The real student of mankind treats no standpoint as absolutely right or wrong. ... The thinker must admit the validity of all, or of none."[6]

Grant that it is an indefensible method to rationalize history as though all earlier societies existed for the sake of our convictions and values and that pluralism means a group of historically limited solutions to questions, how can it be supposed that there are utterly impersonal criteria by which to measure such a group of solutions? To be warned against taking one's own mode of social existence as yielding a universal meaning for perished societies does not free us from the modality of a point of view and of the questions that arise in connection with it. Spengler's thesis is a sophisticated relativism in comparison with what he calls the "innocent relativism" of Nietzsche and his generation. Although his interpretation may be said to have freed itself from earlier prepossessions, it cannot, by the very nature of his historical pluralism, be completely free from time-place limitation. Yet Spengler asserts so complete an escape, which is attained by the

---

[4] Vol. I, p. 20.

[5] Vol. I, p. 24. "It was never seen that many questioners implies many answers, that any philosophical question is really a veiled desire to get an explicit affirmation of what is implicit in the question itself, ..."

[6] Vol. I, p. 25.

"godlike insight" of a historical method as an "intuitive vision" yielding an "immediate and inward certainty."[7]

By assuming an inner certainty of intuitive vision Spengler transcends the bounds of relativistic perspective though still claiming to stay within them. He insists that the "picture of world-history" brought before his readers could only be delineated and framed at this time in Western society. The picture "is natural to us, men of the West, and to us alone." It should follow that value questions are necessarily perspectival and the answers relativistic. When Spengler asserts that "every Culture has *its own* Civilization" and that the relation is periodic, "a strict and necessary organic succession" in which Civilization is the inevitable destiny and finale of Culture, the assertion should carry the qualification, namely, that it is made as a historically conditioned interpretation. Spengler admits as much in the Preface to the revised edition of his book: "A thinker is a person whose part it is to symbolize time according to his vision and understanding. He has no choice; he thinks as he has to think. . . . I can then call the essence of what I have discovered 'true'—that is, *true for me,* and as I believe, true for the leading minds of the coming time; not true in itself as disassociated from the conditions imposed by blood and by history, for that is impossible." If Spengler adhered to this admitted limitation, he could not claim to transcend a historically conditioned standpoint. When he introduces a way of knowing by insight, he lays claim to a historical "vision" which is attained "not from this or that 'standpoint,' but in a high time-free perspective embracing whole millenniums of historical world-forms."[8] This is superhistorical mysticism. It enables Spengler to have his pluralism and transcend it too. As a pluralist, he rejects the ideas of the unilinear development and common content held by a unitary or "Ptolemaic" interpretation of history. It should, then, follow that his own work is subject to the rule of limited questions and answers. The most that could be claimed is a critical awareness of perspective, and thus a recognized relativity of criteria employed in forming judgments and making valuations.

---

[7] Vol. I, p. 25. "In opposition to all these arbitrary and narrow schemes, derived from tradition or personal choice, into which history is forced, I put forward the natural, the 'Copernican,' form of the historical process which lies deep in the essence of that process and reveals itself only to an eye perfectly free from prepossessions."

[8] Vol. I, p. 34.

Relativity is not subjectivity of judgment. Spengler makes a distinction which seems to me to be essentially sound when disentangled from its metaphysical trappings. This distinction is one between an "accidental" or subjective standpoint and a proper or critical standpoint.[9] An accidental standpoint is that of precritical judgment in a twofold meaning. It is precritical in the sense of antedating methods of selection and organization, and tests of evidence and judgments now held to be essential for historiography. Much eighteenth-century history writing is precritical by late nineteenth-century standards. Accidental standpoint is precritical, in a second sense, as a failure to recognize or to think through the implications of historical pluralism, once plurality of histories and of civilizations is generally attested by the records of the past. Thus historians continue to write as though the "modern period" had a special and privileged status with respect to preceding history, and as though that preceding history, staged in ancient and medieval periods by a Christian calendar, were the history of the world.[10] A proper standpoint is a critical detachment from the prepossession that our position is a privileged station on the main line of history. This detachment, expressed in historical relativism, is itself the outcome of many decades of historical study, and constitutes a contemporary time perspective of our own civilization in relation to that of other societies.

A reputable contribution of Spengler's historical work consists in taking the art, architecture, and literature of a past society as a symbolic expression from which to recreate its biography.

[9] Vol. I, p. 94. "To liberate History, then, from that thralldom to the observers' prejudices which in our own case has made of it nothing more than a record of a partial past leading up to an accidental present, with the ideals and interests of that present as criteria of the achievement and possibility, is the object of all that follows."

[10] Vol. I, p. 17. "It is not only that the scheme circumscribes the area of history. What is worse, it rigs the stage. The ground of West Europe is treated as a steady pole, a unique patch chosen on the surface of the sphere for no better reason, it seems, than because we live on it—and great histories of millennial duration, and mighty far-away Cultures are made to revolve around this pole in all modesty. It is a quaintly conceived system of sun and planets! We select a central bit of ground as the natural centre of the historical system, and make it the central sun. ... We have to thank that conceit for the immense optical illusion (become natural through long habit) whereby distant histories of thousands of years, such as those of China and Egypt, are made to shrink to the dimensions of mere episodes while in the neighborhood of our own position the decades since Luther, and particularly since Napoleon, loom large as Brocken-spectres."

"Everything whatsoever that has *become* is a symbol, and the expression of a soul."[11] The attitudes and motivations toward the possible and to-be-accomplished are the "soul" of an individual, a group, a society. The historian seeks to ascertain the nature of the effort expended (the becoming) which eventuated in the product (the become) surviving as evidence. The product is the embodiment and actualization of an "idea" which the historian endeavors to discover by interpreting the product as a symbol and not as an end in itself. A critical standpoint puts us on guard against the supposition that any production in its original setting had the same meaning and value that it now has for us in our inheritance of it.

Spengler recognizes that his kind of historical representation relies on aesthetic sensitivity and a method of analogy. We directly experience tensions and strivings in our own productive efforts. We infer that other men in societies that have long since perished underwent an experience similar in kind but not in content. An unchanged biological nature is not an unchanging human nature. When we assert that other men have experienced the conflict between a desired possibility and actual happenings, the analogy does not extend to a community of meanings and values. The directional character of human actions in line with interests, desires, and expectations is known to us directly and affords a clue for understanding the incentives of men who lived in presents and toward futures peculiar to their time and place. The content of our societal experience affords no immediate insight into the content of theirs; but just as we understand the answers we reach by the problems for which these answers stand as solutions, so we may proceed to study the remains of perished societies as answers and try to

---

[11] Vol. I, p. 101. Spengler in his usage of the term "soul" is guilty of the idealists' fallacy, namely, the fallacy of converting a possibility to be actualized into a "real being" which dominates the "becoming." "Real being" has either the timeless priority of a Platonic Form or the temporal priority of an agent. Spengler exhibits the latter version in converting the definition of soul as the possible to-be-accomplished into soul as a kind of Hegelian Spirit or Agent infused through and operative within the individuals of a society. The metaphysical conversion buttresses Spengler's argument about the inevitable destiny of a society. Men can only effectively will that which conforms to the stage of life reached by the social "organism." The attempt to comprehend the motivations and purposes of producers from the art and literature they produced is not vitiated by Spengler's metaphysical conversion, since it does not depend upon the conversion as a premise or necessary assumption.

recover the questions which had these resolutions.[12] So far as we understand the questions, something of the hopes, fears, conflicts, tensions, aspirations, and ideals of these strangers become appreciated.

Questions and answers are situational and in a changing tradition. One maintains a critical standpoint in recognizing this pluralism and his own perspectivity of understanding. Far from rendering knowledge of the past precarious, a proper historical standpoint is a safeguard against misrepresentation. We have no initial warrant for supposing that the ethical and political questions we ask are perennial, and that answers from all times including our own can be put on the same footing. For a historian cognizant of the situation within which his questions arise and the tradition which sets his historical perspective, the plurality of histories is a challenge to understand questions arising for other men in other times and places. He will comprehend them, not from a superhistorical vantage point, but as a time-conditioned interpreter. If his standpoint is critical and not subjective, his representation will attempt to describe the lives men led in past situations by what was peculiar and indigenous to them. Success and failure, good and bad, civilization and barbarism will pertain to human enterprises in meanings indigenous to contexts. When the productions of past enterprises are valued relative to his own society in its inheritance of them, this pertains to what they have come to mean and not to what they once meant. To ascertain what men once preferred and prized requires a histrionic identification on the part of the historian with obligations and aspirations that differ more or less radically from those now prevalent. Hence, to depict these alien worths without prejudging them by those localized in his own society, he must suspend valuations obtaining within his own "world" for the sake of understanding those within another. There is no society, history, or civilization-as-such which affords a transcendent universal for comparative judgments of value. The terms of valuation are set within each cultural context and have a different currency or no currency at all beyond their localization.

---

[12] Vol. I, p. 364. "Infinitely more important than the answers are the *questions*—the choice of them; the inner form of them. For it is the *particular* way in which a macrocosm presents itself to the understanding man of a *particular* Culture that determines *a priori* the whole necessity of asking them, and the way in which they are asked."

III

There remain for discussion the second and third ways by which an absolute as over against a relative valuation of civilizations is argued: the escape by an objective scale of values, and the escape of ideal civilization-as-such. Both of these derive from a differentiation of civilization-as-fact from civilization-as-ideal. The differentiation was originally introduced by Guizot in 1828 (*Histoire générale de la civilisation en Europe*). His work can be said to have set the problem of whether with many civilizations, each one of which is a complex fact for historical description, it is possible to hold a unitary meaning of civilization-as-ideal. Before Guizot, French thought attributed civilization to mankind and regarded its historical development as the unilinear sequence of stages toward a single, morally ideal state as the goal. If discussions disputed the treatment to be accorded to religion and the church, or gave differing selections of traits definitive of the ideal state, their oppositions were over detail rather than over premises. The disputes were subordinated to the ideas of universal progress and ideal purpose common to all mankind.

Guizot shifted the discussions to new grounds in defining civilization as a general, complex fact to be studied with respect to its constituent parts. Industry, science, morality, art, letters, politics, and religion make up a civilization, and none of these constituents is to be set apart from or above the others. There are and have been several such general facts or civilizations. In each, the historian will discriminate two juxtaposed and interplaying orders, the social and the intellectual "states." The social state is the material civilization, the set of limited and limiting conditions both institutional and physical. The intellectual state is the individual civilization, the conditions experienced and undergone by men as borne out in their intellectual activities. Every part of the general fact is to be dealt with in both its exterior and its interiorized status. The progress of the various parts within a material civilization is held to be the work of individuals, and the humanization of the individual is the justification of a material civilization.

The development in each civilization of the two orders does not answer the question, Is there a meaning of civilization which can be asserted of all, a destiny of mankind? Guizot believed one could affirm a universal meaning if there had been a transmission from one people to another, and from century to century, of human contributions in an accumulating sum. For if there has been this kind of continuity, we can then assert a goal of humanity to which each people contributed and can view history as the progress of mankind toward its realization. For Guizot, the perfection of the civilizational process will occur when the two orders are mutually adjusted and fully harmonized with each other. Civilization-as-ideal is the unitary, absolute norm for all civilizations by Guizot's assumption that the idea of the universal progress of mankind is a fundamental and legitimate idea to be accepted along with the word civilization. The problem is "solved" by falling back upon the idea of a uni-linear development of civilizations to support the idea of a common content.

The search for an objective scale of values desiderated as the prop of universal progress gives way to a pluralistic description of civilizations. Three aspects of civilization make up the range of meaning attached to the word when used descriptively. In a first aspect, by civilization is meant the moral and social-political state of a society: the developing institutions and practices with the affective beliefs, volitions, and preferences of men connected with them. In a second aspect, civilization is economic and technological: the developing skills and powers of production for the control of the physical environment. Third, civilization is the intellectual and humanized: art, literature, science, religion, and philosophy in their cultivation and dissemination. The three aspects are characteristic, in widely different ways, of a number of societies past and present. Unless it be assumed *a priori* that European civilization since 900 A.D., or from the time of the Renaissance, or since the eighteenth century, is not only superior to all other civilizations, but that any question of superiority is to be decided upon the basis of European traditions, there is clearly a problem of valuational comparisons.

A contemporary writer, Alfredo Niceforo,[13] states the problem by asking whether an objective scale of values is possible. Since a civilization is a type of organized social life undergoing transformation in time, the problem breaks down into two questions:

---

[13] *Civilisation. Le Mot et l'idée* (Centre International de Synthèse, Paris, 1930), pp. 113–128, "La Civilisation. Le Problème des valeurs."

How may the superiority of one civilization to another be judged? and How can we judge whether a society is progressing or retrogressing? The questions cannot be answered objectively unless there are indices of superiority of type and of direction of advancement.

Niceforo reviews two solutions both of which are fraught with unsurmounted difficulties. There is, first of all, the theory that societies pass through the same successive phases each superior to the one preceding. If every society necessarily develops through this sequence of stages, then, to make a comparative judgment, it is only needful to compare the level reached in each of several civilizations. Comte's law of the three stages is such a formula, postulating a succession of theological, metaphysical, and positivistic phases, each phase in turn having its substages of progress. The index is intellectual. A moral-political index is asserted by Herbert Spencer in his account of transition from a regime of constraint to one of liberty. For Karl Marx the progression is economic: from slave through feudal and capitalistic systems of production into future socialism. Unless these are mutually compatible with each other, which signs of superiority are the reliable indications? Furthermore, each of these indices involves some degree of abstraction in assuming the intellectual, the political, or the economic status as a measure of other aspects.

A second solution attempts to find the specific characteristics of a high civilization. But when one says of some characteristics that these are the better or the superior traits, the question, Better for whom? is often begged. It is no answer to say, Better for mankind, for this is to evade the problem set by pluralism by falling back upon the unitary interpretation of history. One can, indeed, reply by generalities: It is better for men to be fed than to go hungry; It is better to have medical skill to relieve pain than to suffer from lack of it. When we turn from generalities of this kind to the cultural values, political relationships, and moral ideas of a society, we are confronted with incompatible alternatives and diverse contents. Before one proceeds to judge, for example, that the art of Cézanne is superior or inferior to the art of Titian, there is a prior question: whether sameness of technique, purpose, and problem can be supposed. If it cannot, the judgment of progress or retrogress is otiose.

A refinement of this second solution is to break down the aspects of civilization into ingredients. Niceforo lists some of the indices that have been taken as definitive:

Material indices—mortality rate, wealth, increase of population.
Intellectual indices—publications, literacy, genius.
Moral indices—sentiment of justice, of piety, of honesty or honor.
Social-political indices—the status of the family, the form of government, the quality and number of rights accorded the individual.

Unless increase of population, a greater number of books, or a longer life span is necessarily a better condition, statistics establish a fact but not a value. Niceforo points out that there is no general agreement on the relative importance or essentiality of the sets of indices and of the items in each set. There is apparently no escape from judgments involving incommensurable preferences. In default of any general agreement among valuers, there is no objective standard that is decisive or conclusive in regard to value judgments of civilizations.

Failure to establish an objective scale of values by means of indices reduces to a relativity and not to a subjectivity of value judgments. By an objective scale, as Niceforo uses these words, is meant a measure or standard which is universally acceptable and thereby generally applicable. Subjectivity of judgment would arise in valuation from an accidental standpoint, the taking of values which we preferred as having a special and privileged historical status. From a critical standpoint, value judgments are delimited to conform to situations in which they arise, situations that are historically pluralistic. What is morally imperative within one society is not the less so for not being imperative in another. The admission of valuational relativity surrenders a claim to a common standard. Relativists are then committed, as Professor Adams has charged, to the position that they prefer what is theirs because it is theirs. I grant the charge, with qualifications, and will go farther to indicate the price that has to be paid. But if Professor Adams has found a way, beginning with a plurality of civilizations, of escaping by ideal civilization-as-such, I shall be glad to welcome it. I do not regard valuational relativity as a doctrine to cherish, but as an intellectual obligation to be carried until there are reasons for giving it up.

The duality of civilization-as-fact and civilization-as-ideal is

Guizot's gambit which Professor Adams replayed for an end game of a nonrelativistic content and meaning of civilization-as-such. Let us study the moves. The general societal fact of European civilization is the historically existing system of structures and relationships made up of special facts: morality, industry, art, religion, science, and politics. It is this system in its workings, its governmental policies, its clashes of interest, its nationalistic rivalries, its wars, its modes of production, its forms of ownership, its institutional patterns and practices, that make up civilization as fact, "the container." The container is not the content of civilization as lived and enacted by participation in the legacy of the past. Civilization-as-such, if I understand Professor Adams correctly, is ideal in a twofold meaning with respect to content. This doubleness of meaning, when related to the container, leads unavoidably to a third meaning of ideal, that of civilization as future.

In the first meaning, the content of civilization is ideal as an inheritance, a sharable endowment earlier produced by but absolved from original agents and occasions, and transmitted through symbols and traditions. There is far more in the legacy of music, religions, arts, philosophies, sciences, letters, and written histories than any one of us can hope to participate in within our lifetime. But it is only as we do participate and to the extent that we do share in the legacy that it is living. The content of civilization is ideal, then, in this second meaning of a living, enacted, participated in, and shared inheritance. There is the sharable and the sharing, the inheritance and the inheriting, the legacy and the beneficiaries. The duality of container and content, of civilization-as-fact and civilization-as-ideal, becomes the tension and tragedy of a society when sharing is frustrated by the existing structures and relationships that make up the container.

What, then, of the question bequeathed by Professor Adams at the end of his essay on the grounds set forth within it? Affirming the content as ideal both in the sense of sharable in its absolution from origins and shared in our life participation, the frustration of sharing is our civilization problem. If the container thwarts participation, we are driven to question its adequacy and desirability. The firmer our affirmation of the ideal content, the more vigorous must be our rejection of the structures and relationships which inhibit men from coming into their inheritance. For if the content is ideal in both meanings, frustration of the sharing without which the inheritance is idle and dead is indicative not merely of a bifurcation of ideal and fact, but of an opposition between inner meaning (call it Christian community, the brotherhood of man, freedom, the abundant life, liberalism, democracy, or what you will) and the societal system. If civilization-as-fact, the present container or system, frustrates fulfillment, are we not driven to a position which commits us to a struggle for future civilization, namely, for a societal system that will be instrumental to a general and generous sharing and not the fettering of it?

There is, of course, the alternative of affirming the container and scuttling the ideal content. This alternative is clouded by taking absolved content, the inheritance, legacy, or sharable endowment, to mean absolute civilization-as-such. By sharing in absolved content, our lives though local, parochial, and episodic seem to attain an absolution from relativity. We seem to transcend a time-place limitation in our valuations. What would it mean, however, to say that civilization-as-such is being destroyed in Europe? If we mean the ideal content as a legacy, there is the destruction wrought by war of irreplaceable things; but much remains for later generations—the books to be read, music to be played, art to be enjoyed. If we mean that the conditions of sharing are being drastically restricted and in ways that are antithetical to a humanistic tradition of sharing, then it is not civilization-as-such that is in question but rather the way in which content has been, now is, and should be shared. We seemed to escape relativity when we heard of absolved content and of our sharing by which civilization exists as lived and enacted. For there is transcendence in two meanings: first, by inheritance that confers detachment upon a participant— the detachment of mathematical study, or of a tragic conception gleaned from Aeschylus; and, second, of the content detached from its original occasion, producer, and audience. Preserved in a material which bears man's mark and enduring as artifact and symbol, this content is readable, viewable, interpretable, and sharable century after century and from one society to another. But admitting these two meanings does not establish a third meaning of transcendence, namely, that when reading, viewing, interpreting, and sharing occur in a particular time and place, civilization as there lived and enacted is detached from its specific ways of appropriation and commitment. As Professor Adams indicated, he did not mean by absolution of ideal content any floating, self-subsistent reality; nor by civilization as lived, any Bergsonian life principle evolving through many forms. If, then, absolved, sharable content is only any individual's or any group's content in its participation, does it not follow that how men commit themselves, the derivation and direction of their desires, and the questions and enterprises pertaining to their time and place all point to a relative and not an absolute meaning of civilization?

Not only is there the relativity enjoined by a pluralistic description of civilizations in making historical value judgments about them, but also a further relativity of relationships between material civilizations and an ideal content. The structures and relations that make up a container are limiting conditions of the appropriation and sharing of goods made available to classes of men within that societal system. Thus the economy of a society in terms of what men do and what they get affects in turn their interests and preferences. Changes in material conditions will be accompanied by revisions of interest. Any one connection of this kind is not in itself relativistic, but is historically relative to precedent and subsequent conformations. Relativity of this kind would be subjectivistic, by the meaning already brought out in the discussion of Spengler, if the limited occurrence and persistence of one set of relationships—for example, those of a capitalistic economy—were absolutized in theory as pertaining universally to every civilization, past and future. There is, however, a second meaning of subjective which is often taken to be a concomitant of historical relativism. Where the first meaning refers to a historical standpoint by which a set of values current within and limited to one society are predicated as universal, this second meaning refers to the psychological reduction of values to objects of interest for some individual or group. Psychological subjectivity is charged against relativism as follows.

If preferences are materially conditioned, then the interests expressed in preferences reduce to the conditioned subjects who have these interests and beyond whom there is no appeal. They prefer what is theirs, in what they value and how they value, because it is theirs. Values as objects of interest are subjectively absolute. Relativity is simply the recognition of diverse and unmediable congeries of interest.

If this were the position to which a historical relativist was committed, he would be reproved by a criticism that could be brought to bear from Professor Adams's argument. The position, it could be said, fails to demarcate the conditions of material civilizations and their historical occurrence from an absolved, ideal content. The latter is not characterized by the interests, for example, that an industrial working class has or is enabled to have in this legacy of the past. The conditions and occurrences of sharing pertain to civilization-as-fact. Further, the material civilization and not the ideal content is the locus of changes to be made in providing for a better sharing. Materially conditioned interests are variables as compared with a content which, in its absolution from historical localization, is a constant or historical absolute.

In reply to both the charge and the criticism of subjectivity, a relativist holds that alternatives are not restricted to either a psychological reduction of values or the objectivity of ideal civilization-as-such. The interests and preferences of an individual or a group are not self-instituted, but socially instituted. To ask how a serf in France in the thirteenth century was engaged in the civilization of that time and place is a question having its historical answer from what prevailed in that society as its material conditions and value orientations. Even though it is psychologically correct to say that what were values to the serf were objects of his interest, we are not advanced in our understanding of these interests until we find out how he came to have them. An ideal content, no less than a container of structures and relations, is exhibited when we ascertain that the serf was a Christian, that he was concerned for his soul in a life to come, that his lot was believed to be ordained by God. What is objective and determinate is this limited, historical situation in its interrelationships.

It is from the study of such limited, historical situations that the relativity of relationships between a material civilization and an ideal content is impressed upon us. An absolved content inherited from the past may be in part an encumbrance upon the recognition and actualization of opportunities arising from changes in material civilization. Thus some religious ideals detached from a society in which they expressed hopes and aspirations compatible with its actualities may subsequently be incompatible with and obstructive to the working out of desirable possibilities of technological discoveries and their utilization. It is in this connection that one can affirm the container and deny the viability of that part of the absolved content which, if its perpetuation should go unchallenged, would hinder the reformulations of purpose and ideal in keeping with the changed conditions. Some of the most pressing and difficult problems of valuation have to do with how to reach a decision affirming, on the one hand, that material conditions are in defection from ideals with which they should be compatible, or, on the other hand, that the ideals have lost a relevance they once had and are now without a past justification so far as further perpetuation is concerned. We may in many instances be right in insisting that it is the material civilization which needs to be changed to secure more share for more men in a historical inheritance. That we are not in every instance right is warning enough that an absolved content is no inviolable absolute. Nor is the challenge to its ultimacy a plunge into a subjectivity which sets new values with every change of interest. It is, rather, for historical relativism, the recognition of time-limited compatibilities. An absolved, ideal content, or ideal civilization, bears always a relation to material civilization; but the relation varies. Decisions have no universal formula either from ideal content or from material civilization in an order of priority of the one to the other. They are relative to a culture, in the ethnological meaning of the word, and relative also from one culture to another.

I think there is only one historical way of transcending valuational relativity,[14] once we have entered upon the Guizot gambit and the Adams development, and that is to assert, after the precedent of Hegel, that there is a World-Historical Spirit persisting through every container and expressing itself in parochial and local moments. Plurality then has a master continuant, an inner, metaphysical spirit-as-such for content-as-such; and our valuations though apparently relativistic are, in the reality of the Spirit, expressions of its unity.

Escape from historical relativity, could Hegelian persuasion convince us that escape were possible, would be a signal for great rejoicing. For if we had escaped, consider the assurance we would now have in dealing with "Europe's revolt against civilization."

---

[14] A second, nonhistorical transcendence would be a Platonic reification of ideal content as independent in its being from any becoming of living and enacting.

Grant that the British and the American containers leave much to be desired and contain much that should be changed for the sake of civilization to be lived by participation in absolved content. Still, unless civilization as lived in these nations is false in spirit and traitorous to the ideal, our justification is absolute. The issue is drawn between civilized and barbarous states. Yet how far does the assurance carry us, grateful though we might be to have it? Suppose that Russia becomes engaged in the present war as an ally of Great Britain.[15] Was the soul always there but slumbering? Or shall we admit only that civilization-as-fact is manifested to be welcomed watchfully by those societies which are keepers of the spirit? And what shall we say about the struggles in Spain with regard to Britain's policy of nonintervention? Was the spirit divided against itself, or frustrated in this instance by the container? These doubts and many more will not stay us if our partialities are inhabited by a World-Historical Spirit insuring that whatever is real is rational, and that one who speaks in metaphysical tongues can find a synthesis for every contradiction. Short of taking refuge in a spirit-as-such of civilization, civilization as lived and enacted is not absolved from valuational relativity.

IV

The import of pluralism for both descriptive and valuative identifications of a civilization has so far been presented in connection with the criticisms of attempted escapes from the relativity enjoined by it. This concluding discussion essays a brief positive formulation. The identification of a society as a civilization is by a "nuclear" description. The three aspects of civilization—the material-economic, the social-political, and the intellectual-humanized—are the elements of the nucleus; but it is the persistence of these in their interrelationships through time that constitutes the historical process and occurrence of a civilization. The more generally defined the elements and relations, the more extensive the geographical area and the longer the duration of the societal configuration identified as the place-time of a civilization. Spengler's Western society, for example, is European from the tenth century to a predicted decline that will be in its final stage in the twenty-

---

[15] This was written in the spring of 1941 before Germany's attack upon Russia and the subsequent return to a modified grace of Russia, which W. H. Chamberlin had damned as "lost" to European civilization.

third century. As identification is more specific, a nucleus of relationships in western Europe constituting the medieval synthesis is judged to have broken down and a new set of relations to have taken its place. An industrialistic and nationalistic civilization is thereby contrasted with a feudal society. A further limitation is the identification of civilization with the nation, the familiar French or American civilization.

As long as the continuities of relationships making up a specified configuration predominate over discontinuities and over emergent developments which are not assimilated, we can speak of the persistence of the same civilization. The cumulative consequences of new ways and the discontinuance of relationships and practices previously holding, whether in gradual or in rapid change, necessitate the eventual judgment of the ending of one civilization and the onset of another. A civilization continues in character only so long as no radical redistribution of elements or reordering of relationships occurs.

Starting with this historical identification of civilizations, itself relativistic, at least two interpretations of a breakdown of European civilization can be made, assuming that a breakdown has taken place. On a first type of interpretation, what is occurring is the outcome of a system undergoing destruction as a result of its own internal contradictions (a Marxist argument); or it is the decline of a society which has played out its internal, spiritual potentialities of cultural development and is now necessarily committed to the external expansions of imperialism in an age of Caesars (Spengler's argument). We need not accept either argument to recognize that the nucleus of eighteenth- and nineteenth-century civilization in Europe has been largely disintegrated by discontinuations of its social-political and intellectual-humanized traditions. We might further argue that material-economic relationships as they have been constituted were incompatible with the ideals attached to the other two aspects of a civilization, and that tensions and frustrations generated from this incompatibility have eventuated in revolutions and wars. "It is an incident of human history," Dewey writes, "and a rather appalling incident, that applied science has been so largely made an equivalent for private and economic class purposes and privileges. When inquiry is narrowed by such motivation or interest, the consequence is in so far disastrous both to science and to human life." The "serious and fundamental defect of our civilization" is that "our technique and technology are controlled by interest in private profit." If defect has led to disaster, what is our judgment to be?

By this first type of interpretation, the value judgment that the contemporary revolutions in Europe are barbaric is double-edged. We can call them barbaric because they break with and are opposed to ideals of democratic humanism and the traditions of intellectual freedom. In our own community, we can call ourselves civilized so far as these traditions are still in force. Yet the barbarism is nonetheless that of our Western society in consequences ensuing from its own mode of economic development in the last two centuries. The practices that eventuate in the debacle are discernable also in our own conduct. By confining the designation of nucleus to the nation, we tend to hide the unpleasant fact from ourselves and to engage in exaggerated self-justification. Nevertheless, this first mode of interpretation provides a ground for commitment. We have values to conserve in our intellectual-humanized tradition, and actions to be taken to maintain and to further the social-political instrumentalities that administer affairs in behalf of a more general and generous sharing.[16]

A second interpretation of the revolutions in Europe would be to say that in the breakdown of the older configuration there are now taking shape new orders which are, or may be, new civilizations. Is there a basis for designating a new order in Soviet Russia or in Germany as in part or in whole a civilization? The answer is relative to the identification of valuers in answer to the question, Civilization for whom? Men will here speak for themselves and through their groups. They will avow or disavow traditions, loyalties, and professions; interests, sympathies, and

---

[16] Here, I believe, is where Professor Pepper's machinery of administration and management is the means of control for shaping futures in line with preferences. Yet relativity also exacts its price from him. When Professor Pepper, after arguing that management can be effected by techniques now available, goes on to say that we should proceed to employ these resources for desired ends, the impression is conveyed that a community unified in interest and purpose is being summoned to action. The merely editorial is innocent, but when a program is proposed which we are to carry out, who are *we?* Until the editorial "we" is broken down by specific references to individuals, groups, and classes, questions crucial for practice are begged by its use. A unified community is itself an ideal as an objective of education in a democratic society, but one resorts to a solution by exhortation in summoning the ideal to realize itself.

pursuits. From a critical standpoint, a pluralist is forced to the price of historical relativism in admitting that National Socialist Germany may be a new civilization; but he is nonetheless consistent as a relativist in repudiating and opposing this new order in his allegiance to ways of life which it would replace. His justification is limited. It affirms what he would continue to live and enact so far as it lies within his power to prevail in the execution of his purposes.

A relativist cannot lay claim to a justification by an ideal, absolved content. He would lack historical piety if he did not acknowledge a debt of gratitude for the labor and care which left this legacy to him. He may well believe that the debt is not honorably discharged unless he in his turn acts as a trustee for future heirs. He is enjoined by this historical role to be a caretaker; but the endowment does not obligate the heirs to accept it by his valuations. What the content means for him is not what it once meant, nor what it will continue to mean thenceforth. As interiorized in life and enactment, it has no unitary or universal meaning. In the persistence of a nucleus, which is the historical occurrence of a civilization, there is a limited prevalence and community of valuations. The hopes of perpetuation and fears of cessation are indigenous in the form they take in the historical performance of the actors. There are perished civilizations, histories played out to their end and no longer the theater of hopes, fears, and enactments peculiar to them. For Spengler, this information portends the destiny of our civilization. Pluralism need not be abated to deny this conclusion based on precedent. Only in our time has a war become worldwide. The conquests of space and time that have made possible this extension could be the instruments of a world civilization. Nor is it paradoxical to assert that a conviction of valuational relativity holds more promise for efforts to realize such a civilization than a conviction of absolute justification when claimed by any class or nation of men.

A. I. MELDEN

JUDGMENTS IN THE SOCIAL SCIENCES

PROPOSITIONS about society are propositions about individuals in respect of the variety of relations, associations, and transactions in which they engage and by virtue of which they are constituted as social beings. And just as these relations and associations are various and restrictive, so the adjective "social" calls to mind many things. The society to which all belong is distinguished from the local groups which it comprises—the special associations, communities, corporations, unions, cliques, and so on, each of which is a social unit. The civilization to which all lay claim is not to be confused with the civilizations enjoyed or suffered by individuals as members of particular groups within the total social framework; nor can we identify the democracy of which we are all members with any of its real or spurious representatives in local groups. Society, civilization, and democracy are many things within what we are pleased to call "society," "civilization," and "democracy"; and the fact that they are many is of no small concern to us in our attempts to arrive at agreement on social affairs. Political, economic, and social problems of all kinds may affect all, but usually in no single manner; and the opinions and decisions which men recommend are often typed by the special interests reflected in their particular group affiliations. The phenomenon is common, but its importance cannot be denied; for if these differences in point of view are found to be irreducible, then we shall have to revise our conception of the nature, and perhaps of the possibility, of a social science. We may well ask, therefore, whether it is possible for the theorist in the so-called social sciences to free himself from the limiting influences ordinarily imposed by one's social position, and to engage in an inquiry in relation to which his social position is of purely biographical significance. However extensive the influence of his social position upon his preferences and evaluations may be, is it possible for the social scientist, by virtue of the procedures and techniques of his inquiry, to attain descriptive knowledge of the conditions and nature of social existence freed from the limitations, distortions, and biases occasioned by the intrusion of partisan interests? Or are ideas, at least those of society, intelligible only in the light of the specific social context in which they are framed? If the social context is an irresolvable factor, are we not obliged in all discussions of social questions to resort to a kind of socioanalytic technique to disclose the special pleading that masquerades as descriptive and objective inquiry? It is with these questions that this paper is concerned.

The view that social theory is intelligible only if it is related to the social context has assumed a variety of forms in the history of thought. Long ago the Greek sophists claimed to have discovered the "real" meaning of the social and political forms of the day in the self-seeking interests of individuals. The popular social concepts were declared to be based on nothing more substantial than the need of the mass of mankind, who as individuals are weak, for protection from the strong; and the intelligent man of action was advised to see the lofty ideas and ideals professed by educators and politicians as so much camouflage beneath which he, too, might artfully conceal his selfish ends. The perennially fashionable debunking accounts of the lives of the great represent similar attempts to unmask those factors which selfiish interest would keep concealed but which the demands of "realistic understanding" re-quire to be disclosed. And an even more radical type of critique, popularized by some Marxist writers, according to which all ideas, even those of the physical sciences, are intelligible only in the light of the class or economic setting of the observer, has gained a measure of currency in recent years. To describe music, moral sentiments, social theory, and even physical science as bourgeois or capitalist is to do more, on this view, than specify a causally relevant condition of formulation: a perhaps unsuspected but nevertheless constitutive aspect of meaning and intent is revealed. Indeed, the very description is sometimes taken to be a kind of refutation; for to describe anything as bourgeois or capitalist is to unmask it by pointing an accusing finger at the sordid elements that had given birth to it and, in consequence, left an indelible stain upon their offspring. But, clearly, the knife cuts both ways; the class setting, if it is a source of error and distortion in one case, might likewise function in any other. The imputation conveyed by the use of the term "capitalist" is paralleled by the sentiment associated with the word "communist." Thus the reference to the immediate social setting of ideas cannot, except upon pain of inviting the obvious retort, be taken in itself as an unmasking of distorting factors. Unless we grant this, knowledge of society appears a chimerical ideal and all inquiry and discussion an interminable display of special pleading and bickering. We must examine, therefore, the question whether, if the social context is of intrinsic significance for the nature of our ideas and judgments, it is possible to realize the ideal of a social science.

An affirmative answer to this question has recently been given by Karl Mannheim in his book, *Ideology and Utopia*. It is to Mannheim's credit that he is aware of the problem of objectivity raised by an ideological treatment of judgment and that he attempts to clarify some of the underlying issues. It will be instructive, therefore, to consider his views in some detail.

Mannheim distinguishes between several senses of the term ideology. In its "particular" sense "the term denotes that we are skeptical of the ideas and representations advanced by our opponents. They are regarded as more or less conscious disguises of the real nature of a situation, the true recognition of which would not be in accord with his interests."[1] In this sense of the term the suppressed factors are psychological in nature. In the "total" sense of the term, ideology has to do with the character of an age, society, or concrete group, and within this sense of the term Mannheim distinguishes between a "special" and a "general" use. In its "special" use the word is employed for the purpose of discrediting or unmasking an opponent's views, one's own position being regarded as immune against a similar attack. In its "general" use, however, the term no longer serves to suggest distrust, since all positions without exception are considered in the light of the specific social conditions of their formulation. This last use of the term is central in Mannheim's account: "With the emergence of the general formulation of the total conception of ideology, the simple theory of ideology develops into the sociology of knowledge. What was once the intellectual armament of a party is transformed into a method of research.... To begin with, a given social group discovers the 'situational determination' of its opponents' ideas. Subsequently the recognition of this fact is elaborated into an all-

---

[1] *Ideology and Utopia* (New York, Harcourt, Brace, 1936), p. 49.

inclusive principle according to which the theory of every group is seen as arising out of its life conditions. Thus it becomes the task of the sociological history of thought to analyze without regard for party biases all the factors in the actually existing social situation which may actually influence thought."[2]

The "situational determination" of ideas and judgments is of no mere causal significance for Mannheim. Thus, he contrasts propositions of mathematics with those of history and sociology, declaring that "even a god could not formulate a proposition on historical subjects like $2 + 2 = 4$, for what is intelligible in history can be formulated only with reference to problems and conceptual constructions which themselves arise in the flux of historical experience."[3] Questions of meaning and validity with respect to mathematical propositions are distinguishable from questions of genesis, and the failure to preserve this distinction leads to "psychologism," a familiar form of the genetic fallacy. On what grounds, however, can Mannheim maintain that his doctrine of situational determination does not involve a correspondingly fallacious "sociologism"?

Mannheim does present a fair amount of evidence, much of it highly illuminating, for the existence of connections between points of view and historical settings, and the fact that this can be done is, he argues, significant. He remarks that while the proposition $2 + 2 = 4$ "provides no clue as to when, where, and by whom it was formulated, it is always possible in the case of a work in the social sciences to say whether it was inspired by the 'historical school,' or 'positivism,' or 'Marxism,' and from what stage in the development of each of these it dates. In assertions of this sort, we may speak of an 'infiltration of the social position' of the investigator into the results of his study."[4] But this is hardly decisive, for it has to do with the position of the investigator in the historical development of his inquiry and the possibility of recognizing the school represented in his judgment, and these considerations apply equally well to logic and mathematics, where, on Mannheim's own admission, situational determination is lacking. The position of the investigator reflected in his judgments must be the social position—the position of the observer in his class, society, or age. But does the fact, if it is a fact, that theories in the

---

[2] *Ibid.*, p. 69.   [3] *Ibid.*, p. 71.   [4] *Ibid.*, p. 244.

social sciences can be correlated with social positions establish that the social position is of more than causal significance, that it provides a "meaningful genesis" as opposed to a purely "factual genesis"? The point at issue is whether the social context is involved in any consideration of the meaning of judgments, and this, it would seem, is a matter capable of solution only by non-empirical analysis, that is, by logical analysis of the meanings of propositions. For on the view that judgments in the social sciences can be correlated with the social contexts in which they are formulated, we can no more deduce that the meaning of such judgments involves a reference to the correlated contexts than we can deduce from the fact that brain processes can be correlated with the presence of ideas that such brain processes are analytically involved in their psychical correlates. Truisms, apparently, are not always commonplace, for we read as follows: "The historical and social genesis of an idea would only be irrelevant to its ultimate validity if the temporal and social conditions of its emergence had no effect on its content and form. If this were the case, any two periods in the history of human knowledge would only be distinguished from one another by the fact that in the earlier period certain things were still unknown and certain errors still existed which, through later knowledge, were completely corrected. This simple relationship between an earlier incomplete and a later complete period of knowledge may to a large extent be appropriate for the exact sciences. ... For the history of the cultural sciences, however, the earlier stages are not so simply superseded by the later stages, and it is not so simply demonstrated that early errors have subsequently been corrected."[5]

The argument is as follows. If the conditioning factors in the social context were of purely causal significance, then the formulation of successive opinions would consist simply in the correction of earlier views and in the addition to previous knowledge; but since this is not the case, the conditioning factors are of more than genetic significance. The hypothetical premise is alleged to follow from the proposition that the conditioning factors would have no effect upon the content and form of ideas and opinions if they were mere causal conditions. Mannheim would seem to hold, therefore, to a singular view of the nature of the causal relation in view

---

[5] *Ibid.*, p. 243.

of his suggestion that the causal relation is one in which the "content or form" of the effect cannot be correlated with the character of the causal condition or conditions. For what Mannheim is asserting is that, if the social context is of purely causal significance, it can throw no light upon the character of the resulting opinion. But it is paradoxical, to say the least, to assert that the discovery of causal relations provides no basis for correlation, explanation, or prediction. Mannheim does provide other arguments, and to these we now turn.

In reply to the charge that the doctrine of situational determination involves the genetic fallacy, Mannheim declares that the theory of knowledge presupposed by those who maintain that the doctrine is a kind of sociologism exactly analogous to the familiar psychologism must itself be examined in the light of the conditions in which it arose. "Every theory of knowledge," he declares, "is itself influenced by the forms which science takes at the time and from which alone it can obtain its conception of the nature of knowledge. In principle, no doubt, it claims to be the basis of all science, but in fact it is determined by the conditions of science at any given time. The problem is thus made the more difficult by the fact that the very principles, in the light of which knowledge is to be criticized, are themselves found to be socially and historically conditioned. Hence their application appears to be limited to given historical periods and the particular types of knowledge then prevalent."[6] The argument is not without persuasive force; the theory of knowledge upon which the charge of sociologizing is based is declared to be situationally determined, for "there exists a fundamental although not readily apparent nexus between epistemology, dominant forms of knowing, and the general social-intellectual situation of a time."[7] The conception of a sphere of "truth as such," we are told, is implicit in the rejection of the doctrine of situational determination, but, since it is itself situationally determined by such forms of knowledge as mathematics and the physical sciences and, indirectly, by the historical conditions in which these arose, its application is thus limited to these conditions and cannot be extended to the more recently appearing "social-intellectual situation" of the social sciences.

The argument is curious and deserves careful attention. Mann-

---

[6] *Ibid.,* p. 259.   [7] *Ibid.,* p. 261.

heim's critics deny that judgments in the social sciences are situationally determined or perspectival, on the epistemological ground that truth is nonperspectival. Mannheim argues, however, that this proposition of epistemology is itself situationally determined or perspectival. Assuming for the present the correctness of Mannheim's assertion, does it follow that truth in the social sciences is perspectival? If this is Mannheim's argument, it violates the vicious-circle principle. For a judgment about all judgments in the social sciences cannot be identified with any of the judgments about which it is a judgment; hence the meaning of "truth" in the statement that the truth of judgments in the social sciences is nonperspectival is different from the meaning of "truth" in the assertion that the truth of this latter statement is perspectival. Thus, from the alleged perspectival nature of the truth of the judgment that truth in the social sciences is nonperspectival it does not follow that truth in the social sciences *is* perspectival. There is no logical inconsistency whatever in asserting (*a*) that truth in the social sciences is nonperspectival and (*b*) that the truth of the judgment (*a*) is perspectival. All that does follow from (*b*) is that if the perspective in question differs from our own, we are not obliged to accept (*a*). But Mannheim's critics, in charging that his sociologizing involves the genetic fallacy, will naturally deny (*b*), namely, that the epistemology upon which the charge is based is itself perspectival. Mannheim might then attempt to sociologize this *new* statement, but in that case he will be met, inevitably, by a new charge of fallacious sociologizing. The logic of the situation is by no means so simple as Mannheim's argument suggests; but fortunately there are more decisive considerations, to which we shall turn when we enter into a critical examination of the doctrine of perspectivism.

In an attempt to establish a relevant point of difference between psychologism and his sociologism, Mannheim argues that while the character of the psychological processes which condition judgments are irrelevant, in general, to considerations of meaning and truth, the social conditions of judgments in the social sciences are somehow "meaningful." "Social position," he writes, "cannot be described in terms which are void of social meanings, as for example by mere chronological designation. 1789 as a chronological date is wholly meaningless. As historical designation, however, this date refers to meaningful social events which in themselves demarcate the range of a certain type of experiences, conflicts, attitudes and thoughts."[8] To describe the social context as meaningful is, apparently, to direct attention to the interests, evaluations, and attitudes involved in the description of social events. So far, however, the analogy between the social and psychological conditions of judgment would seem to hold, for we do include interests, attitudes, and so on, among the psychological conditions of belief. So long as Mannheim confines his attention to the processes of association he may argue with some plausibility that the psychological conditions of judgment are, in this odd sense of the term, meaningless, but associations by no means exhaust the psychological processes involved in judgment. Why, then, are the conditions of judgment irrelevant to their meaning in the one case and not in the other? Why is a psychological analysis of judgment in terms of purely personal preferences, desires, and attitudes to be eschewed and a sociological analysis of judgment in terms of social position and the interests and attitudes these involve to be advanced? To these questions no answer is to be found in Mannheim's discussion.

By far the most important argument advanced by Mannheim in support of his doctrine of situational determination has to do with his conception of knowledge in the social sciences as "activistic." This view is proposed in opposition to the "idealistic" conception according to which knowing is regarded as "theoretical" or "contemplative," and which, according to Mannheim, can be understood in the light of "the prehistory of scientific logic and . . . the development of the philosopher from the seer, from whom the former took over the ideal of the 'mystic vision.' "[9] In the social sciences, however, knowledge and action are declared to be inseparable, for "knowledge arises only when and in so far as it itself is action, i.e., when action is permeated by the intention of the mind, in the sense that the concepts and the total apparatus of thought are dominated by and reflect this activistic orientation. Not purpose *in addition* to perception, but purpose *in* perception itself reveals the qualitative richness of the world in certain fields."[10] Leaving aside the questionable sociologizing of the "idealistic" conception of knowledge, the statement is of interest since it gives us some indication of the meaning of Mannheim's assertion that

---

[8] *Ibid.*, p. 264.   [9] *Ibid.*, p. 265.   [10] *Ibid.*, p. 267.

the social context is meaningful. Social practices involve attitudes, interests, and evaluations, and these vary from group to group. Knowledge, however, is definable only in relation to practice. In some sense it is directed at certain ends; it is purposive, that is, its meaning lies in the social practices it promotes along with the interests and attitudes which these involve. "Activism," therefore, seems to be another name for instrumentalism. Ideas, in the social sciences at any rate, are not simply had or contemplated; a deity who is not, in the fullest sense of the term, made flesh must remain everlastingly ignorant of the basic concepts of the social sciences. For man is regarded as an organism responding in perception and judgment to the conditions of his social environment, and ideas are viewed as tools or instruments to be measured by their success or failure in permitting adequate adjustments to the conditions of the social environment. Perception is regarded as one type of response, the character of the response being molded or determined in part at least by the specific interests and attitudes shared by the observer with other members of his particular social group. Ideas and judgments which are formulated in consequence of such responses thus bear the stamp of their social origin, for they are the theoretical expressions of the practical requirement of active participation in a social environment. Hence Mannheim remarks that it is both right and inevitable that the theoretical findings of the observer should contain traces of his social position. And it is in consequence of this fact, according to Mannheim, that individuals in different social strata or historical periods will differ so radically in their conceptions of freedom, democracy, and civilization, and even in their descriptions of practices, institutions, and societies. There is therefore an irreducibly perspectival character, for Mannheim, in all perceptions, ideas, and judgments of social phenomena.

This, then, is the theory of knowledge and the central support upon which Mannheim ultimately rests his case for his conception of ideology or situational determination. But before we examine it closely let us first turn to the consideration of the doctrine of ideology itself. We shall then return to the basic issue of the relation between the interests and evaluations reflected in group participation and the theoretical results of inquiry in the social sciences.

Mannheim is most concerned to maintain that his conception of ideology or perspectivism does not erase the distinction between propaganda and description. The social sciences are concerned with matters of fact—there are individuals engaged in social activities and these are capable of exact description. Unless this is conceded, the notion of a sociology of knowledge must be regarded as impossible; for the sociology of knowledge, in its examination of the ideological character of judgment, attempts to disclose the particular situational determination involved, and if there are no "situations" that "determine," no knowledge of situational determination is possible. Two questions arise: (1) Does the notion of ideology entail a sweeping relativism? and (2) If relativism is an unavoidable consequence, is a sociology of knowledge possible?

To begin with, we find Mannheim most anxious to disavow relativism. He distinguishes between what he calls "relativism" and "relationism," rejecting the former and accepting the latter. "Relativism," he says, "is a product of the modern historical-sociological procedure which is based on the recognition that all historical thinking is bound up with the concrete position in life of the thinker. But relativism combines this historical-sociological insight with an older theory of knowledge which was as yet unaware of the interplay between conditions of existence and modes of thought, and which modeled its knowledge after static prototypes, such as might be exemplified by the proposition $2 + 2 = 4$. This older type of thought which regarded such examples as the models of all thought, was necessarily led to the rejection of all those forms of knowledge which were dependent upon the subjective standpoint and the social situation of the knower, and which were, hence, merely 'relative.' Relativism, therefore, owes its existence to the discrepancy between this newly-won insight into the actual processes of thought, and a theory of knowledge which had not yet taken account of this new insight."[11]

It would seem, from this account of relativism, that the relativist is asserting a flat contradiction; for the relativist, on this account, asserts that judgments are ideological, and, since he retains an older theory of knowledge, that they are not ideological. By definition, therefore, the statement that relativism is inadequate becomes a masterpiece of understatement, and it appears that instead of avoiding relativism Mannheim is avoiding an objectionable label.

---

[11] *Ibid.*, p. 70.

Not even the extreme Protagorean relativism which Plato examines at length in the *Theaetetus* may be described as a flatly self-contradictory view. What, then, does "relativism" mean? Historically the term has been used to designate doctrines according to which apparently conflicting statements are logically independent. Thus, on the Protagorean relativism the perceptual judgments "This is red" and "This is not red" may both be true even though they are about the same object, for the reason that each statement is about the given object only with respect to the given percipient. The statements are incomplete as they stand, and for purposes of explication should be completed by the addition of some qualifying phrase of the form "for A," where for "A" we may substitute a personal pronoun or name standing for a percipient. If the percipients are distinct, the two statements will be logically independent; for in each case the relation to the percipient is an intrinsic element in the meaning of the judgment. The question, therefore, is whether the reference to the social context, if it is an essential factor in the meaning of judgments in the social sciences, does not entail a precisely similar situation.

Relationism, which Mannheim advocates, consists in relating judgments to "a certain mode of interpreting the world which, in turn, is ultimately related to a certain structure which constitutes its situation."[12] To understand a judgment is to understand the "principles of interpretation," the "modes of thought" or "categories," in accordance with which objects are viewed, and ultimately to relate these to the social context from which they spring. Since these terms to which judgments are related provide an understanding of their import, all judgments in the social sciences are incurably perspectival. While Mannheim considers it possible to deal with judgments on an abstract level independently of considerations of perspective, such an approach suggests what is, strictly speaking, impossible on his own view, namely, a "sphere of truth as such" in which objects possess intrinsic properties. It would seem, therefore, that so far as the social sciences are concerned there are no facts except those determined within given perspectives by the social position of the investigator. Mannheim compares the present situation with that of perception. Just as "the controversy concerning visually perceived objects (which, in the nature of the

---

[12] *Ibid.*, p. 253.

case, can be viewed only in perspective) is not settled by setting up a nonperspectival view (which is impossible), "[13] so, we are told, objectivity in the social sciences can be defined only within the framework of a perspectivism.

Clearly, relationism so defined is nothing more nor less than relativism. The close parallel between Mannheim's theory of judgment and Protagoras' relativism is apparent. In both, there are no objects apart from the points of view of observers. In both, a simple declarative sentence which ordinarily expresses a judgment is an incomplete expression of the intended meaning. For Protagoras the sentence "This is red" really expresses that the object in question is red for the person uttering the sentence; and for Mannheim the sentence "Russia and Germany are totalitarian" really expresses that they are totalitarian for one who is a member of the society to which the person uttering the sentence belongs. In both declarations the judgment is really about the judger, the important difference being that for Mannheim the judger is involved only so far as he exhibits a point of view or perspective characteristic of any member of his social group. But, in either case, statements made from different perspectives are logically independent. If, for example, a fascist tells me that democracy is doomed, then my judgment that it is not is logically irrelevant; for what may be true for one who is a member of a fascist state will not necessarily be true for me. This, surely, is nothing more nor less than relativism; to call it "relationism" is merely to substitute a new label for one that is old and no doubt disreputable.

But however this view may be described, is it possible to reconcile this position with the necessary requirement of objectivity? Mannheim's answer is as follows: "In the case of situationally conditioned thought, objectivity comes to mean something quite new and different: (*a*) there is first of all the fact that in so far as different observers are immersed in the same system, they will on the basis of the identity of their conceptual and categorical apparatus and through the common universe of discourse thereby created, arrive at similar results and be in a position to eradicate as an error everything that deviates from this unanimity; (*b*) ... when observers have different perspectives 'objectivity' is obtainable only in a more roundabout fashion. In such a case what has been

---

[13] *Ibid.*, p. 270.

correctly but differently perceived by the two perspectives must be understood in the light of the differences in structure of the varied modes of perception. An effort must be made to find a formula to discover a common denominator for these varying perspectivistic insights. Once such a common denominator has been found, it is possible to separate the necessary differences in the two views from the arbitrarily conceived and mistaken elements, which here too should be considered as errors."[14]

What is involved in the first meaning of objectivity is the agreement between social scientists who share a given perspective. But it is not clear whether Mannheim defines error as that which deviates from the commonly accepted view or whether he merely intends that erroneous judgments will as a matter of fact diverge from the commonly accepted opinion. Neither alternative is satisfactory; the first reduces objectivity to mere agreement with the commonly accepted opinion, and the second involves the questionable proposition that the commonly accepted view is invariably correct, and furthermore, it leaves undefined the notions of truth and objectivity. Precisely what it would mean to say that a judgment formulated from a given perspective is true or false, Mannheim nowhere states. Indeed, he generally falls back upon the common nonperspectivistic meaning of truth. To test this, let us consider the second meaning of objectivity. This consists, first, in relating a number of judgments, each of which in some unspecified sense is valid within its particular perspective, to their respective perspectives, and then in seeking a common denominator or formula in accordance with which each judgment may be translated into any other. To begin with, the expression "common denominator" conveys an impression which is quite inadmissable on Mannheim's own grounds, namely, that it is possible to extract something common to several judgments each of which is perspectival and no two of which are framed within the same perspective. The second suggestion is that it is possible to find a formula by means of which perspectival judgments may be translated into one another, and it is derived from the consideration of perception. Just as the differences in the perceived shape of a given object can be explained by the differences in the points of view from which the object is seen, so we should be able to "translate" each of

____

[14] *Ibid.*, p. 270.

several perspectival judgments into any of the others in the sense that we could explain how from the several perspectives the common object is judged in each case as it is. And, as with respect to perception, we should be able to predict, given any judgment within any given perspective, the kind of judgment which would be made from any other perspective. The objection, however, to this account is that the procedure outlined presupposes precisely what is denied on Mannheim's perspectivism. The perceived shapes of a penny, for example, may serve as an illustration. How do we explain the differences in the perceived shapes of the coin from different perspectives? Clearly, by assuming that the penny really has a shape of its own and, by appealing to considerations of optics, thus explaining the various elliptical appearances of a round disk. Similarly, we can explain why, for example, employers and employees differ on the question of the closed shop if and only if we know the facts—the interests of employers and employees, and the supposed consequences for each of these groups of the unionization of labor. We presuppose, in short, nonperspectival knowledge in our explanation of the differences in point of view or perspective. That Mannheim himself falls back upon a nonperspectival or common-sense view of judgment is evident from the following passage: "As in the case of visual perspective where certain features of the object have the advantage of revealing decisive features of the object, so here preëminence is given to that perspective which gives evidence of the greatest comprehensiveness and the greatest fruitfulness in dealing with empirical materials."[15] In what sense Mannheim can give a meaning, on his own perspectivism, to such phrases as "the decisive features of the object," "the greatest fruitfulness," or "the greatest comprehensiveness," I find it difficult to understand.

I turn now to the consideration of the question whether, in view of the relativism which Mannheim's conception of ideology entails, a sociology of knowledge is even possible.

We might be tempted to argue: if all judgments are perspectival, then this one is likewise perspectival; hence, if our perspective differs from that of Mannheim, we are not obliged to accept the judgment that all judgments are perspectival. To argue in this way, however, would be to argue fallaciously, for the argument

---

[15] *Ibid.*, p. 271.

violates the vicious-circle principle by identifying the judgment that all judgments in the social sciences are perspectival with one of the judgments about which it is a judgment. Nevertheless, if there are good reasons for asserting that judgments in the social sciences are perspectival, then there are, correspondingly, good reasons for asserting that this last judgment is perspectival. And, as a matter of fact, this is conceded by Mannheim, for he writes that "the concept of truth has not remained constant through all time, but has been involved in the process of historical change."[16] But what is the process of historical change that defines the perspective of the judgment that all judgments in the social sciences are perspectival? A new perspective would seem to appear at this point, for the knowledge of the historical process is, presumably, perspectival. Thus the sociology of knowledge begins by discovering the perspective of particular judgments in the social sciences, another in the discovery, still another in this last discovery, and so on *ad infinitum*. The regress is vicious for the reason that the perspective is involved in the meaning of our original judgment, and the analysis of our judgment cannot possibly be completed; for the sociology of knowledge which performs the first step of the analysis must be sociologized in its turn, and this new sociologizing by a new sociology, and so on endlessly. If the vicious regress is to be avoided, the analysis must be capable of completion at some point in the series of sociologies, in which case a "sphere of truth" appears; but if a "sphere of truth" is possible anywhere, then there is no reason for denying its possibility elsewhere and there is no reason, in particular, for denying it to judgments in the social sciences. Consider a simple report of an incident occurring in a past civilization written by one of its members. This report, according to Mannheim, is existentially determined and therefore a proper subject of investigation for the sociologist of knowledge. The sociologist of knowledge attempts, therefore, to understand the report in the light of the historian's account of the social conditions of the formulation of the report; but the historian's information is generally based, in part at least, upon the data supplied in our original report; and the procedure is therefore circular. Assuming, however, that the historian's account is based upon independent data, we are bound to recognize that it is likewise

---

[16] *Ibid.*, p. 262.

perspectival and that, in order to understand it, we must now turn to the sociologist. Is it possible to discover a terminating point in this series of conditions, each of which is necessary if our initial report is to be understood? For suppose that we have at last arrived at our own period, and that the sociologist of knowledge has at last found in our own social position the perspective in the light of which we view the findings of the sociologist, in the light of which, in turn, we view the account of the historian through whose report we understand, at long last, the meaning of our initial report. If we *have* discovered our own social position and are thus able to retrace our steps to the initial report, then we have abandoned perspectivism. But if judgments in the social sciences are perspectival, then those of the nature of our own social position are perspectival and require, therefore, further explication, and there is no limit to the number of successive steps required for the completion of our understanding of what seemed initially to be a self-contained and simple report.

The hopelessness of Mannheim's case for a sociology of knowledge may be illustrated by the consideration of apparent conflicts of opinion which arise out of differences in social position. According to Mannheim, the sociology of knowledge, by discovering the perspective of each of several such judgments, will "particularize its scope and the extent of its validity."[17] For the sociology of knowledge provides more than an interesting sociological description of the background of judgment; it provides an analysis of judgment by disclosing the position and perspective of the observer. In controversial matters, according to Mannheim, difference in perspective and social position are generally unrecognized or considered irrelevant, with the result that each claims his position to be exclusive of the others and each demands that the others accept his position. But the sociology of knowledge, by relating each of the several apparently conflicting judgments to its social context, will particularize the scope and validity of the several judgments in the sense that they will be shown to be logically independent of one another; for all that may be claimed for each of the judgments is that it is valid or true only for the point of view of the particular social position represented in the judgment. The apparent conflict of views will thus be resolved; the

---

[17] *Ibid.,* p. 255.

differences will be neutralized by exhibiting the logical independence of the several positions. The sociology of knowledge will thus arbitrate disputes between employer and employee, for example, by disclosing the differences, and since these differences are definitive it would seem that the sociology of knowledge will disclose that arbitration is neither possible nor necessary—for the employer speaks for his own class, the employee speaks for his, and neither may say nay to the other. The particularization and neutralization to which Mannheim refers reduces to the disclosure of the inevitable phenomenon of special pleading involved in judgment. Each judgment expresses the conditions of membership in a class or society, and only the understanding of the meaning of an assertion is required to prevent the subversion of one's interests by assenting to judgments formulated under social conditions different from our own. Indeed, we must not say even this much. The employee cannot really assent to the view of his empolyer; to do so he must understand his employer. But this is impossible since his employer's judgment is perspectival and the perspective of his employer is irreducibly opposed to and different from his own. The conversion of the employee by the employer on the subject of labor unions cannot be described in terms of arrival at a common judgment. It resembles far more the triumph of one will over another, masked by an apparent but purely verbal agreement. The cardinal virtue, for the sociologist of knowledge, if indeed it is possible to possess it, is consistency with the interests of one's class or society; the cardinal vice is to be so confused and bewildered as to mouth the words of those whose social position is different from our own, and, in so doing, to run counter to one's class interests. This is the picture which Mannheim must face, and, sorry as it is, there is no escaping it.

It is unnecessary to pursue this theme much farther, but a few remarks in conclusion concerning the peculiar status of the concept of a sociology of knowledge may perhaps be instructive. The sociology of knowledge, it must now be apparent, presents two incompatible theses: (1) that judgments in the social sciences are perspectival, and (2) that the perspectives of such judgments can be discovered by relating them to the social conditions of their formulation. If judgments are perspectival, then those of the sociologist are perspectival, and the alleged discovery of perspective is therefore no discovery at all. Once we accept perspectivism, we are obliged to accept the consequences and to admit, therefore, that it is no more possible to discover the perspective of our own judgment than to discover the perspectives of judgments the social situations of which are different from our own. For in either case we must be able to formulate nonperspectival judgments of the nature of the social context and to understand, given these objectively real conditions of judgment, the interests, the evaluations—in short, how the whole perspective is possible. But in order to arrive at this understanding the sociologist of knowledge must make use of those very judgments about the social context with which social scientists are concerned and which, by hypothesis, are perspectival. The perspective becomes, therefore, an elusive will-o'-the-wisp: the sociologist of knowledge may be confident of its existence, but its character must remain unknowable. The difficulty may be summed up as follows. The case for a sociology of knowledge rests upon the presumed fact that (1) judgments are ideological or perspectival. The possibility of a sociology of knowledge presupposes that (2) the judgments formulated by the sociologist of knowledge about the social contexts of judgments are exempt from the limitation of perspective. But if the second supposition is correct, then the first is false and there is no need for a sociology of knowledge. If, on the other hand, our first supposition that judgments are perspectival is true, then the second is false and a sociology of knowledge is impossible.

In spite of these considerations it will be maintained that judgments in the social sciences are not quite analogous to those in other fields. The psychology of Pythagoras may be irrelevant to the meaning and validity of the theorem that bears his name, but, it may be insisted, with respect to social and political theories, interests and evaluations play a considerable part in molding ideas and opinions. The selection of data, the interpretation of social phenomena, the value connotation of social concepts, the services performed by theorists in intention or effect as apologists or dissenters—these, like other no less familiar phenomena, illustrate the play of interests and attitudes to which supposedly disinterested observers are subject. These, no doubt, are important considerations, and it is well that we bear them in mind; but we must not at the same time exaggerate their significance and, like Mannheim, draw the improper conclusions. How far interests and evaluations are implicated in factual descriptions is a matter of great practical if not theoretical significance, but we must not be so far misled as to suppose that they are essential or intrinsic factors in factual description. We have seen that an ideological treatment of judgment leads to impossible conclusions. Where social contexts, and therefore interests and evaluations, differ, communication and agreement are strictly impossible; and since perspectivism precludes a sociology of knowledge, it precludes also the possible recognition of the social contexts in which judgments are rooted and of the interests they allegedly express or promote. The social scientist, on this view, would seem to be reduced to something less than the propagandist; for while, like the propagandist, he speaks for his clique, class, or society, he must, unlike the latter, remain ignorant of the service he renders. For the social scientist, the distinction between the content of judgments and the social interests they serve is an impossible abstraction; for the propagandist, the distinction is a necessary condition of success: unless his victims can consider the opinions he promotes in abstraction from the interests he serves, ideas and arguments cannot serve as instruments of propaganda. Thus, even if the status of the social scientist is reduced to that of the propagandist, we must allow at least for the possibility of distinguishing between the content of ideas and the interests of the social scientist as a member of a social group. The acceptance of judgments of fact may promote interests and values, but judgments of fact are at least distinguishable from judgments of interest and value. In short, the property which ideas have in virtue of their relation to interests and values may be important, but it cannot in general be regarded as internal or intrinsic.

Some philosophers, however, have maintained the contrary opinion despite the seeming obviousness of our remarks. Mannheim, we saw, based his perspectivism upon what he describes as an "activistic" theory of knowledge—a theory which bears a strong resemblance to the instrumentalism with which readers of Dewey's writings are familiar. It may be instructive, therefore, to examine this view in order to determine more closely the relation between the social scientist's interests and position in society, on the one hand, and the character and results of his inquiry, on the other.

One of the distinctive characteristics of activism or instrumentalism is the emphasis placed on such fundamentally biological concepts as organism, environment, response, and adjustment in its account of the nature of ideas. Man is seen as an organism responding and adjusting himself to the varying conditions of the environment. On a purely biological level, these responses and adjustments may be instinctive; but, somewhere along the biological scale, perception and intelligence emerge to play their parts in the responses of organisms to their environments. Indeed, perception is one type of response; so far as it is the response of an interested organism, it is somehow permeated with, or expressive of, interests, purposes, or evaluations—as Mannheim put it, "not purpose *in addition* to perception but purpose *in* perception." Ideas, like percepts, are not simply had or contemplated; their significance lies in their function in accommodating the organism to the changing conditions of the environment. Intelligence is purposive or directive, not contemplative; it represents an evolutionary development and has its own survival value. And the significance of intelligence lies in the means it affords not only of securing adjustments but also of transforming the physical and social environments and of promoting enormous developments of new interests and satisfactions. Social institutions, like the interests they embody, exist in consequence of this active and directive function of intelligence; they represent the successes or failures, the satisfactions or frustrations, by which the adequacies or inadequacies of ideas are measured. As Dewey says: "If ideas, meanings, conceptions, notions, theories, systems are instrumental to an active reorganization of the given environment, to a removal of some specific trouble or perplexity, then the test of their validity and value lies in accomplishing this work. If they succeed in their office, they are reliable, sound, valid, good, true. If they fail to clear up confusion, uncertainty and evil when they are acted upon, then they are false. . . . Confirmation, corroboration, verification lies in works, consequences. Handsome is as handsome does. By their fruits shall ye *know* them. . . . An idea is a claim or injunction to *act* in a certain way as the way to arrive at the clearing up of a specific situation. . . . Its active, dynamic function is the all important thing about it, and in the quality of activity induced by it lies all its truth and falsity."[18]

But in what sense may we say that ideas, theories, meanings,

---

[18] *Reconstruction in Philosophy*, p. 156.

systems are instruments of adjustment to an environment, tools promoting the welfare of interested organisms, means of transforming the environment? To begin with, if ideas, meanings or concepts are tools or instruments, they are tools or instruments in a sense that is different from that in which systems, theories, or judgments are tools or instruments. Ideas, concepts, or meanings are neither true nor false; only propositions or judgments or theories or systems have these properties. If, therefore, truth and falsity are defined in terms of the consequences of enactments, the sense in which concepts or ideas are tools or instruments must be derivative, that is, definable in terms of the sense in which propositions or judgments, in which these concepts or ideas occur, are useful, useless, or harmful tools or instruments. But what meaning can we give to the statement that propositions and judgments are tools or instruments in this primary sense? Surely not that they are tools in the sense in which physical objects of any kind are tools. Can we say that they are tools in the sense in which mathematics is a useful tool in physics, or in the sense in which, according to many recent philosophers, logic is a useful tool in philosophical analysis? Again the answer is in the negative, for the validity of the principles of mathematics or logic can hardly be said to be tested in their applications to special problems in physics or analysis; and the kinds of applications, if we may use this term, by means of which the propositions of logic or mathematics are tested, are quite different from those applications in practice by means of which, according to the instrumentalist, empirical judgments are tested. In what sense, therefore, are judgments, theories, systems, tools or instruments, true if they remove some specific trouble or promote some desired end, false if they fail in this their appointed office? Two quite distinct answers are suggested by Dewey's remark that "an idea or conception is a claim or injunction to act in a certain way as the means to arrive at the clearing up of a specific situation."

1) As claims, judgments have to do with the consequences of action designed to solve problems confronting interested organisms. A judgment p would consist, therefore, in the claim or judgment to the effect that if p is acted upon, the consequences of such action will be useful. For example, the judgment that England will win the war will, on this view, consist in the claim that if we act in expectation of this outcome the consequences of such action will

be far more useful than those which would result from our acting
as if England were sure to lose. To describe the judgment p as a
tool and as useful or useless is to speak somewhat inaccurately. For
it is not the judgment p, for example, the judgment that England
will win the war, but the action as if or in accordance with p, that
is useful, useless, or harmful. And there are very serious objections
against the view, for according to it the judgment that England
will win the war is of the form: if anyone acts in the expectation
that England will win the war, then the consequences of a British
victory will be useful, salutary, and so on. Now this judgment is
rather curious. If our original judgment is p, our new judgment,
which, it is asserted, expresses the meaning of p, is of the following
form: if anyone acts as if p, then the consequence of such action
will be thus and thus. But "acting as if p" means acting as if the
judgment p were true. The analysis is, therefore, circular and
worse than useless. For it was assumed that the judgment p could
not be understood apart from a reference to action and its consequences, but in order to understand what is meant by the phrase
"acting as if p," the instrumentalist must presuppose what on his
own hypothesis he is obliged to deny, namely, that p can be understood apart from all reference to action and consequences. If the
instrumentalist's assumption was correct, his analysis is meaningless; but if judgments are not analyzable, in general, in terms of
enactments, then, while the analysis is intelligible, it is quite mistaken. Further, the circularity in the analysis leads to a vicious
regress. The judgment p is the claim or judgment that action in
accordance with p is useful. Let us call this last judgment "f_1p."
We have, therefore, the following: $p = f_1p$. Now f_1p is a judgment;
hence, $f_1p = f_2p$, and so on *ad infinitum*. The regress is vicious
since each member of the series of judgments requires that its
successor be given in order that it may be intelligible.

2) The second suggestion contained in Dewey's statement is that
a judgment is really an injunction. On this view, to describe judgments as useful tools is to assert that they are really injunctions or
imperatives which it is useful to follow or obey. The judgment, for
example, that chickens generally cross the road on the approach of
motorists becomes the injunction to beware the chickens at the
side of the road as you approach in your car, or, if you are a farmer,
to act in a manner appropriate to your interest in chickens or in

remuneration from unwary motorists. The paradoxical nature of the suggestion is evident. To begin with, we are told that there are judgments, but in conclusion we are informed that there really aren't any at all, for what looks like a judgment is not really a judgment, but an injunction or imperative. Now, imperatives or injunctions may be useful or useless, and they do elicit responses; but they can scarcely be said to convey information or express facts. And if for any reason we do, with Dewey, find the adverb "truly" more fundamental than the adjective "true," the fact remains that while we say that someone is judging truly, it is nonsense to say that anyone commands or enjoins truly.

In general, the attempt to define meaning and truth in terms of practical consequences seems foredoomed to failure. To argue that the meaning of judgments is to be found in their practical applications is to put the cart before the horse; for unless the meaning is already known prior to and independently of such considerations, it would be impossible to determine what judgment, if any, is being acted upon. A corresponding difficulty arises in the instrumentalist's conception of truth as utility; for unless the truth of the contention that the consequences of enactments are useful is defined independently of further enactments, unless, in short, the determination of questions of utility presupposes truth as a noninstrumental concept, knowledge must remain impossible. For in order to know that any given judgment is true, it would be necessary to know that the consequences of application are useful; but in order to know this, further applications would be required, and so on without end.

But aside from these difficulties there remains a problem of especial importance for our discussion of ideology or perspectivism. Meaning, it has been alleged, involves interests and evaluations, and truth, their realization and satisfaction. But what interests are implicated in judgments in the social sciences, and what is the utility that constitutes truth? Interests, of course, are always qualified by ends in view, and which of these shall we treat as preferred stock in our accounting of the judgments of the social scientist? As a member of a complex society, he enjoys a variety of interests in consequence of his many associations; for groups within our society are not, in general, mutually exclusive sects or castes. Social groupings overlap, and the interests of the social scientist, like those of our own, represent the effects of overlapping associations. The employer as employer is a member of a distinct group within our economic system, but as a concrete social being his interests and associations expand beyond the limits of his economic position. He may, of his own accord, recognize the right of his employees to form collective-bargaining agencies in the full knowledge that such agencies must restrict his privileges as employer. Such instances may be rare, but they do occur; and to describe such an employer as a traitor to his economic class is but to make the tacit admission of the inadequacy of the metaphysics of class interest. For the interest in profit is one, and only one, of the various interests with which we have to deal; other interests, no less important, are required in order to account for the facts of human nature and experience. There are as many interests as there are types of association. The local society for the cultivation of cactus and other succulents is based upon a community of interest as genuine as that of the association for the increased consumption of California prunes. If, therefore, we are to agree with the instrumentalist that interests are implicated in the course of the social scientist's inquiry, which interests shall we select and what are the satisfactions for which his judgments are tools or instruments? Is it the interest in the perpetuation of the economic group that provides the special endowment necessary for the continued existence of his inquiry? Is it the interest in the perpetuation of any of the social forms, or the interest in the correction of abuses wherever these may be supposed to occur? Certainly the results of inquiry may have enormous practical consequences. Theory can and quite often does serve as propaganda, and even classroom discussions, remote as these may seem, are not without their practical effect in determining the character of opinion concerning current issues. Nevertheless, theory and propaganda are scarcely synonymous terms; the interests implicated in the inquiry of the social scientist cannot, therefore, be identified with those served by propaganda. If the interest the satisfaction of which provides the test of social theory is the interest in the preservation of an economic class, or the interest in the perpetuation of a civilization or society, or the interest in the institution of desired changes in the social system, then the propagandist may well lay claim to the mantle of academic respectability. Some restriction upon the kind

of interest is obviously called for on any reasonable instrumentalism. It will not do to appeal to the interest in the improvement of
human welfare, for what we count as improvement depends upon
our particular interests. If objectivity in the social sciences is
possible, then such hopelessly relative interests and evaluations
cannot be accorded special status. And even if we grant that there
are absolute standards of value, we must still recognize that the
interest in inquiry is different from the interest in the improvement
of human welfare; the social scientist may, and indeed should be,
interested in social welfare, but the activity of inquiry is at least
distinguishable from that of reform.

When, therefore, the instrumentalist asserts that "truth as
utility means service in making just that contribution to reorganization in experience that the idea or theory claims to be able to
make,"[19] what service is intended? Ideas, meanings, conceptions,
theories, and systems are tested by their ability to remove some
specific trouble or perplexity, but what kind of trouble or perplexity is removed by successful inquiry? By persistent reference
to interested organisms, adjustments, transformations in the environment, and so forth, the instrumentalist would seem to be
referring to just such interests, satisfactions, and troubles as we
have examined; but the cardinal interest of the social scientist, the
troubles and perplexities his inquiry is designed to remove, can
scarcely be described in such terms. What is served is the interest
in knowledge, for the troubles and perplexities are those of minds
in their attempt to understand and describe the facts. And however
extensive and important the satisfactions provided by social theory
may be, unless they include the cardinal satisfaction of the interest
in knowledge they are vain and pretentious. Confronted, therefore,
by these facts, the instrumentalist will conveniently shift the meaning of his terms. The biological root metaphor will be dropped.
Service, perplexity, adjustment, satisfaction—these, like the other
familiar keys to instrumentalism, will have to do with the details
of procedure and confirmation in the development of theories and
systems, in complete independence of all practical applications
and consequences. But once the narrower considerations of utility
suggested by the instrumentalist's language have been abandoned,
the "activistic" theory of knowledge has been left behind, and with

---

[19] *Ibid.*, p. 157.

it the only philosophical ground offered for the perspectivistic or ideological conception of judgment. It matters little, for our present purposes, what further points of disagreement remain between ourselves and the instrumentalists, for once the interest in truth, in the understanding of matters of fact, has been recognized, not even the faintest trace of ideology, in Mannheim's sense of the term, remains. For the interest in truth and understanding is the interest in truth and understanding in the quite ordinary sense in which any empirical judgment, whether from physics, geology, or history, can be said to be true, namely, when it just simply agrees with or corresponds to the facts.

It is somewhat paradoxical that the doctrine of ideology, while stressing the function of group participation, misses quite completely the importance of one very important group in determining the character of the social scientist's views; for as a social scientist he is a member of a group whose primary concern it is to promote the development of social theory in total abstraction from all considerations of the special interests of other groups. That the social scientist's interest in knowledge may weaken in the face of contrary inclinations and desires, and that he has not, so far at least, succeeded in realizing the ideal of a science to the degree to which investigators in other fields who share his interest in knowledge have succeeded, are matters with which all of us are sufficiently acquainted. These matters call not for an impossible doctrine of ideology according to which the distinction between fact and value is so far obliterated that common understanding is conceivable only where interests, values, and the social context are shared, but rather for the development of the proper techniques, the clarification of procedures, in short, the development and mastery of the proper instruments of inquiry. How may these be acquired? It would be folly for those who are not social scientists to suggest an answer. Techniques and procedures vary from one inquiry to another, and they are best qualified to determine what techniques must be devised, both to guard against the possibility that error may arise from the intrusion of partisan interests and to increase their knowledge of society, who are most intimately concerned with judgments in the social sciences.

WILLIAM R. DENNES

CONCEPTIONS OF CIVILIZATION: DESCRIPTIVE AND NORMATIVE

THE PRECEDING lectures in this series support the view that if we are to improve our knowledge of social processes and of civilizations, and to render our evaluations of them more enlightening and more helpful, we need to advance along four lines. (1) We need to make the reference of our key descriptive concepts as clear as we can. (2) We need to make detailed studies of the influence of bias and predilection upon men's observations and inferences in their social studies, and to discount this influence. (3) We need to make the meaning of our normative concepts as clear as we can. And (4) we need to determine whether there is a serious basis for wide agreement upon norms, or whether every normative conception of civilization must be restricted to the values emphasized in that particular civilization, whichever it happens to be, of which those who develop and employ the normative conception in question are participants.

Dr. Melden argued (and convincingly, as it seems to me) that the second of these tasks—the determination of the influence of a man's social perspective upon his judgments of fact, and the development of techniques for detecting and discounting such influence—is properly the work of empirical scientists: psychologists, economists, anthropologists, historians. We shall therefore address ourselves to phases of the three other problems. Our questions are: What criteria do we employ—what, indeed, do we mean?—when we say of two patterns of group living that one is civilized while the other is not? And, when we say of two patterns of living, both of which we call civilizations, that one is higher than the other, what norms do we in fact employ? And what norms would be most satisfactory to employ?

We face, at the outset, the fact that there is very little constancy in the usage of the terms civilization and culture, whether by scholars or by laymen. A good many social scientists write that they mean by a culture—I quote R. S. Lynd—"all the things that a group of people inhabiting a common geographical area do, the ways they do things and the ways they think and feel about things, their material tools and their values and symbols."[1] Franz Boas, in his most recent work, defines culture as "the totality of the mental and physical reactions and activities that characterize the behavior of the individuals composing a social group, collectively and individually, in relation to their natural environment, to other groups, to members of the group itself and of each individual to himself. It also includes the products of these activities and their role in the life of the groups."[2] Goldenweiser has observed: "A branch is a bit of the physical environment. Whereas a branch used as a club is culture."[3] Culture so defined includes not only all that we know of man himself; much of it is possessed also by animals other than men.

Other social scientists make more distinctions. They apply the term material culture to the tools and techniques shared by a people, and reserve the name culture (without adjectival qualification) for structures of techniques which are integrated to some degree with tribal laws, myths, ritual, dances, and the like. But it is extremely difficult to establish a clear line of distinction between material culture and culture thus conceived, for nobody has ever observed (still less, inferred) any human tool-using or any human techniques of which he could say with assurance that no elements of symbolizing, of enjoyment of rhythm, or even of ritual, enter into them.

Some writers distinguish a still higher degree of culture—the late Edward Sapir[4] chose to call it "genuine culture"—marked by the fact that within a particular nation every part of life— economic, social, religious, aesthetic—is bound with great firmness to every other, reinforces every other, so that each person, whatever he may be doing, feels himself no isolated, lonely, helpless, and insignificant atom, no insecure casual, but an integral and creative factor in a firmly knit supporting context of living. Some authorities use the term civilization to refer to, and distinguish, the cultures which exhibit such development as Sapir calls genuine

---

[1] Robert S. Lynd, *Knowledge for What? The Place of Social Science in American Civilization* (Princeton University Press, 1940), p. 19.

[2] Franz Boas, *The Mind of Primitive Man* (rev. ed.; New York, Macmillan, 1938), p. 159. Compare pp. 4 and 5 of Franz Boas and others, *General Anthropology* (New York, 1938).

[3] Alexander Goldenweiser, *History, Psychology, and Culture* (New York, 1933), p. 59 n.

[4] See, e.g., his "Culture, Genuine and Spurious," *American Journal of Sociology*, Vol. XXIX, No. 4, pp. 401–429.

culture. But many others, including Sapir himself, use the term civilization to mean the mainly technological patterns of group life, and employ the terms culture or genuine culture to specify the sort of integrated living we have just roughly described. European critics, for example, impressed by America's advanced plumbing and (as they judge) backward arts, have divided about equally between telling us that we have civilization but no culture and telling us that we have culture but lack civilization.

Other social scientists have employed still other criteria to mark off what they call a civilization from what they call a culture. One criterion is that the cultural life of a group be mediated by self-conscious history and by articulate science, if it is to be called civilized. When symbols are so used that the habits common to a group are not only *in fact* transmitted from older to younger members, but also their career, their structure, and their transmission are recognized, reported, thought about—there, and only there, do we have civilization.

Now, when what we call science and history *are* thus developed, it becomes possible for human beings to take a very crucial step: namely, the members of a nation may then advance to the apprehension of similarities and differences between themselves and their neighbors, between their neighbors' histories and their own. They may thus come to conceive of themselves, not as *all* the really human beings, as *all* the people,[5] the rest wholly inconsiderable, the rest as alien as, or more alien than, the brutes—but to conceive of themselves as merely *a part* of humanity able to share with other nations, to learn from them and to contribute to them, as well as to fight against them. A really revolutionary change begins when a tribe thus recognizes that members of other tribes are also men— a change which no human group, I suppose, has carried out consistently or at all completely. Some social scientists and psychologists regard this step as so important that they make it the division point between the cultures that come before it and the civilizations that develop after it and nourish its results.

Still other social scientists[6] would mark off by the term civilization the careers of those nations whose nationals, besides develop-

---

[5] A conception reflected in the fact that in most tribes the tribal name is the general name for men as such.

[6] Among them, Mr. Erik H. Erikson, to whom I am much indebted in these inquiries.

ing history, sciences, and arts, and besides recognizing community with human beings outside the tribe or nation, *conceive the future as processes which will not necessarily merely continue (or repeat) present or remembered processes* (as primitive peoples characteristically feel they must), and which, furthermore, may be modified by prudent choice and skillful action. In a civilized society, on this definition of the term, scientific and historical studies would in part be directed toward the specific goals of (*a*) determining the direction of the dominant *de facto* tendencies in human social development and (*b*) devising changes in patterns of living which will conform to, and facilitate, those tendencies.

Still others use the term civilization, as did Professor Adams, to specify either values themselves, such as truth, justice, and beauty, or else such developments of science, of historical knowledge and insight, of fair practices, and of artistic activity, by a community, as may be objectively adequate to those values. And Professor Mackay, if I understood him, described civilization as no specific stage or structure in the process, but rather as the active process itself of *extending* appreciation, and of perfecting the *communication* and the sharing of objects and activities to be appreciated.

Following the lead of eminent historians, anthropologists, psychologists, and philosophers, I have now directed your attention to eight phases or characteristics of group living which have been taken by them as definitive of the term culture, or of the term civilization, when those terms are used descriptively. Some scholars, as we have seen, use the name culture for the "simpler" phases, civilization for the more complex; others exactly reverse this practice; and still others use the two terms virtually as synonyms. We may observe at this point that none of these eight descriptive notions restricts culture or civilization to any particular pattern of organization. For example, a highly aristocratic or a highly democratic pattern of social living might, either of them, conspicuously exemplify—or fail to exemplify—what is meant by culture or civilization in any of the eight senses. We must note, also, that there are *indefinitely many* other types, phases, and products of social living which can be distinguished and studied, and taken as criteria of civilization;—how many (and which) a man will deal with will be determined by his interests and capacities and by the problems that are felt as pressing at the time. The eight descriptive notions I have selected and brought to your attention are, to resume:

1. Material culture.

2. Culture, that is, material culture conjoined with art, ritual, laws.

3. "Genuine culture" (in Sapir's phrase)—a firm integration and mutually reinforcing development of all the factors specified as constituting culture in sense 2.

4. Civilization as culture (or "genuine culture") *mediated by history and science.*

5. Civilization as tribal or national culture so mediated by history and science as to lead to the recognition of the equal humanity of other nations.

6. Civilization as that special development of sense 5 which is essentially characterized by the employment of intelligence to discern the dominant tendencies of change in men's ways of living together, to predict future changes in these respects, and to accommodate men to (and even facilitate) such change.

7. Civilization as values realized, and particular civilizations as the patterns of social living more or less conducive to, or adequate to, the enactment and experience of values.

8. Civilization as an active process of growth in communication and appreciation.

Now which of these conceptions of civilization is the correct one? Is civilization "really" any one of these, or any combination of them? Or is it "really" something else? Such questions have intermittently plagued philosophers, and seem continually to confuse popular discussion and the oratory of statesmen. But fortunately, with the ground so well covered by preceding lectures, we need not take time for them. For to ask of a conception of civilization whether it is the right one is usually to ask: (1) Whether it repeats, or accords with, some previously adopted definition (tacit or explicit) of the term. Questions about the correctness of that prior definition would refer to still prior definitions, and so on *ad infinitum.* Or (2) whether the conception (or definition) makes central what is most valuable or most valued—what is most worth attention. To some of the problems involved in this question we shall soon turn. Or (3) whether the conception accords with historical usage or with the usage of the most expert, or, if neither, then whether it offers some marked terminological convenience.

On examining the eight descriptive concepts more closely—putting aside the pseudo question, Which (if any) of them is the "correct" one ?—the first difficulty that strikes us is that of distinguishing material culture—material culture *not* as mere artifacts lying buried in clay beds or in museums, but as artifacts actually used and the actual techniques of their use—from culture as the conjunction of art, ritual, and laws with such material culture. It is not *merely* that the two are always in fact associated. Rather, elements of art and ritual seem to be part of the very content of material culture, for tools cannot be used, techniques cannot be repeatedly applied, without exhibiting some elements of the rhythms, and the appreciation of rhythms, which are essential aspects of several of the arts and also of ritual activity. And men cannot live in groups at all, let alone use tools and employ techniques, without maintaining some fairly continuous patterns of coöperation and forbearance—and such patterns and their maintenance are the essential content of jural laws.

Similar comments apply to Sapir's attempt to distinguish "genuine culture" from mere culture. For all cultures exhibit a degree of integration greater than zero between some, at least, of their constituent factors. And no culture exhibits a 100-per cent integration and mutual reinforcement of *all* of its constituent strands. How firm, then, must be the firm reinforcement, how integral the integration of strands, to make a culture "genuine" ?

It is, thus, hardly possible to set up satisfactory criteria to distinguish material cultures, cultures, and genuine cultures from one another. There seem to be no gaps, but continuous gradations, between the sorts of social living meant by the three terms. Unless, therefore, we specify, in each case that we consider, just what the factors are that are found and supposed—how much and what kinds of art, how much and what kinds of ritual activity, how much and what kinds of integration—the descriptive import of the three terms material culture, culture, and genuine culture is nil. Indeed, our predicament is likely to be worse than that. The nomenclature is likely to be not merely theoretically insignificant, but positively misleading. For the mere use of three distinct terms will almost certainly lead us to believe that we have found, and are considering, differences, whether we have done so or not.

Consider the normative use of these notions. What Sapir called genuine cultures do seem to satisfy what are generally regarded as basal human needs, more largely and more reliably than do mere cultures, and those latter more than do merely material cultures. But, as Mr. Adams explained, the satisfaction of a need is merely an event occurring in nature. And admitting the fact that a need has been satisfied never of itself rules out the judgment that the need *had better not* have been satisfied—even if that should entail the death of the man who harbored the need. If we say that it is wrong to asphyxiate a man in the gas chamber at San Quentin, we do not ordinarily mean, by our statement, *merely* that the man has a basal need for air free from cyanide fumes and that that need would be frustrated by asphyxiating him. But, granting all that, what else can we *seriously* refer to when we approve (or, *mutatis mutandis,* condemn) capital punishment, except the probable satisfaction of needs—the prospect, namely, of more adequate satisfaction of what we regard as a more important organization of needs, and a preference for this over the satisfaction of a particular man's need for air? Indeed, unless we mean *something* like this, and unless (besides) we have reasonable evidence that our belief is true, our deliberate execution of a man would be sadism or vindictiveness of the ugliest sort. Similar factors determine any reasonable judgment respecting whether it is better to resort, or not to resort, to war. But ought we to accept, as our normative concept, the satisfaction of basal needs? And can we achieve a serious agreement upon what the basal needs of human beings are? It is always possible to argue that the development, so far as possible, of new and "higher" needs, and a restriction of the satisfaction of basal needs in favor of more attention to such "higher" needs, is a decisive part of the norm by which we ought to judge civilizations. And until we have dealt with that argument, I shall say no more about the normative relevance of the three notions of culture which, by means of one terminology or another, scholars have commonly tried to distinguish.

Of the convenience of the fourth descriptive notion—civilization as culture mediated and sustained by science and history—there can be no doubt. There are, of course, plenty of difficult borderline cases. Paul Radin has argued (and with supporting evidence that is by no means negligible) that it is mainly the provincial dullness and conceit of so-called "civilized" observers and interpreters— and *not* the facts of social history—that have led them to character- ize peoples of primitive culture as devoid of historians, scientists, and philosophers. But at least as a matter of degree the distinction is important between those societies in which activities similar to those we name historical and scientific study do, and those in which they do not, exercise a considerable influence upon the lives of the people—irrespective of whether those activities are widely partici- pated in or are the exclusive province of an elite. Also of great importance *for many human interests* is the discovery that all people, on any widely used definition of "people," are not restricted to any one tribe or nation. As for the use of intelligence to discern the dominant tendencies in social processes, and to conform to them and facilitate them in order to "shape the future," this too is ob- viously important *for many human interests*. But there is no inher- ent authority in dominant tendencies, or in so-called "waves of the future." If they threaten what is precious, the intelligent thing is not to accept them or facilitate them, but to resist and alter them. It is, as Mr. Pepper explained, sheer superstition to hold that any specific pattern, or cycle, of social change is ineluctably necessary. To be sure, we may have grounds for believing that resistance to some changes would probably be ineffectual; but even in that case it remains an open option whether to exert oneself on a slight chance of securing some modification in the impending changes, or of keeping open the possibility of speculation upon alternatives, or maybe only of making as vigorous a protest as one can against what may seem to be the overwhelmingly probable course of events.

There is no logical or theoretical fault in taking as the criterion to mark off civilizations from mere cultures: the achievement of serious history and science, *or* the use of them to recognize human- ity beyond tribal limits, *or* the use of them to anticipate, and to adjust to, future developments. But it is, in every case, more informative to specify, as well as we can, the particular theories, explanations, methods (and ranges of effectiveness) of adaptation achieved in a society than merely to apply the general term civili- zation, whichever of the criteria we employ as determining its reference.

In the immense body of social interpretation represented by Mr. Adams's lecture, achievement of values is made the essential criterion, not merely of the normative, but also and specifically of the descriptive, reference of the term civilization. Civilization-as-such is described as values realized, experienced. And particular civilizations are described as containers which possess more or less objective adequacy to the content, which is civilization-as-such. Now it is quite generally insisted by social scientists, and by writers on its methodology, that we must be confusing (or identifying) description with evaluation if we thus take values, or relations to values, as determining the descriptive meaning of the term civilization. Social science cannot be objective, they allege, unless it defines its central concepts so as to be neutral as far as values go. But their criticism is mistaken. For if one specifies as well as one can—if one specifies recognizably—what one means by values, then it is nothing more (nor less) than a question of fact[7] to what extent the values are enacted, experienced, disseminated, rendered secure, in various civilizations—that is, how "objectively adequate" the particular civilizations are to civilization-as-such. However, neither the conception, nor the fact, of the objective adequacy of a civilization to the realization of values excludes, or presupposes, or even suggests, any one particular theory of values—Platonic, Aristotelian, Stoic, theological, Kantian, Hegelian, intuitionist, hedonist, evolutionary survivalist, or naturalist. For *whatever* may be one's theory of the nature of value, the question how far a given civilization nurtures that which upon one's theory is valuable— the question how adequate, in this sense, the given civilization is— is a question quite as much about objective factual relations as any question could be. The answer to the question cannot be derived from any theory of value, and it does not entail any one particular theory of value as against its rivals. It can be reached only by empirical study and inductive inference. Mr. Melden's analysis has, it seems to me, sufficiently refuted the basic type of arguments to the contrary. Consider, for example, the naturalist value theorists who were described by Mr. Adams as arrested at the intellectual level of college sophomores—all of whom, he says, know that facts are objective but values are functions of subjective interest. For such naturalists the question whether life in the pattern of a particular civilization satisfies certain interests (including, possibly, an interest in variegating and enriching interests in certain

---

[7] Although it may, of course, be a very complicated and difficult question of fact.

specific senses) is a question about *the objective adequacy* of that civilization to values, in precisely the same sense that it would be for a Platonist—provided that the Platonist has made clear to himself and to others (and otherwise than by expressing his loves) what it is that he means by values in his loftier characterization of them.

Similar comments may be made in support of the descriptive objectivity of Mr. Mackay's and Mr. Dewey's characterizations of civilization as growth in appreciation and communication. It is plain, I think, that neither of these philosophers means by "growth" mere quantitative expansion or proliferation—although Dewey has been a thousand times accused of meaning only that. If we understand their conceptions of value—and for my own part, so far as I understand them, they seem enlightening and largely acceptable—then it becomes a task of determining probabilities about objective facts, just as in any other field of study, when we address ourselves to the job of discovering in which patterns of living (actual or possible) valuable communication and appreciation thrive and have thrived (or would probably thrive) and what appear to be the decisive conditions of their growth or of their arrest.

The harvest of our discussion thus far would seem to be this. Of the eight descriptive notions of culture and of civilization considered, *each* specifies phases *or* structures *or* results of social living which are interesting and important in many connections, theoretical and practical. But the notions in no way conflict with one another. If one chooses to define civilization by any one of the eight criteria—or by any other criterion—one's definition will say nothing about, and will entail nothing about, the existence or the nonexistence, the importance or the unimportance, of ranges of social living that are marked by the traits definitive of the selected notion (or of any other of the alternative notions). The upshot is this. If we proceed seriously and carefully in the descriptive use of any concept of civilization, we shall be describing found or inferred phases, constituents, or results of social living and their causes and conditions—descriptions which are bound to be quite compatible with the results reached by persons who are (also seriously and carefully) describing and interpreting, under the name civilization, *different* phases, *different* constituents, and *different* results of social living, and *their* causes and conditions.

Consider a concrete example. If *both* proceed scientifically, the man who explains all civilized activities (including those of science) in terms of their relations to economic processes will not reach results that are different in theoretic content from those reached by the man who explains all civilized activities (including the economic) in terms of their relations to the evolution of science. The choice of one or the other frame of reference not only does not settle, it does not even throw any light on, the question whether economic changes or scientific changes are causally prior, the one to the other. A serious answer to *that* question must be a conclusion, and not a presupposition, of inquiry. The only defensible way to approach it is by exploring the evidence in particular ranges of economic and scientific activities. That evidence will support exactly the same inferences for both inquirers; and if it is in-decisive—if it leaves alternatives open—it will do so for both inquirers. If the two inquirers, with the same evidence, do in fact make different inferences—choose different alternatives—we can-not ascribe this to theoretical implications of their different cate-gories, but only to their different habits, hopes, and biases. If we deny this, we should be on all fours with those who would say that different estimates of the effects of insulin upon diabetic patients are established according as one's "philosophy" of medicine is homeopathy or allopathy.

On the descriptive level, I conclude, it makes no difference what-ever to the theoretical content and the explanatory hypotheses of history and of the social sciences (or to the interpretations of social philosophy, if these are different from such hypotheses) whether one sort of structure or process is taken as the criterion of civili-zation and other sorts are interpreted as variously related[8] to instances of what is thus called civilization, or whether some one of the other sorts of structure or process is taken as criterion and other structures and processes are interpreted in their relations to instances of that.

Now does this mean, as is so commonly alleged, that *anything* which men happen to call—or choose to call—civilization is quite as good as anything else? That a reversion to tribalism, provided a few needed ranges of science were still maintained, would be as good as an advance toward a world polity?—since the partisans of each

---

[8] Related by relations of similarity, difference, causality, constitutiveness, etc.

might (with perfect sincerity) describe them as progress toward what they conceive civilization to be. Does it imply that so-called higher and lower civilizations are simply different civilizations, each precious to those who may flourish in it? Franz Boas has recently written that "any evaluation of culture means that a point has been chosen towards which changes move, and this point is the standard of our own modern civilization."[9] How largely this is, or must be, our predicament, I am about to inquire. But at this stage I want to say one thing apodictically, namely: to recognize that the choice of descriptive concepts of civilization makes no difference in the theoretical content of our knowledge about civilizations and their contexts, and that one descriptive concept is, therefore, theoretically as eligible as any other, most certainly does not mean (or imply) that *any civilization* is as good as any other. It is, indeed, completely to pervert the descriptive use of any notion of civilization to pretend to find in it such implications for evaluation—or indeed any implications for evaluation at all. Even descriptive concepts of civilization (like Mr. Adams's and Mr. Mackay's) as the realization, or the sharing, of values leave quite open the questions (1) whether any particular instance of such realization or sharing should be judged as, under the circumstances, desirable or undesirable and (2) whether further consideration might not induce—and *justify*, in the relevant sense of justification—the preference of other values to those which a man has employed as descriptive criteria of civilization, and, by their relations to which he has determined the "brute facts" of the objective adequacy of various civilizations.

As a matter of fact, all six of the descriptive concepts of culture and civilization, other than Mr. Adams's and Mr. Mackay's, are, *equally with theirs* (although not so explicitly), defined in terms of values—in terms, that is, of activities valued by those who participate in them, or valued by those who interpret them, or, as is most commonly the case, by both. For the patterns of activity taken, respectively, to be definitive of these descriptive concepts, respond to, develop, satisfy, or frustrate needs and interests pretty widespread among human beings.

In order to make out what is involved, not merely in the classification and explanation of patterns of civilization, but (more importantly) in evaluations of them, let us consider examples of

---

[9] Franz Boas, *The Mind of Primitive Man*, p. 205.

such evaluations, particularly evaluations in which participants in a civilization rise up to condemn it as, in whole or in part, needlessly low, or as uncivilized. The examples I have chosen—from a historian, a novelist, a critic, and an anthropologist—are not, except that of the anthropologist, especially learned. I do not, myself, find any of them altogether convincing. And they do not express any particular philosophical theory of what is involved in (or "validates") such evaluations.

First, consider Mahaffy's judgment[10] of the superiority of fifth-century Athenian to modern Christian civilization as epitomized in the difference between the humane and kindly treatment accorded that duly sentenced criminal, Socrates the son of Sophroniscus, in his last moments, as against the "gauntness and horror of our modern executions, as detailed to us with morbid satisfaction by the daily newspapers." Our two thousand years' course, as Christians, of believing the impossible, must, he thinks, be partly responsible for the deterioration of our intelligence and morals.

Take, as a second example, Norman Douglas' evaluation[11] of Western Christian civilization as one of the lowest known, if only because of its degradation of women (who are, after all, the more numerous half of mankind). In many other cultures, he argues, women have roles as restricted; but only in ours have the restrictions been supported by such emotionally extravagant, intellectually pretentious, and hypocritically concealing rationalizations. Hence the restrictions characteristic of our civilization are the most damaging to human personality. He contrasts the Mosaic, and the Hindu, pity for a woman unmarried or without progeny (think of Rachel's cry, "God hath taken away my reproach," when she bore her son) with St. Paul's advice that marriage is better only than burning; St. Augustine's that a fruitful marriage is not to be compared in excellence with the purity of a virgin; St. Chrysostom's characterization of women as "a foe to friendship, an inescapable punishment, an ineluctable evil"—and virginity as superior to married life as heaven is to earth (how the statement would have scandalized Moses!); St. Bernard on women's faces as burning winds and their voices as the hissing of serpents; St. Jerome's calling women the "gate of Hell," men who love their

---

[10] J. P. Mahaffy, *Social Life in Greece* (3d ed.; London, 1877), p. 267.
[11] Norman Douglas, *Goodbye to Western Culture* (New York, Harper, 1930).

wives ardently, adulterers, and his writing to a widow about to remarry in terms of "the dog returning to his vomit, and the sow that was washed returning to wallow in the mire." The effect of such doctrines—worse, in the first instance, upon women than upon men, because their role in the bearing and rearing of the children which are the fruit of sexual expression is so large—was to produce a civilization in which, Douglas argues, more completely than in any other known to us, a basic human need was strangled, or distorted, or hypocritically condemned, so that it sought satisfaction in covert and morbid forms. Even the adoration of women in romantic Western poetry he takes as part of the shocking ambivalence which pays them the highest verbal compliments (all the way up from the dull prose of calling them our "better halves") at the same time that it restricts most of their activities, irrespective of their talents, as men's activities are not restricted—or allows a few to overcome the restriction, but at the risk of extreme neurosis, or worse. He judges that Western civilization thus tends, more largely than any other known, to reduce all women to the status of prostitutes. For, to the intelligent, restriction not based upon difference of capacity is far more degrading than is physical abuse.

Take, as a third example, Lewis Mumford's comparison of late Renaissance European civilization with the industrial civilization of the nineteenth century—two stages in what is ordinarily regarded as the career of one civilization. "The goal of the eotechnic civilization as a whole until it reached the decadence of the eighteenth century, was not more power alone, but a greater intensification of life: color, perfume, images, music, sexual ecstasy, as well as daring exploits in arms and thought and exploration. Fine images were everywhere: a field of tulips in bloom, the scent of new-mown hay, the ripple of flesh under silk or the rondure of budding breasts, the rousing sting of the wind as the rain-clouds scud over the seas, or the blue serenity of sky and cloud, reflected with crystal clarity on the velvety surface of canal and pond and watercourse."[12] By contrast, in the nineteenth century "the realities were money, prices, capital, shares: the environment itself, like most of human existence, was treated as an abstraction. Air and sunlight, because of their deplorable lack of value in exchange,

---

[12] Lewis Mumford, *Technics and Civilization* (New York, Harcourt, Brace, 1934), p. 148.

had no reality at all."[13] "These new economic men sacrificed their digestion, the interests of parenthood, their sexual life, their health, most of the normal pleasures and delights of civilized existence to the untrammelled pursuit of power and money ... [But] outside the industrial system, the economic man was in a state of neurotic maladjustment. These successful neurotics looked upon the arts as unmanly forms of escape from work and business enterprise: but what was their one-sided maniacal concentration upon work but a much more disastrous escape from life itself? In only the most limited sense were the great industrialists better off than the workers they degraded; jailers and prisoners were both, so to say, inmates of the same House of Terror."[14]

"The rich feared the poor, and the poor feared the rent collector; the middle classes feared the plagues that came from the vile insanitary quarters of the industrial city, and the poor feared, with justice, the dirty hospitals to which they were taken.... The school was regimented like an army ... teacher and pupil feared each other as did capitalist and worker. Walls, barred windows, barbed wire fences, surrounded the factory as well as the jail. Women feared to bear children, and men feared to beget them; the fear of syphilis and gonorrhea tainted sexual intercourse; behind the diseases themselves lurked Ghosts: the spectre of locomotor ataxia, paresis, insanity, blind children, crippled legs, and the only known remedy for syphilis, till salvarsan, was itself a poison.... The drab prison-like houses, the palisades of dull streets, the treeless back yards filled with rubbish, the unbroken rooftops, with never a gap for park or playground, underlined this environment of death. A mine explosion, a railway wreck, a tenement-house fire, a military assault upon a group of workers, or finally the more potent outbreak of war—these were but appropriate punctuation marks. Exploited for power and profit, the destination of most of the goods made by the machine was either the rubbish heap or the battlefield."[15]

Consider, as a final example, Sapir's evaluative contrast[16] of genuine cultures—in which, although primitive, great chieftains dance, and their dancing is part of their importance and privilege; and men gain their food, say, by spearing salmon and snaring rabbits—with civilizations such as our own (which, he says, lack genuine

---

[13] *Ibid.*   [14] *Ibid.*, p. 177.   [15] *Ibid.*, p. 195.   [16] *Op. cit.*, pp. 415–429.

culture), in which our chieftains, our captains of industry and finance, may watch the Ballet Russe but, if they dance themselves, generally do so as a "minor amusement, or even as a concession to the tyranny of social custom." And most of our people gain their food by such appalling sacrifices to civilization as are typified by the telephone girl's manipulation of technical routines which answer no felt needs of her own. "As a solution of the problem of culture," Sapir argues, "she is a failure—and the more dismal the greater her natural endowment."

These four are typical samples of evaluative judgments. Each of them appears, *prima facie,* to be more than a man's merely saying of a given civilization, as Boas interprets such judgments, that in such and such respects it resembles, or differs from, his own. For these are, in large part, evaluations of the very civilizations in which the interpreters themselves are participants. Upon what does a man stand—and what is the fulcrum of his balance— when he thus weighs a civilization otherwise than by a merely factual comparison with his own? Or when he evaluates his own civilization?

Mr. Adams offered, by way of answer, a version of the Platonic notion of values as objective norms which have a being other than the being of facts, and have validity otherwise than as in fact satisfying (or being likely to satisfy) needs and as being the objects of interest. Truth, justice, beauty, experienced and realized, were among his examples of such values as should supply norms for the evaluation of civilizations. Surely he is right in saying that the truth of a true statement is objective if there is ever any sense in calling anything objective. For such truth is constituted by the occurrence and configuration of the objects which the statement purports to describe and not by any feeling, wish, or act of persons, of subjects, who happen to believe the statement. But is the truth, which is thus objective, as such valuable? We can, of course, define the words truth and value so that we should have to say this. But in that case we should have to say that it would be better for a human being to know all truths—including those about the locations and paths of motion of each of billions of billions of atoms, and also about the processes by which he knows these, and so on, *ad infinitum*—than to know only such truths as served to explain the events that puzzled him and his fellows, and to guide their conduct when choice was incumbent upon them. If we should take this position we would be very like a late beloved museum director who insisted that, since no two birds are exactly alike, a really good museum of birds would have to have in it *all* the birds there are, or ever were—no single bird left out.

If truth is a fair example of what is called an objective value, an intrinsically authoritative norm, then we must say of such values that they are, in themselves and objectively, just the configurations of events and characters which they are, and unless, in calling them values, we mean to make no synthetic assertion, but merely to say that they are what they are, it is hard to find an alternative to the naturalistic rendering which makes their valuableness consist in their being objects of interest, or contributive to the being of objects of interests. Such interests may be revealed—they need not be explicitly *asserted*—in value judgments.

But I must not rattle the dry bones of the ancient controversy between the naturalistic and the other theories of value. For my own part, I have failed to find in any theory of value a final specification of the differentia of what is generally treated as valuableness—let alone a justification of one—other than relation to interest or preference. I shall not now defend my result, but shall engage instead in a hypothetical inquiry: If one accepts the naturalistic rendering of values, what would be the significance of judgments, such as those we read, of the worth of a civilization?

The naturalist here takes a cue from Plato and Aristotle, namely, the human good is the realization of man's capacities, the fulfillment of his real nature, which both of those ancient philosophers often said was what men *really need*—and *really want*. Plato derived his account of what men *really* need from a theory that one certain formal structure of personality, and no other, is intelligible. Aristotle seems to have derived his account more or less empirically and inductively, but then to have fixed it, and to have claimed extra authority for it, by virtue of a definition. We have just lived through a period in which most psychologists, anthropologists, and philosophers have denied that man has any specific nature, any native needs or capacities—arguing that he is completely malleable and is shaped by the social forces that mold him. But there is now, and with good reason, a convergent interest among serious students in discovering what the needs and interests are which human beings—*not must, but do in fact*—exhibit in their lives in all the cultural patterns known to us, and how different patterns of culture and civilization affect those needs and interests, integrate them, frustrate them, and develop new ones. During the last twenty years psychologists have made great progress in this work. For they have learned the lessons implied by criticism of overspecialized and hypostatic instinct theories, like McDougall's, and, in the other direction, of oversimplified reflex theories. They have come to recognize that there are no sharp knife-cuts in the life of a human organism between one sort of needed activity and other sorts. They have all been influenced by the results and suggestions of psychoanalytic investigations. But those for whom these last-named results dominate theory, and those for whom they do not, have equally learned that what we can specify recognizably as *drives, needs,* and *interests* are patterns of behavior (including, of course, talking) and of the preceding, accompanying, and constitutive fine scale tissue behavior studied by physiologists—and *not* independent powers or forces, transcendent of such behavior but controlling it. In our own laboratories and institutes at Berkeley, particularly vigorous and promising studies are going on toward the more accurate discrimination of such human needs, and of the relations of their manifestations to the maturation, and to features of the physical and social environments, of human organisms. Whether they classify basal human needs as "id-needs," "ego-needs," "super-ego-needs," and "enlarged-ego-needs," as Tolman did in his challenging address on "Psychological Man,"[17] or whether they classify them as "tissue tensions," social needs, and auxiliary needs, as Tolman has done in other connections, or whether as viscerogenic and psychogenic needs, described as much by their developed clusterings as by their locus of origin (as in the work of H. A. Murray and his collaborators)[18]—the serious psychologists seem to me, in all cases, to have described much more specifically and fully than had been done before patterns of activity that appear very early in the lives of human beings generally, and that persist (in varying clusterings, developments, and counteractions) in the lives of human beings in all the cultural patterns that are known to us. More than this, they have learned much about the

[17] *Journal of Social Psychology*, Vol. XIII (February, 1941).
[18] Notably H. A. Murray and others, *Explorations in Personality* (Oxford Univ. Press, 1938).

average chronology of the manifestations of various needs, about their conflicts, about the factors that produce conflicts and deviations from normal chronology, about derivative second-order and third-order interests that develop as new phases of basal needs or as offering substitutes for their satisfaction. And they have learned a good deal, not only about the ways in which basal needs conflict, but also about the ways in which derivative interests conflict— seriously, and often destructively—with basal interests: destructively not merely in the sense of diminishing the satisfaction of those interests, but also in the sense of destroying the health, and even the life, of the organism.

Now, explicit interests and preferences, so far as we have any knowledge of the matter at all, appear to be resultants (and symptoms) of the operations, the conflicts, and the various patterns of integration, of basal needs. It is not surprising, then, that any man, whether he be a naturalist philosopher or not, should, on examining his own and other men's interests and preferences, come to approve those which facilitate the satisfaction and integration of the basal needs that generated them. But logically it is not necessary that a naturalist—or any other man—should advance to this attitude of approval and preference. The question is this: when it becomes clear that alternatives lead to physiological and psychological disease, to war, to untimely breakdown, and to death, *is there any better reason* that can be found (or imagined) in any philosophy to justify a man in taking as his norm for evaluating civilizations the degree to which they, with their patterns of living, their arts and sciences, enable men to understand, and to satisfy more fully, more generally, and more reliably, their basal needs? Such needs include many besides those for air, food, drink, elimination, sexual activity. We know man only as we find him, and we have found him nowhere, and in no epoch, in which he has not manifested cravings to explore, to understand, to affiliate, to coöperate, to be loyal, to play, to imagine, to sing, to dance, to produce and enjoy various rhythms, as well as cravings for air, food, drink, rest, shelter, sex, child nurturance and tendance, sleep, and pain avoidance. The needs for knowledge, beauty, and coöperation are as basal as those for air, food, and sex. And not only in the sense of being as widespread. They are as basal in the further sense that extreme frustration of them leads to the derangement and even the death of the organism. To be sure, if you frustrate totally a man's need for food or for air, his activities are very quickly deranged, and soon thereafter terminate. If you frustrate his needs for affiliation (as our own culture has so largely done) and for understanding, you get, after a longer period, such results as love strangled by aggressions which, in the mistreatment of children and in wars and in other cruel ways, lead to death (a slower and in some respects more agonizing death) just as surely as does asphyxiation or starvation.

Such conclusions of our psychologists, for the most part, confirm and extend, rather than radically alter, the opinions generally held today by men of common sense, of average literacy, and of good will. Something very much like them, though it may be rough and pretty inarticulate, is I believe the ground upon which Mahaffy and Douglas and Mumford and Sapir (historian, novelist, critic, and anthropologist) are standing—and not merely upon the fashions that happen to prevail in their own civilizations—when they pass the critical judgments which we read a few minutes ago. Can we conceive of any better grounds to stand on? Is the notion of satisfaction of basal needs the best normative conception to employ in evaluating civilizations? And would the adoption of this norm transform the task of social intelligence into the objective and scientific one of determining the facts and the probabilities, with respect to the satisfaction of needs, in various patterns of group living? What are the main objections to this normative concept?

One objection springs to mind immediately. If all we know about men's needs and interests is what we observe (or infer) to be, or to have been, men's actual behavior (molar and molecular), then *whatever* men do, *whatever* patterns of civilization they develop, will all equally be outgrowths, expressions, and satisfactions of their needs—and all equally good; for what is not, in this sense, *needed,* just does not come into being in human history. Therefore, it is urged again, we need norms and criteria independent of the facts of human behavior in order to evaluate those facts significantly.

This criticism is an example of the sort of partial insight for which there ought to be a name, as there is a name for half-truths. The criticism rightly recognizes that no naturalistic evaluations are final or immune to modification. But it falsely infers from this fact a principle very dubious even respecting its meaning—the principle that, if we are to criticize and modify naturalistic evaluations, there *must* be a higher and more authoritative type of evaluation than the naturalistic from the vantage ground of which we can carry out our criticisms and modifications. The difficulty is that attempts to specify what the higher type is have not succeeded in demarcating it, seriously and recognizably, from the expression of preferences. The critics are quite right in pointing out that the judgment "It is good that hunger should be satisfied" is not the same thing as—and does not mean—an occurrent need for food or the satisfaction (by eating) of such an occurrent need. The judgment is rather (*a*) the verbal symbolization of our having, and recognizing, many, many needs and interests besides the need for food, and (*b*) the symbolization of the conviction that if the need for food is not satisfied, all (or most of) these other needs will, in various ways and to various degrees, be frustrated.

Many answer that it is not by its bearing upon the satisfaction of other needs that we evaluate the satisfaction of a specific need, but by its contribution to the realization of ideals like those of truth and justice, or to the achievement of an integrated personality, which is no mere organization of needs and satisfactions, but a metaphysical or moral presupposition of their significance, on a level higher than theirs and with a justification which does not depend upon them, *their* justification, on the contrary, depending upon *it*.

Now, unless we choose to demonstrate our love for truth by preferring speculation to the painstaking, and also highly critical, studies made by psychologists, we shall have to take seriously the conclusions of the latter that in the process of the forming of ideals in children's development and maturation and in social history they find only varying developments and clusterings of needs and satisfactions conjoined with various symbolizations of them, verbal and other. And when the verbal symbolization takes the form of asserting absolute validity for an ideal—that is, validity otherwise than as satisfying *de facto* human needs—they find that the behavior exhibits all the traits that define what in other ranges of behavior is called activity exhibiting strong needs for dominance, for recognition, and for succorance.[19] It seems to be one of the more sublimated expressions of those needs.

---

[19] I follow, here, H. A. Murray, *Explorations in Personality*, as on p. 152.

Can we answer here that the genesis of an ideal is irrelevant to its content and its validity? That at some stage in the natural history of thought an event of discernment occurs, having a content which is no part of natural history, and an authority which does not depend upon any spatiotemporal events? That what supervenes, in this act of discernment, is insight into objective excellence?

If we do say these things, would there be any serious grounds for anybody else to accept, or comply with, what we report as our insight, except whatever empirical evidence there might be that such compliance would probably open the way to a fuller satisfaction of human needs?

No. The evaluation of men's cultural patterns in terms of the satisfaction of their needs does not oblige us to say either that all are equally good, since all satisfy some needs, or that, if some are really better than others, it must be because they approach some other norm than the satisfaction of needs. Where what satisfies some needs nevertheless leads to conflict, frustration, and the judgment that all is not well, it is precisely because other needs are blocked by it; and it is these others that are speaking out in our criticisms.

It is well known that different patterns of civilized living develop, satisfy, and frustrate different interests and needs, and that men have managed to survive in the various patterns of group living for longer or shorter periods. Not only have they survived! The influential and articulate participants in each pattern have been happy, and have celebrated theirs as the best of civilizations. For obviously, or even truistically, it is persons who are well adjusted to a given social order that rise to eminence in it. The badly adjusted drop into relative insignificance, or migrate, or even die, unless by an exceedingly aggressive drive to overthrow and transform it they succeed in altering the social order to one that better fits their pattern of personality. Of those who survive and thrive, each sincerely finds the pattern of his own group life admirable. It is these facts that prompted so many critical minds, from the ancient sophists to Aldous Huxley (of the day before yesterday, not today) to veer away from every doctrine of native human needs, to develop the myth that man's nature is infinitely plastic, and to adopt a cultural and historical relativism according to which the most we could ever say is that some patterns of living nourish some interests, and others—others!

Such conclusions are intolerable to a serious intelligence. That is why we all sympathize with the motives, and the efforts, of those thinkers, ancient and modern, who have sought by various metaphysics of authoritative norms to do two things: (1) to escape such relativism as is illustrated by the statement that all we can meaningfully say, when we evaluate National Socialist policies, is that to the Nazis many aspects of our ways of living are offensive, whereas to most of us many of theirs are, and (2) to defend the conviction that the higher values, such as those of science and fine art, are those in relation to which the satisfaction of biological needs is to be justified, and not *vice versa*. The rendering of values as functions of human needs is plagued by the *reductio ad absurdum*: whatever anyone says that human needs require for their satisfaction, anyone else can totally dismiss, simply by saying that he has needs which require its elimination or even its reversal. But the metaphysics of objective norms—developed in the course of a quest for a kind of certainty—do not seem to have answered this *reductio* effectively. On the other hand, empirical studies of human behavior in various patterns of civilization, while they give us no authority to say, "You are absolutely wrong irrespective of relations to human needs," to the man who holds that his very special and distinguished needs ought to take precedence over the needs of the many, of the vulgar, or over the basal needs of all mankind, nevertheless do give us grounds for saying that (*a*) unless he can integrate with the needs and interests of others the special needs which he seeks to satisfy, he will not be able to satisfy them at all fully or securely, any more than a poet writing in a tongue known only to himself can achieve the expression which he craves, and (*b*) that the frustration of the basal needs of others leads to resentments, aggression, breakdowns in health, war—from the results of which, if they are widespread in the world, no man can escape.

Let us turn our attention, in closing, to the second major objective of many of the nonnaturalistic metaphysics of value. That objective has been to establish that the higher values, mediated by reflection and symbolization—such values as those of science and art,—are those in terms of which the satisfaction of biological needs is to be justified, and *not vice versa*.

Would that civilization be desirable in which higher mathematics, music, jurisprudence, painting were brought by an elite to what experts called exceptionally high development, but in which most of the population were not only ignorant, but also ill nourished, overworked, and sexually starved or degraded? On the other hand, would a civilization be desirable in which all the participants were perfectly comfortable, their "biological needs" satisfied, but their imaginations unstirred and unexpressed in song and poetry and plastic art, their curiosity not developed into what we should call serious and extensive science? Are the "higher civilized activities" best regarded (1) as instrumental to, or (2) as quite independent of, or (3) as inimical to, or (4) as the justifying ends of, the activities by which men satisfy their "simpler" biological needs? Mr. Dewey's view on this issue is so enlightening that, familiar as it is, we cannot recall it too often. He has held that all four of these positions are theoretically unsatisfactory and also actually dangerous both to the so-called "ideal interests" and to the satisfaction of simpler biological needs. In order to be effective *in their own terms,* he has argued, the highly civilized activities must be firmly rooted in men's basal needs, and must deal in large part—directly or indirectly—with the concrete tensions and conflicts which develop in the struggle to satisfy those needs. Art and science that cut themselves off from such roots become trivial, however technically expert their development may be. But the arts and sciences, when thus healthily rooted, are not merely instrumental to the enlightenment and the satisfaction of preëxistent basal needs; they also generate new interests—interests especially precious to many men. But these new interests can never, without disastrous consequences, be taken as eliminating (and replacing) the basal needs, their conflicts, and the problems thus engendered, which were in all cases their foundations, and also the ladders of their ascent.

The four alternative views which we formulated—all rejected by Dewey—may sound like merely dialectical variations upon the possible relations between ideal interests and the commoner human needs. But they are much more than that. They are tragically serious alternatives—and every one of them is misleading. What are usually called the higher civilized activities—coöperation in the development and dissemination of the sciences, the fine arts, criticism, philosophy—all depend upon (and some of them are largely constituted by) a marked development of activities of symbolizing. It is by means of these, as Mr. Adams explained, that human beings emancipate themselves from the tyranny of the present and the local, share the experience of other ages and of other nations, preserve and interpret their own observations, consider possibilities unbounded in range, predict the future and guide themselves in shaping it. We do not see things clearly if our eyes are pressed smack up against them. The effectiveness of symbolization depends in part upon the distance introduced, by general notions and by rules of procedure, between us and the concrete events and objects we want to understand. The magnificent convenience of some mathematical constructs, when used in science and in technology, illustrates this point; and, except for the satisfaction of a kind of aesthetic curiosity, I suppose that such convenience is *the* serious justification of mathematics as a theoretical discipline. By means of it, forces can be reckoned, of magnitudes so immense or so minute (and so complex in structure) that the measuring, remembering, or imagining of them as concrete individual factors would be too much for our powers.

But the risks which accompany such symbolizing are every bit as great as the convenience; for by means of symbols we can take account of other symbols, as well as of nonsymbolic experiences and actions. That is, in some respects, a very useful job to do. But since symbols are generally so much better behaved—so much easier to get hold of and manage—than are the sorts of processes originally symbolized, it is very easy for us to transfer our whole interest to the symbolizing devices, which may thus become substitutes for—instead of instruments for use in the explanation of—the concrete processes which we need to understand and to control. This mischief is much worse if (as is very commonly the case) we do not recognize our activities as merely intrasymbolic, but imagine that we are still dealing—though at great symbolic distance—with materials other than symbols. And even if we maintain a reference outside of symbols for our symbolizing, there is always the further danger that, where our thinking achieves extensive symbolic distance from its referents, we shall become insensitive to the human importance (as serving or not serving basal needs) of the concrete processes thought about.

Could generals carry on wars if they were constantly as vividly aware of thousands (or millions) of tortured human beings—wounded soldiers, drowning sailors, starved, diseased, and mutilated civilians—as when those generals may encounter, let us say, the broken bodies of their own sons? But the principles of strategy are *another* matter. By virtue of them, generals can consider dispassionately the disposition and combat assignments of hundreds of thousands of men, as may be most likely to destroy the enemy. If we have been doing a good (and that means an improving) job of civilized living, and are invaded or threatened by a destructive aggressor, we may well rejoice that symbolization—in the forms of strategic theory, of charts, and of maps—enables our generals to plan effective (if bloody) war, as they could not do if the individual agony of every victim were vividly before their attention. But, if no leaders on any side were able to substitute symbolization—theoretic, artistic, religious, along with talk of racial destiny and national glory—for dealing directly with the horrible straining and the hideous actions and sufferings of individuals, it might well be that *none* could plan and carry out a war. If a military aviator were commanded by his superior officer to land his plane on a specified field, walk into an adjacent hospital, bash in the brains of one-third of the sick children, gouge out the eyes of another third, and cripple the arms and legs of the rest, the chances are a thousand to one that he would refuse—would prefer to be shot, or even tortured, rather than obey. But give him commands in terms of latitude, longitude, altitude, instant of bomb release, and he will feel few qualms about obeying; although he might realize, on reflection, that while he hopes to hit military objectives, there are definite probabilities that the results will be just such as in the first case, which he would die rather than produce. For in the first case too there are only probabilities; since the aviator, if he entered the hospital, could not be sure in advance how much resistance might arise to block his execution of commands. Nurses and doctors are, on the whole, courageous people, and their lancets very sharp. His difference of attitude to the two cases is partly a matter of different intention; but it seems also to be in part a difference in the symbolic mediation of the instructions given him.

It is not at all my purpose to deal in horror, but only to bring home vividly the dangerous as well as the useful way our symbols have of cloaking from us the concrete actual effects of many of our most important actions and the concrete actual referents of our most ingenious theories. And it is not in juvenile and inept theorizing, but precisely in our most highly developed thought, that we are most in danger of being cut off by our instruments of symbolization from the very things that we are, or ought to be, trying to think about. When and if a situation exists in which greater evils can be averted only by inflicting and suffering horrible and brutalizing tortures, then it is best to inflict and to suffer them, and to use all the symbolic instruments of detached, cool-headed strategy in preparing them. But the point is this: the fact that our leaders and their influential advisers—and to a less extent we ourselves—deal in highly theoretical and symbolically mediated considerations of strategy, and of relations of political, economic, and military forces, is all too likely to prevent us from conceiving adequately the concrete individual experiences involved, so that we can judge whether the balance of satisfaction over frustration of human needs justifies the decisions we take and the policies that we may be willing to support at the cost of many lives.

But this is all a familiar story. We learned the grammars of foreign languages in order to understand the science, literature, history, philosophy, expressed in them. But comparative grammar may easily come to monopolize our attention and actually stand in the way of our understanding anything else. The same comments apply, *mutatis mutandis*, to symbolizing in art, ritual, government, philosophy, metaphysics. *All* these have been developed by animals who are unusual (*a*) in the complexity of their needs and the sensitivity of their reactions and (*b*) in the long period of their infantile dependence upon adults—parents or others—which, some students conclude, engenders the emotional ambivalence of love and resentment toward those who so long support—but also control—us, and also toward the institutions that later serve as parent substitutes. In civilized communities, economic dependence upon parents, and consequent control by them, commonly continues long after the young are psychologically and physiologically fit for—and in need of—a larger measure of autonomy. Our very long infancy and adolescence, it is held, induces a strong feeling of insecurity when finally we do emerge from the guidance and control of our elders. So far, the most effective remedy for this insecurity has been the sense of solidarity nourished by life in some tribal cultures. In the last few millennia the civilizing activities, particularly the scientific, have broken down, for the intelligent, such tribal solidarity. But these civilizing activities have yielded, in the form of reliable knowledge of the immense impersonal world, a partial substitute for what they have destroyed, and, through the arts, they have rendered some parts of the surface of the world more immediately satisfying. They are capable of developing programs of coöperative work for the better housing, better health, better education of mankind, which would be complete and magnificent substitutes for tribal solidarity. But where civilized, symbol-mediated activities cut us off from what they began by symbolizing—still more, where they become barriers to the satisfaction of basal needs, barriers either as substitutes, as compensations, as escapes, as rationalizing denials of the existence of the needs, or as means of unduly strengthening taboos and restraints which may, in proper measure, have been indispensable to the development of civilized activities—there civilized activities contribute to making us more anxious, more insecure, more estranged from one another, more aggressive, more violently destructive, not only than are some primitive tribes, but than is compatible with physiological and psychological health. A good example of a highly civilized activity which seems to imperil human values is the second-order symbolizing activity which constitutes theories defending the higher civilized activities as ends-in-themselves. Of such theory Dewey is right (I think) in arguing that it tends, in fact, to promote that potentially destructive factor in all civilization which we have been discussing. Another example in Western democracies has been the verbal celebration of human brotherhood, of sharing, of communication, of coöperation. There is no doubt that this verbal behavior has reflected some genuine devotion to these values. But to far too great a degree it has been compensation, façade, escape—or (at the best) a symptom of devastating conflicts. For while we have talked of brotherhood we have been meaner to one another in many important areas of our living (notably the economic) than are almost any of the brutes within their kinds. Another example is our high-flown verbal appreciation of women, which all too often reflects a bad conscience about the ungrounded discriminations we make against them. Six days ago the dean of a great university (some thousands of miles from here, I may say) inquired about literary scholars to fill a post. When a woman was mentioned to him, he doubted that *any* woman could be qualified. When assured that one was, he answered that, in that case, she must be "far too precious, far too much the poet, far too fine," for us men to expose her to the tarnishing routine of university work!

One of the most gifted of living psychologists has suggested that a key difference between the roles of men and women in all societies known to us is the degree to which the former are preoccupied with language (with symbol structures) whereas the latter are preoccupied with life. My very general characterization of his theory cannot but distort it. But if there is anything at all in it, it may well be that the restriction of women's influence is considerably responsible for the degree to which our symbolizing activities have become the enemies of human life instead of the instruments of its enhancement. Or, have the very restrictions they suffer been the cause of women's better comprehension of human values? Would women, if the restrictions were removed, become just as preoccupied with symbol-mediated activities as men are—and as women who now enter learned professions, arts, business, are commonly accused of becoming? Or would childbearing and child nurture keep their thinking closer to human values? Another leading psychologist—a woman, as it happens— assures me that women are in general much more mature, more reasonable, and more realistic than men, and that the best of women are much more humanely mature than the best of men. It would probably not be becoming for me to challenge this opinion. For quite apart from considerations of courtesy, can a man be competent to judge degrees of maturity and reasonableness from which he is, himself, quite cut off?

Where civilized activities are injurious in the respects we have considered—and so often in the nasty sense of compounding and condoning injury—is there no alternative but relapse into a partial tribalism, which may galvanize a nation into solidarity and give its members a sense of security by reviving superstitions about racial superiority and destiny and by embarking upon programs of military (and other) subjection of neighboring nations? We do not need to accept the dialectic of Hegel or of Marx in order to be impressed by the extreme pendulum swings of action and reaction in this, as well as in so many other, aspects of human history—the reversion to tribalism when civilized activities neglect, or strangle, some of men's basal needs.

It was the insight—and also the fervent conviction—of some of the Pythagoreans, of Plato, and of the modern idealists that genuine civilization is the fulfillment (and cannot be the frustration) of the real individual. Thanks to philosophers like Dewey, and to the work of the anthropologists and psychologists, we are today in a far better position than ever before to implement this insight. For we have come to see that high (but viable) civilizations and "real individuals" are not on some level metaphysically higher and axiotically more authoritative than the brute occurent needs and appetites of men. And we now know pretty well what we have to do if we are to integrate the higher activities called civilized with that social solidarity and coöperation and affiliation (achieved in some primitive tribes, and, in some respects, in totalitarian societies)— the solidarity and affiliation without which men are the victims of anxiety, neurosis, superstition, and war. What we have to do is to understand, and to develop, our civilized activities responsibly, as exploring basal needs and contriving developments and satisfactions for them, and not as if they were autonomous activities upon some higher level.

The *faith* that men can move in this direction is the faith of democracy. The *ideal* is that which Tolman has sketched as Psychological Man. The *method* is experimental intelligence. The norm is physiological and psychological health—a flexible norm, indeed, but no one can say it is a meaningless norm unless he is willing to deny *a priori* what empirical scientists have made out concerning men's almost invariable wants, and concerning the breakdowns, the wars, the incapacity to act and even to live, that follow upon the serious blocking of any of them. Seriously, can we make out a case for a better norm, a better faith, a better ideal, or a better method? Is not every one of our troubles (and every one of the theoretical faults we find with these conceptions themselves, and the evils we resent in our working democracy) due to the half-hearted practice of this method and our less than half-hearted devotion—for all our lip service (perhaps we do "protest *too* much")—to this faith and to this ideal?